I WON'T SAY A WORD

A NOVEL

JOE CLIFFORD

Square Tire Books, Austin, TX.
Book cover by Christian Storm

Author contact: joe@joeclifford.com

First Edition 2024

Dedication TK

PART ONE

THE BEGINNING

ONE MORE CUP OF COFFEE BEFORE YOU GO

Today, Josh would put flowers on their mother's grave.

Jobs seldom delivered him this close to Bennington, Vermont, the small town where his mother Toni was born and now buried. Josh kept meaning to visit. At the end of each grueling day, he found new reasons not to. Sciatica flaring. Daylight fading. Depth charts to log, AA meetings to make. Bullshit excuses. Josh didn't visit Toni's tombstone because it would hurt too much. Especially sober. He didn't want to deal with the emotions it would dredge up—about his dead mother, his dead father, his big brother, who though technically alive was stuck in a hospital three thousand miles away with little hope of getting out.

The large diesel truck lumbered into the Shell Station on Farmington Ave., shuddering to idle in front of pump number eight. The early dawn sky glowed vibrant. Purples, reds, rose, orange. Sand layered in a mason jar. Like an art project when Emily was in elementary school. Now their baby girl was in college. White Mountain University. Her number one choice. Didn't even need a fallback. God, she was smart. A helluva imagination, too, a real gift for storytelling. Must've inherited the talent from her uncle, who had the way with the words. At least until the accident broke his brain. After work, Josh needed to help Em finish that family tree project—providing the motel's wireless was working, which was no guarantee. A brainiac,

Emily was already in New Hampshire, getting a head start on freshman year.

Slamming the door shut, Josh caught the company logo. For a second, he expected to see the familiar insignia for AC Victor.

You fucked that up.

These days Josh was back to being a regular employee on the clock. Paul was a good boss, JP Construction a good outfit. But JPC wasn't AC Victor, the drilling and splitting business Josh started and co-owned with his best friend, Freddie. Until drugs and alcohol grew into a beast too wild to tame.

Why was Josh doing this to himself? First thing on a Monday morning? Addiction, dead parents, brain-addled brother. Josh was staring at a long haul. Why add extra fuel to an already exorbitant guilt trip?

Josh slid the AmEx through the slot, flipping the gas cap, and jamming in the nozzle, prepared for the insatiable monster to gobble up a hundred-and-forty bucks' worth.

Stalking between islands, weaving beneath buzzing fluorescents, Josh shoved open the mini-mart door.

"What'll it be, pal?" the cashier, a man in his late fifties, asked. Must be new. For years, the same old lady, Betty, had greeted him behind the register. Why does everything have to change?

"Pack of Marlboro Lights." Then as if remembering he'd forgotten to take his heart medication, Josh added, "And a bottle of Advil," which was the strongest drug he was allowed to take for his perpetually barking back. "Oh, yeah, and a coffee."

An odd expression contorted the cashier's face. This early, they were the only two in the store. A strange tension filled the air. Probably sleep deprivation. Twelve-hour shifts were taking their toll.

The cashier pointed over the big guy's shoulder to the coffee station.

"Made a fresh pot." He waited for a reaction. "Hear me? *Fresh* pot. For you!"

Josh flicked a thumbs up. *Okay, weirdo. Hazard of working the grave-yard. That much time in your head, you go insane. Just ask his brother.*

Outside, with his fresh coffee in hand, the early morning chilled, August dawn slow to warm. Josh toppled four Advil, popping them in his mouth, washing down the ibuprofen with scalding coffee. Replacing the nozzle—one hundred, thirty-nine dollars, and ninety-nine cents—Josh chuckled to himself. Back when his brother could read numbers, that figure would've triggered the hell out of his OCD.

The big guy climbed back into the big rumbler, pulling out of the lot, and making for the highway. GPS clocked the trip at three hours and change. Josh hated being away from his wife Amy, but it was nice knowing he wouldn't have to spend six hours behind the wheel. During the week, Josh stayed at motels up north, sparing himself the round trip back to Berlin, the heart of Central Connecticut—Berlin, like the one in Germany, but pronounced with the accent between syllables, like "pearl" and a preposition. And God forbid residents hear you pronounce it any other way.

Considering how badly he'd screwed up, Josh knew he should be grateful. To Paul, for giving him a second chance at JP Construction; to Debra, his father's second wife, and the closest thing to a mom Josh had left—his stepmother found the Bay Area Institute for People with Traumatic Brain Injury, paying for his big brother's care. Room, board, medical bills. A burden that lands on Josh's shoulder without Debra. He should be thanking her, not holding a grudge. That was the tough-est aspect of AA to stomach—besides the spiritual shit—gratitude. Josh didn't trust his stepmother, not after that funny business with the will. And once money is involved, family business only gets funnier.

Hitting the onramp for Route 9, Josh tamped down his pack of Marlboros. Thinking about family dynamics was giving him a headache. Even when his older brother *was* writing stories, he couldn't have dreamt up a crazier plot. Amy's maiden name was Fortman. It was a made-up family name, only a couple generations old; all Fortmans around here were related. Her father Andy started Fortman Brothers Construction, one of the biggest construction outfits in New England. Andy and his brother Ari—yes, *that* Ari Fortman. It was also the company his father Neil worked for when he contracted the myelofibrosis that killed him. Yeah, barbeques and family reunions were a blast.

Josh wished he could pin his dad's death on Ari—but by the time Neil was diagnosed, the slimeball attorney turned lobbyist was down in D.C., making in-roads, ascending Capitol Hill. And by the time Ari reached the promised land of Mar-a-Lago, Neil was dead. Truth was, there was no one *to* blame. Everyone got screwed on that deal, Andy included. The company charged with testing the soil failed to detect the radioactive materials. So, Dad and a lot of other workers had to die.

Shit happens. Then you die.

Gratitude? Fuck that. We survive.

If Emily hadn't sent those questions for her genealogy course, Josh wouldn't be thinking about any of it. Poking around the web, he'd expected to uncover a great great grandmother with Cherokee blood. Not this. Maybe it was inevitable, given the prominent stage his uncle-in-law Ari currently enjoyed. Is "uncle-in-law" even a thing? *Who knows? But "asshole" is.*

Connecting to Interstate 91, the big guy cracked the lid, steam rising. He fired up a smoke, first one of the day and the only high he was allowed to enjoy. Josh dialed in Howard Stern on Sirius XM, taking long, slow drags, waiting for the jolt that weirdo cashier promised. The more coffee he drank, the more disoriented and sleepier he felt.

Caffeine ain't got nothing on methamphetamine. Still, wasn't coffee supposed to *wake* you up?

Around Hartford city center, traffic slogged, lanes clogged. Riders and racing rats with the same idea to get an early start and beat the morning glut. Gridlock. Any delay would put a dent in the schedule. Paul would be pissed. This job had a hard deadline. Josh's new boss Paul was bankrolling a small empire in ski country. Vermont, New Hampshire, Southern Maine. Bretton Woods. Pats Peak. Sugarloaf. This current gig outside Magic Mountain? Third housing development this year. No rest for the rich. A lot of money to be made in those hills. Josh was hoping to see some of it. As soon as he finished crawling out of the red. What didn't go to Amy and family expenses got sucked up by bill collectors and whittling down credit card debt. Josh planned to start paying back Freddie the money he stole from AC Victor—as soon as he *had* extra money. When do we ever have "extra" money?

A wave of dizziness washed over Josh, and his lids fell heavy. Images, memories, invasive thoughts flooding…

Josh snapped to in time to slam on the brakes, only to have some nerd in a hybrid toot his tiny horn, shaking a furious fist. Looking down at the Connecticut River, Josh considered pulling over for a quick power nap. Power nap? At six in the morning?

Stop being a pussy…

Dad's voice never left his head. Just because people die doesn't mean they stop speaking to you.

Josh pushed aside the voices and memories. Only way to survive. You last long enough, you start to miss everyone. Not that forty-three was old.

Josh had his whole life ahead of him.

CHAPTER ONE

THE PLANE TOUCHES DOWN

When I step off the plane, the first thing that hits me is the heat, a hot, wafting wall of melting asphalt, bubbling tar, and car fumes. Napa, California, where I live at the Bay Area Institute for People with Traumatic Brain Injury—rolls off the tongue, doesn't it?—gets hot. Nothing like this. I moved in about thirteen years ago. Don't ask me for an exact date. I've had trouble with my numbers for a while. I grew up here in Connecticut. Nothing oppresses like a New England summer. I've encountered hotter temps, more humidity but nothing rivals Central Connecticut's ragweed asthma and pollen-imbued summers. Makes breathing feel like asphyxiation, as if you're huffing fumes from a self-cleaning oven through a very narrow straw.

Stepping out of Bradley International with my single rolling bag—I travel light—I pause at Arrivals to look for Debra's car. I sent her the flight information. At her insistence. I told her I could Uber, but she refused. I relented. Not that I don't appreciate the ride—it will be nice to see my stepmom. It's her money that keeps me alive. The Institute, world renowned for cases like mine, does not come cheaply. I hate for people to think I can't handle ordinary, everyday tasks. Not being able to read, write, or speak doesn't make me a less than. This oversensitivity also adds unnecessary weight to the already mammoth chip saddling my shoulder.

Ultimately, I consented to Debra's offer because it was genuine. That's what I appreciate most about my stepmother—and my younger brother, Josh: they don't look down on me because of my condition. Despite my limitations in terms of communication, I am as smart as you or anyone else. That part of my brain still works swimmingly. I have clear *thoughts*. I can't get them *out* clearly. Big difference.

Since agreeing to live at the Institute, I've fought hard to maintain autonomy. You see many residents, sad sacks who feel sorry for themselves. They give up. Let the staff feed them, rotate them to avoid bedsores, wipe their behinds. About half the residents are recovering from motorcycle accidents. Our dad got Josh hooked on those suicide machines. When the old man died, he left *both* Harleys to one of his bastard kids. Josh had been riding dirt bikes since he was nine. Broke my baby brother's heart. Neil, our father, tried to get me into riding. Not for me. I fell off my bicycle. Can you imagine me on one of those organ donors? Not a chance. Stuff like not riding motorcycles was one of several reasons Neil and I didn't get along: he didn't consider me as manly as Josh. Even before the accident. I might be the big brother, but Josh is the *bigger* brother. Six feet, two hundred plus isn't small. But when your father and brother are both six foot six and built like brick shithouses, one of our father's favorite expressions, it's hard not to develop an inferiority complex. At least I got a few tattoos. Maybe it meant something to the old man before he kicked it.

I check my phone for a text. No, I can't read it. But I can push buttons. Giant red ones. They have devices for people like me, apps that translate text to voice. I'm not color blind.

By now I'm sure you've figured out I have … different abilities.

That's what they call them at the Institute. Which is bullshit. *Differently abled.* I *hate* that bullshit. Call it what it is. I'm fucked up. But I'm not stupid. And I'm not fucked up from doing too many drugs, no matter what you've heard. I can't speak, write, or communicate like you because one tiny part of my brain, the one that interprets numbers and letters, assigns meaning, fires signals to your hands and mouth, allows you to count or speak, is damaged. The result of a freak accident.

A text dings and I hit translate.

Getting off the Windsor Locks exit now. Sorry. Traffic. See you soon. Then she adds, *This is Debra.* I don't let her needless clarification bring me down. My stepmom means well.

My real mother, Toni, passed away from scleroderma when I was thirty-four. When I knew she was dying, I gave up self-medicating and sought professional help. I wanted her to see her oldest son sober before she went.

But she's gone now. Without Debra, I'd be homeless.

I center myself—a technique encouraged and reinforced at the Institute. Because of my condition, I can lose chunks of time, get displaced, forget where I am. It's important for me to ground my person. Operating from a one-way, communicative void, I must reassure myself I exist.

Not a cloud in the sky, sidewalk fried-egg-hot, heat rising from the tarmac. Today's date is August twenty-first, two-thousand seventeen. My calendar announces that. *Have a nice day!*

I'll do my best, computer.

Although it's hard to "have a nice day" with your brother missing. That's why I am back in Connecticut. The detectives want my laptop, to analyze the recent electronic communication I had with my brother. Josh has been missing for five days. He emailed me three days ago. I conveyed this to authorities. Josh must be okay. I offered to FedEx my laptop. Detectives wanted me to hand deliver. You might be wondering why detectives are involved in the disappearance of a guy who digs ditches for a living. When your wife's uncle works for the president of the United States, you get special treatment. Fine by me. Ari Fortman is hot shit. They flew me back first class. I could use a vacation.

I don't hate it at the Institute. Set in the lush valley of wine country, the architecture boasts a Tuscany motif, with slithering vines and fresco-painted walls. But institutional living can leave one feeling shackled—regardless of independence, which, as a long-term resident, I am afforded. Hence, this unaccompanied leave. And at forty-seven, I'm not asking *anyone* to take a trip to see my family.

The black Acura pulls up. Debra hops out of the car and wraps me in a big hug. I'm not a hugger. I relent. I haven't seen her since her since last Christmas, when she flew out to San Francisco and drove up to visit. After my father passed, Debra could've easily washed her hands of me. For years, I'd been a thorn in her side and the bane of her existence, a constant source of agitation, my addiction a never-ending parade of arrests and other abhorrent behaviors. Debra used to work for the town as a clerk and notary. She's retired now. My stepmom should be enjoying her golden years without having to worry about taking care of a grown man pushing fifty.

Yes, I got clean. With eighteen trips to rehab, I didn't make it easy.

There is one thing I loathe about the Institute: being this far from Josh. The rational part of my brain knows I needed to get far away from my brother. If I'd have stayed in Connecticut? No way either of us stays sober. We were each other's best friend and worst influence.

"How was the flight?" Debra asks, after we've stashed my rolling bag and I've climbed into the car.

I act out a slow-motion airplane ride with my arms, putting my head to sleep in my hands to indicate how boring it was.

Debra laughs.

The Institute keeps pestering me to learn sign language. I'm not deaf.

In that rolling bag, the one we stuffed in the trunk, I have a device called a "Prologue2Go." It's like a Kindle but designed to aid communication. The pre-sets are generic. "How are you?" and "I'm doing well," the homogenized American version of asking Juan where the *bibliotheca* is. Perfunctory. The P2G's tech is sophisticated enough to program unique phrases to suit your personality. It's also a pain in the ass to set up, impossible without a normie's assistance, and I find it frequently easier to play charades, even if doing so, as I've just done, can leave one feeling infantilized. It's the path of least resistance, which leads to the garbage heap over there. I think Lou Reed wrote that. I used to be a singer in a rock band.

On my phone, I pull up a photo of Josh as Debra winds our way out of Bradley International, making for the interstate, holding it out for her to see. She shakes her head no.

"Still no word," Debra says.

Tilting my head, I point at me. I know he's okay because he emailed me after he went "missing."

"There's that," Debra says, accepting irrefutable math. "Which is why the police want to talk to you. They want to read those email exchanges."

I am glad to be home, even if I hate the local rumors that persist. I keep waiting for Berlin High to invite me to share with the senior class, prop me up as a living "Just Say No" cautionary tale, like that suicide survivor flapping pretzelled arms, speaking through a tube, and sharing his newfound appreciation for life.

What a joke.

Unrolling the window, I stick out my head, a dog happy to be taken for a ride.

I inhale ragweed and pollen. My eyes tear up.

I've forgotten how bad my allergies get back here.

CHAPTER TWO

THE ACCIDENT
Sunday, 1985, August 23, 6:52 p.m.

There are multiple reasons why that specific date and time is important. First, it's one of the few dates I can recall without needing a prompt. I know my birthday of course. I've memorized my social security number. I used to know my childhood phone number. Nobody forgets Christmas. I know today is August two thousand seventeen. But confirming that required tapping my pad, and the specific day has already slipped from my cerebellum. More than thirty years have passed since what we call the accident, and I'm still not sure it makes any more sense.

The effects were gradual, implications lasting and grave, permanent, irreversible. What do I have specifically? In terms of a name? Dysarthria, which falls under the big, parent umbrella of aphasia, a poorly understood affliction at best. Some are born with the malady. Most grow into it. The disorder primarily affects the elderly, a complication of dementia. For others, like me, the onset can be … trickier. Doctors say my condition took root in the forests around Dead Man's Curve (yes, Berlin really has a Dead Man's Curve), the afternoon my brother and I were riding bicycles home, trying to beat a day's dying light.

Dead Man's Curve was up the road from our house on Old Farms Place. My friends Tab, Tim, and Mike lived around there, off Elton and Orchard, backyards without borders, vacant lots and boundless fields, ideal for makeshift ballparks and the future superstars we were all destined to be. This was before developers bought up and developed any extra green space in Berlin to pack in more suburban dream homes. Last I heard Tim worked for the movies in Hollywood, which is the closest any of us got to the stars. I think Mike and Tab ended up with utility companies. As for me? I became this.

Josh had ridden to fetch me because it was dinnertime. This was before the internet or cell phones. When your mother wanted you, she sent your little brother on his bicycle. Although Josh had never been "little." Even at eleven, he was taller than me.

Later that evening, I'd learn a bomb exploded on a flight over India.

Most of the dead hailed from Canada, our friendly neighbors to the north. Sad as the loss of life may be, the moment proved paramount on a personal level, dividing my life neatly into before and after. The correlation between the two tragic events, forever stamping date and time on the cerebral cortex.

Before the accident, I had friends, played baseball, golfed, and crushed like crazy on a girl named Annabelle.

After the accident, my world began to unravel, a thread pulled from a sweater. By the time I'd be diagnosed, we'd crossed the point of no return, and what I'd lost could never be recovered.

They say before you die your life flashes before your eyes. Not true. Aside from my head bashing against the rock, I don't remember much. Tremendous headache. Ears left ringing. Equilibrium throwing off my balance, which meant I'd ruptured an eardrum. Didn't bleed much.

Concussed for sure. Nobody worried about head injuries in the 1980s. If you wore a bicycle helmet back then, you'd get called a pussy and have your ass kicked.

What I *do* recall, as vivid as I recall anything, are the immediate moments leading up *to* the accident. The sun still out, high in the sky, even though it was almost seven o'clock. One of those endless childhood days of summer. I remember feeling good, joyous, free, alive.

Josh and I, delaying orders to return home, took a detour to race down the tortuous, steep incline of Dead Man's Curve. We were only a mile from our house. By this point our parents were separated. Dad, Neil, was already living with Debra, who at the time I didn't like. I'd always been a mama's boy.

That fat old sun bobbed in the sky, the horizon a charcuterie of pale pink and meaty reds.

Then it all gets pummeled, pounded, fried to shit.

I can recap my memory, how it unfolded to *me*: a special news report interrupts our regularly scheduled programming. No one knew it was a bomb set to go off, designed to kill. But I'm not at home; I'm on my bicycle, and it's hours earlier. Which might mean nothing—memory is strange like that, the passage of time reshaping order of events. Except sometimes, when I can't sleep, I get funny thoughts. Like what if that plane crash did happen sooner in my world. What if in my timeline I rode my bicycle after the accident, time space continuum hic-cupping, displacing my existence, plucking me from that fate and tossing me on this one, cursed to spin forever on a perpetual loop, out of sync and sorts. I know how nutty that sounds. Time goes forward. Everyone knows that. But what if I got unstuck in time, like Billy Pilgrim? I'm a huge Kurt Vonnegut fan—I used to think one day I'd be a writer.

Slaughterhouse Five was the last book I was able to read before I'd need books read *to* me. It's comforting to believe my condition isn't real. I'm trapped in the wrong verse of a song, half a chapter behind in the book of life, peddling to catch up to a moment that has already passed, while you sit around and I languish, unable to speak your language, a wrongfully imprisoned man awaiting trial, my case perpetually delayed. I know. Nutty.

My other option is the truth, which is far crueler. Bad luck. A fluke. The gods were not shining on me that evening. I'd rather chalk up failings to fantasy than personal shortcomings.

At the bottom of Dead Man's Curve, there was a stream with a rock ramp. Josh and I—and every other kid in the neighborhood—raced it, tire grooves slicking stone into a summer ice rink and luge track. We'd kick off this giant hill, taking flight on our bikes. "Wiping out" was considered "cool." Josh and I made a few jumps. Then the sun was down, and it was time to leave.

Like the career criminal ready to retire, I uttered those famous last words: "Okay, one more time."

Unsteady from the start, I was going too fast. My front tire landed wonky. Instead of sending me ass over handlebars and scabbing my knees, my bike wheel locked tight in a levee, bicycle wrenched ninety degrees, flinging me portside and smashing my skull against a boulder.

My head didn't split open. Like I mentioned, there wasn't a lot of blood. Even though I have no recollection of the immediate aftermath or walking on my own, Josh said I seemed fine.

At home, Mom, after chastising us for being late, found a tiny cut at the base of my widow's peak. Half an inch. Maybe less. Didn't need stiches. She covered it with a band aid and sent me to bed.

No one could appreciate the magnitude of that tiny incision.

When I hit my head that evening, a fissure opened. Like drilling and splitting a fault line, it would continue spread, widening into a chasm as it ran up my skull, through my crown, and down into my stem.

That's how the madness seeped in.

CHAPTER THREE

MY BROTHER'S KEEPER

Debra delivers us to Josh's house on Christian Lane, where his wife Amy, their daughter Emily, and a pair of detectives wait. I haven't seen Em in person in—what's it been now? Four years? Since then, she's sprouted bean sprout tall and roller skate skinny. Amy smiles at me, trying her best. I know it's hard for her. My brother still struggles with issues I helped start but couldn't stick around to resolve.

You can talk about bicycle crashes at fourteen all you want. Hearing someone was shooting speedballs in a skeezy hotel along the Berlin Turnpike trumps it. Drug addiction is the sexier story, as crazy as that sounds. Folks glom onto sensational. If I could say I was sorry, I would. Maybe that's all this is, my reason for being here: one last attempt to apologize for all the pain and trouble I caused.

Amy and I hug, and she says it's good to see me, which, though a lie, is nice of her to say. I wish we were closer—she's my brother's wife and the mother of my niece, my only flesh-and-blood lineage.

I can feel her recoil when our persons touch. I might as well be a leper.

Emily's reaction is different. Seeing me, she radiates, face lighting up. My niece and I have a very good relationship, or as good as a relationship gets when it's separated by three-thousand miles and one of you needs a robot to speak.

Em darts up the drive, throwing her arms around my neck. We FaceTime often. Even though I can't offer much to the conversation, I'll twist my expressions to exaggerated Mr. Bean proportions, which cracks up Emily. I'm still the cool uncle. Now that she's off to college, I don't know how long I'll enjoy that mantle.

The pair of detectives approach. I pass along my laptop, as requested. The pair bags, tags, seals, and thanks me. Unlike most, I'm not worried about browser history. I use that laptop for calls to Josh and Em, my speech and physical therapy homework, emails with my brother. Nothing else. I don't have much need for the internet or social media.

Paul, my brother's new business partner, pulls in the driveway in his shiny white JP Construction truck. A short man, he interrupts the detectives to give me a hearty handshake and bro hug. Unlike Josh's (equally short) former partner Freddie, Paul likes me. He sees me as a *good* influence, because now I'm on the straight and narrow. Seeing Paul and Amy together illustrates how differently people view me in the before and after. Never mind the accident. Another event defines my person more: the drugs.

Although I was trying to get clean when I met Amy, I was still using—the path to sobriety is seldom a straight line. When I met Paul, I was already sober. To one I was the root, the other hope for a cure. Neither depiction is accurate. There was goodness in me when I was using, just as there are still rotten parts in me now. It's clear from Paul's warm embrace that he only sees a man who, despite hardships and handicaps, managed to get his life together. I'm not sure living in a brick building, repeating daily schedules with arts-and-craft therapy, and having someone pay my bills is crushing it. Compared to the alternative? The reflection of that ogre in Amy's eyes? I'll take it.

With all parties now present, the detectives state where we currently stand in their investigation. Like *Dragnet*, it's just the facts: Josh was last seen filling up his company truck at the Shell Station off Farmington Avenue, five-whatever in the morning. There is toll road footage of my brother driving through Hartford, on his way to the job site in Northwestern New England, the upper Vermont mountains, where he was staying during the week. A motel near Bennington, the town where our mother is buried. Coincidence. He never made it. Not to the job site or motel.

Detectives ask about Josh's most recent drilling project. I don't see why that's relevant. As Paul fills in authorities, my attention drifts to the birds soaring in the sky. I catch a few details. A new development in the foothills of Magic Mountain, one of the best regions for skiing. Upscale community. No one saw anything. That was five days ago.

I know the cops have a job to do, but I'm not worried. I heard from Josh three days ago. Simple math. Subtraction using fingers. Once detectives check my laptop, they'll have the time-stamped correspondence. And before anyone goes all conspiracy theory on me: no one was masquerading as Josh. These communications contained the personal particulars only brothers share. Furthermore, as his brother, I can *feel* his presence. He's fine. I know I've been in hippy-dippy Northern California a long time. Doesn't mean I'm wrong.

The detectives' attention returns to me. Aware of my condition, they ask questions slowly, which is condescending and irksome. Also nothing new. I don't get offended. I could drag out my Prologue2Go. Instead, I answer via pantomime, or Debra interprets for me.

"Did your brother sound like himself in recent emails?" one of the detectives asks.

To which I'd love to joke, "No. He sounded like a robot." Because *everyone* sounds like a robot when you translate text to speech. But I don't. It's a serious situation. Debra is worried, so too Emily and Amy. I wonder who else suspects the same as I do: my little brother got the itch again, and that he is off scratching it under an assumed name somewhere on that Turnpike.

While detectives speak with Amy, Paul pulls me to the side.

"Think he's doing it again?" Paul asks.

At first, I worry he means the drugs. Josh has been off them, working hard to stay clean, attending meetings. That's what he's been telling me in our email exchanges. I *want* to believe it. If Josh experienced a slip, there's still time to prevent full-blown relapse. Like so much of life, recovery can be one step forward and two steps back. Even if I knew my brother was using again, do I want to tell Paul? I have faith my baby brother is going to follow my lead. Eventually. Will Paul, his boss, understand? Addicts don't adhere to conventional patterns and time-frames. After Josh's flame out with Freddie, he needs Paul's faith and financial backing.

When I don't answer right away, Paul, making sure Amy remains out of earshot, adds, "Piece of ass on the side?"

That implication is crass, but not without merit. Josh cheats on his wife. I know because he tells me. I know because he is our father's son. Our father cheated. My brother cheats. Shitty, lousy. I try to get him to walk the line, but in the end, he's going to do what he wants to do, and I'd rather he got his highs with new lays than needles and pills. Again, I'm forced to question my motivation. Is this lackadaisical attitude toward infidelity because I want to see my brother sober? Or because I don't like his wife?

I shrug, but, yeah, sure, Paul, the thought has occurred to me once, twice, or half a dozen times. Occam's razor, the simplest explanation. I would never cheat. Then again, women aren't lining up to marry damaged goods. *Even if he's this good looking and witty?* Please, don't take the easy shot. I've heard that joke as often as a guy named Joe gets asked where he's going with that gun in his hand. It's tired, played out.

Our parents fought endlessly about Dad's numerous affairs. Mom would receive calls on our old landline, some new woman saying, "Tell Neil he's got another son/daughter," before hanging up. My parents divorced ages ago. My mom got those calls till the day she died. But that's what we do as grown-ups, isn't it? Spend adulthood repairing the damage from childhood. As much as I'd love to separate current fates from dysfunctional pasts, we are composed of the same genetic materials. Nature vs. nurture. Maybe Skinner was right and we're all blank slates, *tabula rasa,* computer codes yet to be written. No one's asking me to contribute an article to *Psychology Today.*

Paul doesn't have to add the other part, the drugs. It's implied, the two forever connected, My brother has a pattern. First, it starts with the affairs, the girlfriends, mistresses, "pieces of ass on the side." Sometimes it stops there. But if the cheating goes on too long…

"He's been working his butt off," Paul says. "Calls in every night." Another stolen glance at Amy. "Last time we talked … I thought I heard a girl in the background." Paul shakes his head. "Could've been the TV." We both know he doesn't believe it was the TV.

I groan, the suggestion ludicrous—Paul grabs my arm, stopping me from being so demonstrative and tipping off Amy. Like me, Paul wants to protect Josh from further aggravation. Maybe he does it because Josh works for him—my brother, for all his faults, has always been a hard worker. I do it because he's my brother. Different agenda, same end.

"Let's keep this between us." Paul takes one look in my eye, and he knows I'll never tell.

I don't want to get my brother in more trouble—with his wife *or* business partner. The question, however, hits me deep. My main concern isn't my brother's wandering eye; it's that if he is using again, I won't be able to catch him before he goes off the deep end. After days of radio silence? I fear we are on the cusp.

"Whoever she is," Paul says, "he'll get tired of her." I don't know who he's trying to convince. "Guy's up there all week, alone in the mountains…" He winks. "A man has needs."

Yes, a man does. For my brother that means chasing highs forever out of reach, like trying to catch smoke. It's a dream unattainable.

Paul says he has to get going, but he gives me his card. He knows I can't read. I already have his number; the card is a reminder to use it. The look he gives is sincere. We're on the same side—*Josh's* side. He says goodbye to Amy, assuring her everything will be all right, before climbing back in his big truck.

For a moment, we all gather—Debra, Amy, me—as detectives end on a positive note, urging us to keep hopes alive, they're on it, it's going to be okay, say a prayer.

Then it's over. A detective passes along their card. Unlike Paul's, which I stuck in my pocket, this one I hand off to Debra. If "anything comes to mind," I'll let my stepmom know.

Amy can't get rid of me soon enough. My brother is an addict. My presence here is a reminder of that. My brother is missing. My presence is a reminder of that too.

I turn and make for the Acura. I'll be staying with Debra.

Em bolts out the front door, running down the front steps. My niece grabs her mother's hand.

"Dad would want him to stay here," Em says, before peering up at me with anime-wide eyes.

I wish it were that easy, kiddo…

One look at Amy's face says she'd sooner see me rot under a bridge.

CHAPTER FOUR

THE LONG LONESOME ROAD HOME

Before Emily lets me leave, she insists I wait, running inside the house before darting out again with a stack of stapled papers and a small tape recorder, a device you don't see much of these days.

"This is a story I wrote for class." She passes along the items. "I know you can't read, but I recorded me reading it. I thought maybe, if you were bored, maybe you'd want to …" She says it so meekly. Em bites her lip. I remember the sensation well, back when I considered myself a writer. Opening your heart to create art to share with the world, and the paralyzing, gripping fear to show anyone and be judged.

I smile wide, stashing the recorder in my pocket, clutching the papers to my heart. I'm touched she cares enough to share her dream with me. And when you first begin writing, trust me, those words are more precious than gold.

Back at Debra's, sequestered in one of the several guest rooms—the house is a grand Colonial in the town's historic district—I sit on the bed and listen to Em's story. I *wanted* to be a writer. She's going to *be* a writer. Her command of language is deft. Good writing hinges on parallelism. Think: it was the best of times; it was the worst of times. Balance. The rule of three, this, that, and the other thing. Good writing resides in its syntax, which is the offensive linemen of prose: you only notice it when it's done wrong. Good writing is alliteration and sibilance, rhythm, the musicality of language—an internal beat—and of course the practical applications: limiting adverbs, metaphors, and similes.

The story is about a man who hits his head and loses the ability to speak or write, but who does not give up; he rises above his disabilities, refuses to quit, and in the end perseveres. It's an American story, the *Rocky* ethos, where the only talent that matters is the ability to take a punch, stay on your feet, and go the distance. Our father was an amateur boxer. Josh no doubt shared a hearty dose of Rocky Balboa with his daughter.

The rest of the story is … surprising. It takes turns I don't expect. I'd assumed Emily, being a girl, would write something more romantic, less plot-oriented, with more allegories, feelings, thoughts, lighter on external action, heavier on sentiment, the poignancy of eating breakfast alone in Japan on a rainy Christmas. Literary fiction.

I feel guilty for my misguided prejudice and unfortunate sexism.

The story is dark, violent, twisted. The protagonist finds himself in a remarkable situation. That's a cornerstone of genre. Mystery, suspense, thriller. An ordinary man faced with an extraordinary situation.

The rest of her story reads like film noir. The landscape bleak, we are transported to the cold snow, terrain hostile and infertile. Duplicity abounds. People lie, get hurt, double cross, are arrested, with fantastic (if improbable) escapes. There's nefarious institutions, malevolent powers that be, and unexpected antagonists. Elements of science-fiction and horror get thrown in as well.

In many ways, it's a mess—she's still seventeen—but big picture? It shows promise and excites in that raw, early draft fashion, like a band's first take of a killer track before it's polished too much to shine.

I dissect books all the time, and it's rare an ending surprises me.

This ending surprises me. Although looking back, I see she played fair, hiding clues in plain sight. There's a multi-layered mystery, which I missed the first time, distracted by the mechanisms employed by its architect.

Some reading it might be worried about the author—the ending is *that* savage, brutal, and shocking. I am not. Emily is a sweet kid, albeit one with a hearty, vibrant imagination. I'd like to believe, at least in part, she inherited that skill from her uncle.

I should be flattered. Her "hero" is clearly based on me. It's funny how others see you. In Emily's eyes, I am a survivor, a fighter, a good man.

Problem is, like any work of fiction, it's a lie.

I'm not an inspiration.

I'm the reason Josh is missing.

————

Returning to high school in the fall of 1985, I wasn't the same, and teachers started to notice the change. More of an English major, I'd never been good at arithmetic. When I couldn't make the jump to Advanced Algebra or Calculus with the rest of my class, no one panicked. They placed me in remedial courses. I focused on my art. I liked to write, but I could draw and paint as well. A musician, I started a band. I was voted Most Artistic by my graduating class of '88. Demented and sad, to quote John Bender, but social. Or in my case, the highlight of an artistic career not meant to be.

That fall, my parents, Toni (short of "Antoinette") and Neil, always at each other's throats, finally divorced. Flunking pre-algebra had nothing to do with it. My mom was sixteen when she got married, my father nineteen. Shared interests: trying to escape alcoholic mothers. A fighter, my father had a temper, and was quick to act on it. Till the day he died, the old man was getting in trouble for punching people in the head. I only witnessed the end. But I can picture it. This wizened, chemo-balding, former pugilist throwing a left hook or dropping a right hammer because someone outside the gas station disrespected him.

The divorce wasn't finalized before Dad was living with Debra, the woman on the side (this time). The nicest thing I can say about my father? He was a hard worker. He was also ruthless and vindictive. Guy made six figures working as a high school dropout. Supervisor in charge of explosives. My father got his employer, Fortman Brothers Construction, to pay him under the table to screw my mother on the child support. A stay-at-home mom since nineteen, my mother got a full-time job, taking night courses, eventually landing in medical coding, all the while paying for the room, board, and care of two boys. We paid her back by becoming junkies.

I had plenty of excuses for using. The big one being self-medicating. My brain was like a balloon with a small, pinhole leak. Unless you had time-lapse capabilities, you'd miss the slow, steady progression of its collapse.

It's hard to describe what I saw on the page—and doctors would later ask, unrelentingly. Best response? Letters were letters. Wasn't easy, but with concerted effort I could string enough of them together to read. Numbers? I recognized 1 and 0. The language of a computer. After that? A jumbled hodgepodge of hieroglyphics, mangled cats and dented urns shaped like snakes. I didn't admit this to anyone at the time because I thought I was going crazy. No one wants to be different in high school. Hollywood makes different seem cool. They churn out movies about iconoclasts named Duckie (and John Bender). But in high school, if you are different, you're earmarked with a target on your back. No one connected my learning difficulties to the accident. Not even me. My father, with whom I had little relationship, chalked it up to laziness. My mother, leaning harder on Jesus, vowed to pray more.

In retrospect, I should've asked for help, said, "Hey, I can't seem to count anymore," but I wanted to get a girlfriend, at least cop a feel before graduation. Turns out its easier to flunk pre-Algebra and earn a diploma than it is for a teenage defect to get a handjob.

I'd always been a reader. I possessed a "fine flair for writing," as my tenth-grade English teacher, Mrs. Virostek, told me. My journaling project netted an A with accolades I was "a natural born storyteller." I can still quote it because it was the last time anyone praised my academics.

Later in college, I'd attempt writing a book—I probably ended up *writing* four or five books' worth—though I wouldn't finish before that part of my brain stopped working. It was about a lonely handyman on a cold mountain in New Hampshire, a high school dropout quick to throw a punch. Those butchered words are in a box somewhere.

Though I hated my father, I wanted to be like him. How weird is that? To aspire to be the very thing you despise? It tears you in two.

I scored high enough on my SATs to get into Central Connecticut State University—back then a fallback school—going four years, without a degree, GPA hovering around the Mendoza line. Unable to count, I avoided math courses with bubonic ferocity.

That last year was hell. Story ideas dried up. I got kicked out of the band. My creativity was shot. My penmanship, always elegant, grew illegible. Professors complained they couldn't read my writing. This was before students printed out every paper from a computer.

I didn't drop out. I stopped showing up.

I could feel my brain cracking. Like an egg. There were all these PSAs about your brain on drugs, and I might be the only person who interpreted these advertisements as sound career advice. I started using drugs to self-medicate. I'd pop any pill. Up, down, sideways. Anywhere it took me was better than here.

My mom had to sell the house, moving us across town to a tiny condominium. In the beginning, I kept my drug use secret.

Secrets eventually outgrow their shadows. My mother and I fought endlessly as my drug use worsened, weekend warrior act bleeding into weekly horror show. I'd work some shit factory job, earn enough to stay afloat, until I'd screw up and get fired. I don't want to sound vain, but I've always been good looking (my father, for all his faults, *was* a handsome man). By this time, I'd figured out how to get dates. I milked that bad boy trope dry, wringing pocketbooks with it. Girls came and went, a new one always willing to take a flyer, but I was growing increasingly frustrated.

My brother, a terrific football player and wrestler, was nailing life. Despite partying like a high school, senior star athlete, Josh got a full ride to Boston University for football. I packed up and moved west to San Francisco, like Jack Kerouac, still planning to fulfill my dream of being a writer.

I know: how can you write if you can't … write? In a word? Speed. Methamphetamine. Crystal. Crank. Ice. At first, speed helped me focus. If I didn't do *too* much. The stuff's basically Adderall, which they pump into kids these days. I still couldn't count. Then again, the only time I needed numbers was deciding whether I wanted a teenager (sixteen grams) or an eight ball. I landed a good-paying job in the bindery department of a print shop. Half the guys working there were either drunk or high. Life was okay.

Then something strange happened. Josh quit football and college, returning home. Had nothing to do with me. He was going through his own crisis of faith. He and his high-school girlfriend (Amy) broke up, and my brother reached out to me. He said he felt lost, empty and aching and didn't know why, like Cathy boarding a Greyhound bound for Pittsburgh. Josh wanted to fly out to San Francisco to visit me.

Growing up, my brother and I weren't close. Not like we hated each other. We didn't have much in common. By the time we reached Berlin High, we hardly spoke. Now in our twenties we were learning how alike we were. Bonding over a shared enemy, our father, we became what we'd never been yet were all along: full-blooded, biological brothers.

After a long night of drinking, Josh said I *seemed* better. I shared the secret to my success: methamphetamine. I asked if he wanted to try it. I know how awful that sounds. But I was twenty whatever, with a traumatic brain injury. Consider the source.

"What's it feel like?" he asked.

"Let me show you," I said. "Give me your arm."

I was the first person to inject my baby brother.

That brings us up to speed. Sorry. My bad. We started using heroin as well. Speed to lift you up, dope to calm you down. A perfect cocktail.

When Josh returned home, he'd have me mail him meth—junk he could score in North Hartford—concealed in unscrewed cassette tapes (which should tell you how far removed from this digital age we were). Josh joined our father at Fortman Brothers Construction. My brother reconnected with Amy. Soon they'd marry.

When you first start using drugs, it's not like the movies where you're in an alley, pants at your ankles, eating out of dumpsters. With a little finesse, you can pull it off.

Then I learned Mom was dying. I returned east, admitting I had a problem. I wasn't letting my mother die with me being a junkie. I went to rehab and got clean. She still died. Off the meth, my glued-together brain fell apart. A blessing in disguise, as doctors began connecting my condition to the accident, prescribing FDA-approved medications to treat my worsening symptoms, even if no one yet had a name for it.

Mom wasn't in the ground a week before we learned our father was sick, too. Unrelated. He'd be gone six months later. Myelofibrosis from a contaminated job site. Our father's death was big news. This was the Erin Brockovich era. Fortman Brothers won a huge settlement against the company that was supposed to have tested for hazards, Blackguard, Blacksmith, something like that. A stand-up guy, Andy Fortman matched that settlement, helping care for victims and their families, paying out *millions*.

Neil left all his money to our stepmom.

Josh never liked Debra. After that, he hated her. He said she was a greedy, bad person. I stuck up for her—how could I *not?* It wasn't her fault our father cut us out of the will. Debra was the closest thing to a parent I had left. She tried to fix me, paying for specialists. CAT scans showed a small shadow on my frontal lobe. A scar from the bike accident. It would take a while before an official diagnosis. Within a year, I'd lose the ability to read, write, or speak.

Debra found the Bay Area Institute for People with Traumatic Brain Injury in Napa, an hour north of the city that nearly proved my ruin. Now it was my only hope.

That was thirteen years ago.

I've been living there since.

Until now.

CHAPTER FIVE

THE BODY IN THE RIVER

After a power nap on a bed too soft with an abundance of pillows, I wake to a quiet house. It's dark. I'm not expecting to be fed dinner—I can feed myself—but I feel overwhelmed. It was light when I fell asleep. Now it's dark. I find that switch over, from day to night, unsettling. I am fine if I *see* it happening, witness the transition. But if I fall asleep when it's light and wake in the dark, I arouse disoriented, out of sorts, discombobulated. We've covered this in therapy, and practitioners all agree there is a deeper, psychological underpinning for this emotive response. It represents a liminal moment, crossing over. Before, after. One life of light, and another existing in the dark.

I quickly check my email, hoping Josh has caught wind I am back in town. Even if he's on a run, dropping anchor in another port, to use a polite euphemism, I'm hopeful he'll let *me* know all is well. Nothing to worry about. Even if it's a boldface lie, I'll gladly buy it. After my meeting with detectives, their urgency is rubbing off on me. I want reassurance my baby brother is okay. When I open my email and find nothing, I accept my wishful thinking was never realistic. Even if he were stuck up at a job site with lousy cellular service, he's not leaving his wife and daughter to worry. For five *or* three days. Josh might need a suitable lie to cover tracks, or track marks as it may be, but it is I who has been lying to himself. Josh did write three days ago. He sounded fine. It's been almost a week since his *family* has heard from him. I can't explain that. Or maybe the answer was there all along. I'm lousy with numbers. Five days. Three days. You've been relying on my math? I'm forced to admit willful ignorance. Something has been wrong the entire time.

I poke my head out the doorway, peering up and down the hall. The door to Debra's room is open. I creep to the threshold, knocking lightly, easing it open. Empty.

Descending stairs, I find no one there either. It's eerily still, like the calm before an earthquake. We get those frequently out west. Right before the ground shakes, rattles, and rolls, the wind stops blowing, leaves cease trembling, and then … nothing. For an infinitesimal second, the world seems to stop spinning. The only movement: birds fleeing higher into the sky. Then: boom! It feels like that now, as if the floor beneath my feet is about to tear apart and I'll need to seek shelter beneath a table. Is this my anxiety speaking? Or my sixth-sense premonition picking up on imminent danger? I'm not worried about an earthquake—the East Coast seldom experiences them. Thunderstorms, cloudbursts, torrential rains, nor'easters, bomb cyclones, sure, but the ground here remains sturdy.

It's unlike my stepmother to leave without telling me. I know I can help myself to whatever's in the fridge. I am less hungry and more restless, propelled by the need to be moving. When I get anxious, I find moving, in any direction, walking, running, climbing hills, helps calm my worried mind. Plus, I don't want to eat Debra's food. I can take care of myself. I have money and credit cards.

I don't want to go into town because I don't want to be recognized, but I have nowhere else *to* go. I can only pace around the kitchen and stare out dark windows so long.

Like many, when I look in the mirror, I see the same kid I did in high school. I don't see the wrinkles or ravages, the forehead furrows. My crow's feet are still faint enough to be hinted at rather than a confirmed sighting. I have a full head of hair. I see a young man. Until someone snaps my picture, presents photographic evidence in unflattering lighting. I'm not what I once was. I'm turning into an old man. I'll be fine going into town. No one will recognize me. It's the lies we tell ourselves that let us keep on living.

A change of scenery will do me good.

It's only a mile or so to the town bar, Sliders, well within walking distance. Then again, as the joke goes: everything is if you have the time.

Tramping down Worthington Ridge, I trace the Turnpike, past Micky Finn's motorcycle shop, left on Deming, before slicing right in front of the old ghost house.

When we were kids, we convinced ourselves the house was haunted. The abandoned gothic home looms like a set piece stripped straight from *Psycho*. The Bates Motel with steeper rates. The unruly yard sprawls tall and rebellious, corndogs on sticks, cattails swaying in the soft summer breeze. The night is warm but cooling fast. The house sports cracked windows and splintered doors, imposing its gothic aesthetic. I haven't seen this house in over a decade. Doing so now unnerves.

Before. After. Light. Dark.

I make my way toward the town's favorite watering hole, which is down Episcopal Road. If you're sensing religious overtones, ding ding. In Berlin, you learn to lean hard on Jesus.

The bar, Sliders, was established in 1993, around the time I left. I had soft drinks with Josh last time I was back. I don't want a drink, but there's food. Not particularly *good* food. I didn't eat when I landed, which means I haven't eaten all day. I'm not a big eater. Never been much of a foodie. I eat to live, not live to eat. I guess that (and the long walks) keeps me in shape.

Stepping inside, I feel out of place. My collared shirt, dark jeans, and nice shoes scream pretentious among the throng of flannel, cords, and trucker caps, the beer-bellied men and pear-shaped women with frosted wedges. So many red hats. Several large televisions broadcast competing baseball games—Yankees, Red Sox. Equidistant between Boston and New York, the town's allegiance is divided. It's not uncommon to see NY Giants jerseys and Boston Red Sox caps, Yankee hats with Tom Brady tees.

Eyes flash on me. Not because they know me. I am different.

Berlin has always been insular. I worry I carry myself with inflated airs, personifying the dreaded coastal elite stereotype. Not everyone here leans right—you can find liberals if you look hard enough at the library—but the red hats outnumbering blue extends beyond baseball loyalty.

Maybe I sound pompous, overselling my lifestyle. I'm not Prince William or a Hollywood movie star. I don't live in villas on the Mediterranean Sea, even if the Institute's predominant architectural scheme feels Italian. I operate in contrast to the rest of these people, who are happily inebriated, flinging darts over pitchers of Bud Lite. This isn't political affiliation. I don't belong here. Not then. Not now.

Sidling to the bar, I take a stool and motion for a menu, gesturing at the picture of a Diet Coke, an easy logo to spot.

In between the ball games, John Mellencamp laments about living long after the thrill of living is gone. How many times have I heard this song—and that line—on classic rock radio? This might be the first time I truly get it. For me, the thrill has been gone for a long, long time.

"You want anything to eat?" the bartender asks.

I point at a picture of a chicken sandwich. I'd prefer a burger but don't feel like playing charades to get it delivered medium rare. Cooking meat beyond medium rare is barbaric. Ordering food, I've learned to keep it simple.

Stealing side-eyed glances, I can name several former classmates. Jim, Ron, Jack. If they know me, they don't let on. My meal arrives faster than I'd think it would take to cook a chicken breast. The first bite tastes microwaved, which is fine. It fills my belly, will keep me going, kill time. When the clock hands hit the top, I pay my tab, head out the door, and make my way back to my stepmother's place.

The walk gives me too much time to think, and it takes concerted effort to stop my brain from going places I don't wish to visit. At the haunted house, I run down the list of women I wouldn't mind seeing again, the ones from high school, my all-time, desert island top five. It's a game I play to distract myself. I mentally recite Super Bowl winners, making it backward to 1983, confident I've gotten most correct. I am not obsessed with football, sports, or lists. I don't want to learn what is coming next. I am not prescient. I don't own a crystal ball. But I can *feel* it.

I refuse to think about my brother. Three days is nothing. Jesus Christ was gone that long, *died*, and still got half the streets in this town named after Him.

A week is too much.

Taking a different route, I head toward my brother's house on Christian Lane, which cuts through the center of town. Before that, a crest, a knoll, a few industrial outlets and factories. Behind me, nighttime traffic whizzes on the Turnpike, receding in the background, roaring engines and chugging motors lost to the night. Like a

Springsteen song, the mills are closing, jobs are leaving and they won't be coming back. I distract my racing thoughts by singing these songs in my head about my hometown, wishing I had my brother's life. I would've liked a little one to sit on my lap, tousle his hair, tell 'em to have a good look around. This is your roots. This will always be where you are from no matter how long you run.

I convince myself this distraction is why I don't comprehend the flashing blue and red lights in Josh's driveway.

Josh is just partying, getting high. He wouldn't run out on his family. He'd never leave Emily. Why do these detectives have to keep prying? This is the narrative I've bought into, the story we are going with, ignoring any evidence to the contrary.

Which is why, even as I walk up the driveway, see the three new shiny Berlin PD vehicles and the sullen, morose officers with their heads bowed beside them, I refuse to panic. Everything is going to be okay.

When I see Amy and Emily outside, sobbing, I can't lie to myself anymore. The illusion is shattered, centers can't hold. I catch Emily's eyes, filled with the questions I cannot answer.

Details and specifics don't matter.

I'm briefed anyway.

They found Josh's truck, submerged in the Connecticut River.

That's where Debra has been.

With Amy.

Identifying the body.

CHAPTER SIX

THE CHOCOLATE CHIP EFFECT

A jogger found my brother's dead body, bloated in a truck, while getting in some cardio along the Connecticut River during afternoon rush hour. Inhaling diesel fumes from the 84 and 91, working up a good sweat through the thrush and shoreline foam, weaving between the egrets, herons, and other one-legged birds. The jogger spotted the rusted metal shimmering in the sun. Authorities determined the truck had been there several days, plugged in the muddy silt and slimy sludge of the grimy river. With the recent sweltering temperatures, enough water had evaporated to reveal a license plate.

I've spent most of my adult life numb. Everyone in this town knows my history. I did drugs. Lots of them. When the money came in, I found a new address to do them. With money, drugs come legally. I'm prescribed the same drugs I abused when people considered me a scumbag. My dysarthria grants me license, a lifetime script to a multitude of mind-numbing agents. Diazepam, muscle relaxants. The migraines and brain trauma add opiates to the mix. Once upon a time, had police found any of these in my possession, I'd be sent to jail. Now? I receive written permission, via doctors' illegible signatures; I'm a compliant, respected member of society, a patient in good standing at one of America's most esteemed institutions. Back at Debra's house, in amber bottles, sit powerful narcotics, with the ability to swipe the slate clean. How much blanker can blank go? Right now, I'd love to fry every nerve ending. I've lost my brother. My best—only—friend. Better living through chemistry has its limits. I could pop every one of those pills and not feel any number than I feel standing in this driveway.

And, because life is a study in contrasts, at the same time, that numbness is equally matched by pain. Inaccessible pain. Like an itch buried underneath several layers of epidermis. Tangible, tenable, within my reach. Yet … like my words, I just … can't … get … to it.

Amy glowers at me. It doesn't matter how many years I've been on the straight and narrow. I'll always be the lowlife POS who got his baby brother hooked on drugs, which is what killed him in the end.

Even now, I'm full of shit.

I'm not worried about their judging Josh; I'm worried about their judging me.

Soon, Paul arrives in his JP Construction truck, followed by Amy's dad Andy in his bigger Fortman Brothers' one. Everyone hugs and laments the tragic loss. So young. So senseless. Like thoughts and prayers after another mass shooting, so … meaningless.

How arrogant to think that I, a mute dummy, would need to rise up in Josh' defense? Even the cops weep. Everyone here is a friend. Everyone here is part of the same community.

Everyone that is except me.

No one tells me, his *brother*, the full story. Instead, I slink along the shadows, a silent observer, piecemealing together my baby brother's final hours.

The story goes like this.

Highway patrol has my brother stopping off for a handle of vodka after work somewhere in Hartford. Again, *after*, not before. Several days ago.

"Coroner says at least four days," a cop tells Amy and Paul. "Maybe more."

Outside a liquor store on Park Street, Josh scored some pills from a guy who sold them. My brother was a big man with a bad back. Who doesn't pop the occasional Percocet or Vicodin? What goes better with liquor than opiates? For an addict? Like milk and cookies. Think about how big Josh was—close to six and half feet tall and over three hundred pounds? The big guy—that's what our mom used to call him—worked in the trenches, bending, hefting, wrenching, tearing his spine to shreds. Given his history, doctors weren't prescribing pain meds, and my brother wasn't the type to grovel. Maybe if they'd helped Josh manage his pain, monitored his in-take with urine tests…

The few times Josh could get a doctor to give him a break, the handful of pills they'd ration wasn't enough. He was a *giant*. With the opioid crisis, the FDA had been putting on the squeeze. Guys like my brother would never receive the relief he needed.

I know I am justifying, rationalizing, and making excuses.

Maybe Josh knew the pusher. Maybe the man was a stranger. They found an empty amber container, name and Rx number scratched out. Josh popped a perc. Only it wasn't a perc. Not all of it, anyway. The pill contained fentanyl, the trendy new filler dealers are using to extend the high of homemade stock.

"These pills," I overhear a detective say, "are like chocolate chip cookies. Think of the concentration of fentanyl like the chocolate chips in the cookie. Maybe you take a bite and miss the chip. Maybe you take a bite and get a mouthful. And by then? It's too late."

The poison kicked in between the 84 and 91 split. Josh probably felt funny, pulled off the highway and headed down to a vacant lot, planning to steal a power nap, concealed by black knot fungus on birch branches, cotton-webbed, fuzzy white beech blight and aphid nests, shrouded from passersby, semis and tractor trailers barreling down the boulevard, all oblivious to a man slowly dying alone. After he over-dosed, he fell on the gear shaft. With no means to engage the brakes, the truck rolled into the river. Which is where my brother drowned, out of sight. And where he'd remain submerged, dead, until that jogger found him.

This is all speculation, a detective reiterates.

"Any leads?" Paul asks. "About the scumbag who sold him that shit?"

The detective—this time I catch his name, at least his first name, Gary—turns his head enough for Paul to follow his gaze, their eyes landing on me.

I wasn't even in town until today!

"Truck was extracted earlier this afternoon," says the other detective, who still hasn't given his name, or maybe he did and I was too late and missed it.

"We're sorry for your family's loss."

Every cop says it.

"Please accept our thoughts and prayers."

No one looks at me when they say it.

I'm standing right here! His brother, the last person to speak with Josh, in a manner of speaking. I hopped on a plane and flew across the country at the drop of a hat. No one loved Josh more than me. So why do I, a man who hasn't ingested an illicit narcotic in over a decade, feel like the main suspect?

The detectives mill and officiate. Amy, Paul, and Berlin's finest converse, hover, huddle, and sign off on formalities.

Emily comes to my side.

"I guess you're leaving, huh? Back to San Francisco?"

I nod.

"But you'll wait for the funeral?"

Of course, honey.

When I look in Em's eyes, I identify what eluded me earlier. It's the look of someone with questions. I have them too.

Chief among them: if Josh had been dead for several days—"at least four," detectives said—who was emailing me three days ago?

CHAPTER SEVEN

YOU'RE ONLY AS GUILTY AS YOU LOOK

The next morning, I shower and shave at Debra's. We don't communicate over coffee downstairs, standing awkwardly at the counter, gazing out the kitchen window, over the still meadows of this quiet town. We are both devastated. The longer you live, the more you lose. Josh wasn't as close to our stepmother as I was. He was still her son. Neither of us were prizes; I didn't see anyone else champing at the bit to pick up the mantle. The regret eats away at her. I can feel it. When people die, it doesn't matter if you had a good relationship with them or a bad one. Death gets the last word. No returns. No exchanges. No do-overs. If you didn't get in that apology before the final bell, tough cookies.

Debra and I drive to meet Amy and her dad at the Erickson & Hansen Funeral Home. I sit on the end, my chair as far from Amy and Andy as possible. Debra is only person in the room who doesn't openly display disdain for me. Thank God I'll be back at the Institute soon. I want my private room with my coloring books, thick markers, and big blocks of numbers, patted on the head for being a good boy.

I wish Andy didn't hate me. Unlike Ari Fortman, Andy is a good man. I don't blame him for hating me—he only knows half the story, the one from his daughter, which focuses on my horrible influence. Moreover, I don't hold the man accountable for our father's death.

Because Fortman Brothers were victims too. The company that was testing the soil? Blackgate. They're the real villains here. I can't tell him any of this.

Blackgate's culpability came out during the insurance investigation. I don't know much about that world, construction, but I *do* know that anytime construction begins on a new project, especially one with potentially hazardous chemicals, they have to test the soil. And this soil? Next door to the Milford Power Plant? It carried higher risk for toxins. If Blackgate does their job, Fortman has a chance to treat the site and make it safe. Can't grease enough palms to bypass safety protocol, even if your brother is a political bigwig like Ari Fortman. This process is overseen by the EPA and liberal organizations, Save the Earth and the Sierra Club, the hippy-dippy tree huggers. I laugh, internally, remembering the time Josh told me about going to a job site and a bunch of longhair bicyclists blocked his entrance, holding mammoth signs to "Save the Rock." This is why people hate liberals.

The company tasked with checking the soil—I need to look up the exact name—it's not Blackgate. Maybe Blackjack? Whatever their name, the company reported the ground was safe to dig and drill. What was Fortman to do? They operated under false findings. The courts agreed. Independent contractors later found pockets of plutonium. If you want an analogy … think chocolate chips in a cookie. Like Josh, our father hit the wrong pocket. The courts ordered restitution. Blacksmith or whatever had to pay.

At first, I wondered why Josh hadn't gone into the family business— the Fortman Brothers are a well-respected outfit. Instead, Josh risked starting his own company. Maybe my brother *did* blame Andy. Except he'd married the man's daughter. Josh seemed to get along well with the entire family. Maybe not Ari. Who could get along with that skee-zeball? I don't know what the guy does for the president. I just know, like most politicians, he's a duplicitous snake. Or maybe I'm wrong about that too. I don't understand politics any more than I do drilling and blasting. I get my news the same way you do. Ninety percent of all media is owned by what? Six companies?

I prefer to focus on the positive. Josh didn't want to work for the Fortmans like our father. He wanted to be his own boss. Every son wants to surpass his dad. It's hardwired from the days of hunting and gathering. There's a great, if tragic, story about Joe DiMaggio's son. The Big Clipper's boy didn't even try. He dropped out, became a hobo, getting drunk and hopping trains. How can you compete with the greatest ball player of all time? I don't know if that story is true. Like so many tales in my personal collection, I prefer entertaining parables over verifiable realities.

For whatever reason—probably thinking about athletic superstars—I remember the time I flew back to see Josh inducted into the Berlin High Hall of Fame for his outstanding accomplishments in wrestling and football. My brother holds several records that will never be broken. This was a few years ago, our parents long since departed.

"I'd like to thank my mom," Josh said, after he'd stepped to the lectern to accept his award, titling his head toward the heavens. Before, with perfect timing, gazing at the floor: "I'd thank my dad too. But I have a feeling he's in the other place."

Recalling the joke, I laugh out loud. My version of a laugh anyway. The shrill screech escaping my mouth is loud enough that the director of the funeral home, Clark Whatever, Amy, Andy—and even Debra— leer my way.

I didn't bring along my Prologue2Go. Even if I had, how could I explain my headspace? I don't want to be part of this conversation.

Clark the Director, Amy, Andy, and Debra pick out Josh's final resting accoutrements. Casket and lining, gold and maroon (so regal), discussing how grand the tombstone will be. Dick measuring in the afterlife. Crass, I know. Josh would appreciate the joke.

You know it, brother.

I whip my head around, swearing I heard my brother's voice, before accepting I imagined it. Josh's voice will always be in my head. Josh doesn't leave this life when he dies. Josh leaves this life when *I* die.

Knowing Amy, she'll erect a mausoleum to make King Tutankhamun envious. The biggest marker in the cemetery so all eyes will be on how magnanimous she is.

Daddy says, "Whatever you want, love."

And when my brother's many affairs come to light—which Amy knows damn well about—she'll win martyr points on that front too. The long, suffering spouse who endured infidelity and drug abuse and *still* stood by her man. In Berlin, the virtuosity of Tammy Wynette's mandate lands somewhere between tying yellow ribbons around big oak trees and overlooking the pedophilia of nearby churches.

I can feel my heart racing, seizing, pounding. I make a show of retrieving my script and toppling a pair of Valium. I don't care what these people think of me. Who are they to judge?

"The mahogany chestnut casket is only twelve thousand and comes with a veneer finish."

Only twelve gee? For that price, you're losing money if you *don't* buy it. What a crock.

Erikson & Hansen is no different than any other funeral home. I'm letting my emotions best my intellect. Angry. Blaming. In denial. I'm hopscotching around Kubler-Ross like an ADHD kid with hotfoot.

By this point, we've all stood up and exited the office. Amy and her dad walk solemn through the venue, Clark the Director highlighting some of the home's finer features. Debra takes my hand, squeezing it.

The act of compassion does little to sooth the raging beast inside. I gesture at my heart, conveying I need time alone.

"Of course, dear."

The funeral home has a chapel where one can kneel and converse with the god of their choice. A sign reads, "All Faiths Welcome." It's plastered beside a photograph of blond-haired, blue-eyed Jesus.

I can't go in the chapel. Like Doc Holliday, my hypocrisy only goes so far. Instead, I stalk these halls, searching for someone to blame. All the walls are painted soothing shades of tan: taupe, buttermilk, sandcastle, biscotti, hazelnut, fawn, eggnog, and of course the Mona Lisa of light brown: beige. I took art classes. Before the accident, I was a very good artist. I'm not overselling that. It's not bragging to say, once upon a time, I could've been what's called "a Renaissance Man." Don't blame me. I didn't make up the term. I could draw, paint, write, compose music. In fact, I was so gifted in the arts, my father was certain I was gay. Which, in Berlin, back then, was the closest he could come to saying he hated me.

When I return from my solitary walk, I overhear Andy telling Clark, "Money is no object," before addressing his daughter: "Honey, you pick out any package you want."

After that, it's choosing thread counts, what type of fancy pillow my brother's head will rest on while decomposing into the afterlife.

Josh wouldn't give a shit. It's how he and I viewed death. Recent hallucinatory delusions aside, I don't believe in Heaven. Or Hell. Dead is dead.

No one wants me here anyway.

I ghost. I think that's what the kids call it.

If anyone sees me cut out, no one bothers with goodbye.

CHAPTER EIGHT

AT EVERY OCCASION I'LL BE READY FOR A FUNERAL

If people were pretending not to recognize me at the bar the other night, they can't pull the same stunt now. My widowed sister-in-law and I stand at the entrance of the funeral home. Greeters. Such an odd custom. Not sure how it all got started, this formality to acknowledge grief with an earnest handshake and empty platitude.

I endure endless variations of "Sorry for your loss" until I want to puke. Surrounded by statuettes of the Virgin Mary cradling an emaciated Jesus dripping bloody from the cross, I've never been happier to be mute. The ritual is garish. There are no words. If I could speak, I'd scream.

Hearing Amy's crying is awful. I know her tears are genuine, birthed from the deepest pits of despair. I loved my brother, faults and all. Amy did too. If there was ever a time for a sincere, heart-to-heart moment, it's now. That river is too wide to cross.

I must shake a hundred hands, those two-handed handshakes, so the guest can let you know how sincerely they share your pain. None of these people share my pain. A wife? Okay. Daughter? Obviously. Of everyone at the viewing, my heart aches most for my niece. Since I've been home, the only person I've felt any affinity toward is Em. Debra and Paul have been kind, and it's meant a lot. But Em is my blood. Her absence from the receiving line is an act of mercy.

The stream of guests flows endlessly, to the point *my* back is throbbing.

I know most of these mourners and townsfolk, even if they avoid my eyes. They goddamn well recognize me. People get weird around others with handicaps and disabilities.

Berlin is not a big town. I could stay gone for another decade. I'd still recognize the entire class of '88, the year I graduated, and most of '92, the year Josh did. I accept condolences from every Rich, Rob, Ron, Jim, Jack, and Jon, before they drift off to gaze at flower arrangements, the tasteful, colorless bouquets for the dead.

While none of these encounters are pleasant, I am touched they've come to pay their respects to my brother.

I can't say I feel the same when I see ... *him.*

Ari Fortman, Mr. Washington D.C. himself. I'm shocked he's made the trip for something as trivial as a funeral, even if it's for his niece's husband. The last time I saw the SOB was at my brother's wedding where he wore, I shit you not, a shiny silver sharkskin suit. What a douche.

Ari mills about, a pair of secret service flanking him. I assume they are security. They make no effort to ingratiate, scanning the room for potential threats. They don't have on sunglasses, and they aren't sporting earpieces. But the matching blazers that stretch at the shoulders give them away. The sight is comical—as if an assassin were coming to the Erickson & Hanson Funeral Home take to out Ari Fortman— as well as sobering. Ari's presence is a reminder of everything grim and unjust. My brother's death. The flailing state of the union. The hypocrisy of the human race. On one hand, Ari Fortman is just a man. He bleeds and shits like anyone else. He also represents a perverse form of idolatry of American royalty. There's a subset of the oppressed that champions the one percent, lauds their greed, celebrates tax evasion as evidence of superior business acumen. Watching that smug prick work the room fills me with a red-hot crimson rage.

If I was half the man I thought I'd be, I'd…

What? What would I do? Nothing. But standing by idly, letting a snake like Ari Fortman slither through the garden feels wrong, too.

I make for the viewing room.

As unpleasant as the gladhanding—or sadhanding as it were—was, I am grateful for the closed casket. Seeing my dead brother in his suit with that mortician's pancake make-up would be more than I could bear. I hate open caskets, the deceased on display. We did that for my mom. Awful. A polka dot dress and pearls. My final impression of the woman I loved most in this world, a gaudy outtake for a Target ad.

Without a pulse or soul, we are meat puppets. You can feel the cold-ness, the absence, the human body but a shell. I don't need to imagine the decomposition, worms crawling through sockets, bones drying until they are dust in the wind. Save it for classic rock radio. I want to remember my brother the way he was: larger than life.

In front of the casket, I kneel and fold my hands in prayer. I'm not religious. I hate the term "spiritual." I'm also not vain or hubristic enough to denounce the possibility of an entity greater than I.

I try to find the words in my head to say goodbye, give my bother a chance to answer. I heard Josh's voice earlier—his *real* voice—talking to me. Now when I need it most? Total silence.

You've always been a stubborn bastard.

Unable to kneel any longer, I rise to my feet, pretending not to feel the stares, and wipe my eyes dry.

The funeral team preps for the eulogy, essentially a practice run for tomorrow's main event at the church. Before he takes the stage, the priest asks Amy for Josh's favorite meal and/or restaurant. It's an odd question. I don't understand why a priest would want to know the answer to either. Who cares what a dead man liked to eat or where he liked to eat it?

The priest ascends to the podium to begin his sermon. "I know it's hard for so many of you. You won't be able to go with Josh to the Great Taste restaurant and share Capitol Chicken with him—"

And then I realize why the priest asked Amy that question. Because the priest doesn't know fuckall about my brother. He's up there adding colorful details to an otherwise generic eulogy, insert name here, pretend to give a shit, collect tithing. It's his job. In ten minutes, this priest won't give my brother a second thought. Not sure why it pisses me off so much. But the charade makes me get up, rattling my chair hard enough to invite stares and whispers as I storm outside.

Light rain falls.

That's your baby brother crying.

Now you want to talk?

Hahahaha.

I know they are not real. These voices. I accept they are a symptom of my illness. What I may have glossed over earlier, or perhaps skipped outright: doctors have warned me it was a matter of time before I broke for good; before neurological circuits rerouted, found new ways to make sense of my surroundings, which is a fancy was of saying eventually I'll go insane.

"How you holding up?"

When I turn over my shoulder, I'm not sure who I expect to find. But among the last on any list would be Freddie, my brother's disgruntled, former business partner. A short man, Freddie stands on the top step of the backstairs. I'm on the bottom rung. Which puts us eye to eye. He lights a cigarette.

"Haven't smoked these cancer sticks in eight years." Freddie gestures over his shoulder, down the hill toward a bright gas station without a name. "Stopped in for a pack. Figured I might need it tonight."

We remain under the awning, rainwater dripping. I get the impression Freddie has more on his mind than bad habits.

He thumbs over his shoulder. "See Ari Fortman in there?"

I nod. It's either that or a thumbs up. Both come across as childish.

"Nice for Mr. Washington D.C. to make the trip." Freddie laughs. "Good for him. Enjoy the vacation before they ship his ass to prison."

I cast a side-eyed glance.

"Guy's a crook. I don't trust him. Your brother sure as shit didn't." Then making sure he has my full attention: "Andy and his brother are closer than you think."

I'm not sure the point Freddie is trying to make. The guy doesn't like me, and last I heard, he and Josh weren't even speaking after my brother siphoned funds from their company to support his habit, leaving Freddie holding the bag.

The last thing I expect from Freddie is a friendly conversation. I *did* grow up with the guy. Maybe with Josh dead, Freddie regrets the hard line he took. Maybe making peace with his dumb brother is the next best thing. I haven't smoked a cigarette in over a dozen years, but I hold out my hand. Freddie passes along the lit one. It feels like the right thing to do. Smoking a cigarette with an old friend as a soft, summer rain falls outside the funeral home.

Freddie and my brother wrestled together. Quiet the odd couple, given cartoonish discrepancies, my brother a giant, and Freddie a shrimp. Those are the terms they used back in the '90s. We're more sensitive now. Josh and Freddie were superstars, dominating their respective weight classes. There were a lot of jokes about Arnold Schwarzenegger and Danny DeVito. That movie *Twins* had just come out.

I take a drag, coughing, but also soothed by the influx of nicotine.

Freddie peers over his shoulder, before descending into the rain, beckoning me to follow.

At his car, we flick our smoldering cigarettes into puddles and climb in the front seat.

Freddie turns on the car, letting it idle. The radio plays "Sweet Home Alabama," which cracks Freddie up. "You remember that band you had? Before… That night you called me and Josh up on stage and we sang this song together? Jesus, we were so wasted. I could barely stand."

I can't get a read on Freddie. First, he shocks me with the friendlier, tender tone. Now bittersweet nostalgia?

As for the memory? How could I forget? I was eighteen. Words still flowed from my mouth. At least when I was singing. Music freed up my voice. Cheap beer, scrawny chicken wings, and townies who thought shouting "Freebird" was funny (until we learned how to play the entire goddamn song, start to finish, eighteen-minute solo included. They stopped pulling that crap after that). It was one of those nights you remember forever, singalong songs scratched into your soul.

"You snuck us into the bar, telling the owner we were your roadies. What were we? Fourteen? Josh, I could understand. He looked twenty-one. But me? You must've stowed me in the bass drum. Or maybe you did a helluva job talking up the owner. Because you … you were a smooth talker back then. Before, it started to, y'know, get a little fucked up."

I catch his eyes in the rearview above us. Freddie's face washes sadder. No one ever knows how to broach my condition. I've heard people say my eyes retain light, a shine that doesn't go out, making it clear I understand, am fully cognizant. Which is true. We never know how we look through other people's eyes.

Freddie looks down, up, stares straight ahead, checks over his shoulder, before turning to me.

"Listen," he says, "I wanted to talk to you."

I figured as much when he invited me into his car. It's the subject matter that has me baffled.

"You know Josh and me had a falling out…"

Not a question. Hardly a secret. It's the hesitation that follows that piques my interest, a means to delay, which predicts pain and remorse, uncertainty. I'm not anticipating an apology. Josh betrayed a trust; Freddie played the hard card. Tough love. If Freddie needs me to absolve him? No problem. You're absolved.

My assessment of the situation is off base.

"You brother called me," Freddie says. "Same day he went missing." He catches himself. "Morning," he corrects.

I'm the wrong guy to ask about timely specifics, but in this case day and night are worlds apart.

"I don't want to stir drama or make shit worse. For you or Amy, or anyone. It's just…" Freddie halts, watching the light rain turn heavier.

"The morning he called me." Freddie blurts a laugh. "I couldn't believe it. We hadn't spoken… It'd been a while. I was surprised. Wasn't his cell—I wouldn't have picked up. Vermont area code. I usually don't answer strange numbers. I don't know anyone from Vermont, no one I want to talk to anyway. Honestly, it was five o'clock somewhere, y'know? I was having a breakfast beer. Maybe two. Caught me off guard. My first instinct was to tell him to get fucked."

Out the window, mourners gather by the back door, smoking under the awning. Seeing them, Freddie's gaze intensifies. He watches them— two men and a woman, none of whom I recognize—as if they were spies.

"What do you know about Blackmill Solutions?" Freddie finally says.

That was the name of the company that tested the soil for Fortman. Blackmill. Not Blackjack, -smith, or -gate. Blackmill. Blackmill Solutions. The name of the company is inconsequential, which is why I didn't commit it to memory. All that matters is their negligence resulted in senseless deaths.

I open my palms, *Sure, what about them?*

"I cut Josh out of my life," Freddie says. "But we lived in the same town. I'd see him, walking out of Stop and Shop. Sometimes at Sliders. He did me the dignity not to make scenes or try talking to me—I told him I didn't want to hear a goddamn word until he came up with a plan to pay back all the money he stole." Freddie regains his composure, having gotten himself riled.

I understand. I'd be mad too.

That's not why we're sitting in his car…

"From everyone I spoke with…" Freddie twists his head around, left, right. I can feel the conflict, how you can both hate and love someone even after they've done you wrong. "I knew Josh since we were eight. I'd check in with people. See how he was doing. Part of it was, sure, I wanted my money. I also wanted to know how he was." He pauses to swallow the hurt. "I missed him."

I don't envy the guy. Forgiveness is … complicated. I'm not sure I believe in it. A nice thing to say, but the gesture smacks of grandiose. Who am I to forgive anyone? Or you? Or vice versa? It's ego talking, believing we hold such a power, as if from this esteemed perch, one can gaze down upon the unwashed masses, and with a wave of the hand decree, "I forgive thee for thy transgressions." Okay, Jesus. It's hubris. We screw up and fuck over. Happens to us. Happens to them. At one point or another we've all been the bully, the victim, the offender and offended. You either accept and move on, or harbor a grudge and … move on. Forgiveness is a word to sell greeting cards.

"Josh was doing good," Freddie says. "He was staying off the hard stuff. Heard he wasn't even drinking." Freddie looks at me. "I guess you know this."

I know what Josh told me. I believed what was convenient. I can't be certain of the chasm between the two. It's nice to have the corroboration.

"The morning he called me," Freddie continues, "he *sounded* okay, but the shit he was saying … I mean, it was out there. Even for Josh. Weird-ass, conspiracy shit. Maybe it's not *too* weird, not when your uncle-in-law works for the president. But he was going on about Blackmill Solutions. He kept saying it was a shell company. For Fortman." He catches my eye. "Know what that is?"

I try not to look offended. Why wouldn't I know the definition of a "shell company"? I listen to audio books and true-crime podcasts.

"Emily was working on a class project. Getting a head start to the semester, I guess. Family tree or whatever. Josh was poking around the web, researching, and he made a connection. Josh says he learned Blackmill was a … subsidiary … of Fortman Brothers."

He waits for me to catch on. I will—once I catch up. This is more than a story about Josh. Our father's death, regardless of my personal relationship with the man, or lack thereof, produced rippling effects. We may not have seen eye to eye, but the man didn't deserve to die. Not the way he did.

"Let's put it in baseball terms," Freddie says. "Having Blackmill test the soil of the power plant is like having George Mitchell investigate whether David Ortiz was taking steroids."

For those of you unfamiliar with a good ol' American baseball analogy, trust me: Freddie knocked that one out of the park. To make the comparison easier to grasp for the non-baseball fan: it's another way of saying the fox was put in charge of guarding the henhouse.

"They—" Freddie again turns, speaking quieter—"Fortman Brothers—both Ari *and* Andy—knew that site, the one that killed your father, was contaminated. They *knew.* They sent him out there to work, knowing damn well that ground was poison. They didn't care."

I'm speechless. (Pun intended.) This can't be true, can it?

Again, like Freddie can read my mind: "Look it up. Easy to do. Right on the web, man. Fortman isn't even trying to hide it. Maybe they couldn't. That's the reason for the huge settlement, why Andy and Ari matched insurance payouts. It wasn't generosity. It was a payoff."

Freddie grabs my arm. He wants to make sure I hear this next part. I don't need the physical prompt, but I turn his way, leaving no doubt that I'm listening.

"I know you and Amy don't get along. But she loved your brother. I don't think Amy knew what her dad had done. He put her through some shit, too. I think your brother's recent relapse, or whatever—he was conflicted. Amy's still a Fortman. They're tied forever by *blood.* Knowing your father-in-law *knew* that ground was toxic? Sent your dad out to die because it was more cost-effective? Must've been tearing your brother apart."

Why wouldn't Josh mention this during our e-mails? He e-mailed me around the same time he was calling Freddie. He brought up *none* of this. He talked about the old days, evoking sweet memories like the time we got those matching daisy tattoos in San Francisco, shit like that. Walks down memory lane, on the sunny side of the street, steering clear of the heavy and morose. If this is true and Fortman *knew* the ground was tainted, *I'm* the one impacted—more than Freddie. I'm his brother. Maybe Josh didn't want to worry me? Or maybe he didn't want to leave an electronic trail? Which is a good thing since now detectives have my laptop and all our communications in their possession. And if Ari Fortman is involved, you better believe the Feds are having a look too. If true, this is huge. *If it's true…*

"They paid off the families and other workers who caught myelofibrosis like your dad. Had them sign NDAs—non-disclosure agreements. Put it in a search engine with your … thing." He means my Prologue2Go. "You won't have to dig deep. Few pages. Why wasn't this a bigger deal?" Then answering himself, Freddie says, "Because Ari Fortman is untouchable. Or was." He chuckles.

Ari's been in the news lately, exposed for the scum he is. The president is washing his hands of him, hanging the guy out to dry. Good. Nothing to do with construction, just your run-of-the-mill collusion with foreign governments. Connecticut is a tiny, insignificant dot on the map compared to Washington D.C. Ari is already in political hot water. Then again, maybe a leaked allegation about criminal malfeasance tips scales of injustice. The only thing worse than bad press isn't no press— it's press so awful and relentless supporters abandon you to save their own hide.

"Everyone signed the NDA. Except one." Freddie pauses for me to appreciate the magnitude. "Your brother."

Yeah, I've figured that out by now.

"He was with Amy, and I guess they thought… I don't know what they thought. Didn't matter. All the money went to your stepmother. I know you think Andy is the lesser of two evils, but he's as big an asshole as Ari. If Josh was poking around, found out that Blackmill and Fortman are one in the same… I'm not into conspiracies, but his phone call and time of death? That's not a conspiracy, man. That's paying attention. The Feds need one more thing to push their case against Ari over the line. Guy was still a full partner with Fortman Brothers when your father got sick. Look up the story in the *New Haven Register*. Your dad had a lawyer, Alice something. It's in there. Maybe she can help you." Freddie stops to shake his head. "Maybe Josh was using again. He seemed to have his shit together with Paul. Maybe this is all guilt on my end. Maybe I just hate Ari Fortman. All I'm saying?" Freddie catches my eye. "Have someone you trust double check that death certificate."

Freddie makes to open the door but stops. "One more thing: those emails from Josh? The ones after he went missing?"

How does Freddie know about those emails?

"Re-read those too." Freddie catches his mistake. "I mean, however, y'know, your computer…" Trying to converse with me must be hell. Freddie cuts his apology short. "If Josh *did* find something last minute? He'd relay that information to you. He trusted you more than anyone in this world."

CHAPTER NINE

DOWN GOES FRAZIER

After the memorial service, we drive back to Debra's house, the ride
subdued and melancholic. If I could speak, I'm not sure what I'd say.
Does it matter that she was awarded all that money? Debra never
shortchanged me. My father never liked me. He wouldn't have left me
a dime regardless. Josh would have the ax to grind. He and our father
were close. A lump sum would've allowed Josh to pay back Freddie and
start another company. Then again? Maybe that much money puts my
brother six feet under six times sooner. Josh was already pissed about
the Harleys.

When we get home, Debra says she's tired and is heading to bed.
She stops by my side and kisses the top of my head.

I sit in the living room, flipping through stations. Scrolling for
Yankee highlights, I land on a twenty-four-news network. Crisis in
the White House. What else is new? Every day is a circus with this
administration. What do you expect when you elect a reality TV star
president?

Upstairs in my room, I grab my Prologue2Go, fishing around
my rolling bag for the USB inputs and cables I'll need to plug into a
computer. The house is quiet, dark. Tiptoeing downstairs, I make for
Debra's desktop computer. I expect to find a locked screen. By now my

stepmom is asleep. I don't want to wake her to ask for the password. Truth is I don't want to confirm what Freddie told me. Nothing good will come of it. My brother will still be dead, and I fear I'll view Debra in a different light. I shake the mouse, surprised to find the computer fizzle to life, unlocked.

How much can one have to hide if their computer isn't password protected?

Before retiring, Debra was a notary. Hardly cause for extra cyber security. Attaching my P2G, I poke around the internet. A couple pages in, I find nothing incriminating on Blackmill Solutions, let alone corroboration of alleged ties to Fortman. I know it's possible to scrub the web. There are services you can hire to, if not eliminate, at least bury bad press, unfavorable Yelp reviews or whatever. That's for restaurant owners. A political bigwig like Ari Fortman would have more powerful tools at his disposal. Would it even be necessary? Yes, sending men to die in pits you know are hazardous is awful. That part makes me outraged. But you don't need to hide it. People can read about El Timor, El Salvador, and Grenada, and still not give a shit. Always struck me as hysterical countries like China censor their internet. You can give the public all the information they need, and people will still vote against their interests.

I sign into my email, looking for a smoking gun when it hits me: just because I received the emails three days after Josh went missing doesn't mean they were *written* three days after he went missing. I'm such an idiot. How many times have I been stuck playing catch-up because my P2G doesn't relay information in real time? No wonder no one else cared about my timeline for the emails. Authorities can trace electronic stamps to the second. The only way I can tell time is whether the big hand hits the top or the cow says "moo." To be thorough, I have my P2G repeat those final emails. Josh is up in Bennington, sharing mundane details of his job. The part about our matching daisies tattoos catches my attention but not because it's a clue; the memory is a nice one from happier if crazier days.

I unhook my P2G from the computer, head back upstairs to brush my teeth, floss, and do my push-ups. I sit on the edge of the bed, too wound up to sleep. Intrusive thoughts flood my head. Amped up, I am unable to power down.

I summon an Uber to bring me to Sliders. Not sure why. If I'm blowing my sobriety, I'm not doing it over fried pickles and schwag beer.

This might be hard to understand, but when you live the way I do—like a Victorian child, seen but not heard—sometimes the best place to hide is in a crowd. Sometimes the only way to drown out the silent screams that fill your skull is with the mindless chatter of strangers.

The rain has let up. A cool breeze washes over the evening, wiping everything clean. When I step inside Sliders, I am disappointed. No one I recognized the other night is here. No one from the funeral home or church or reception. Meaning I can't add the slight of feeling ignored to my list of woes. Like listening to sad songs after a break-up, I ache to ache a little more.

Loneliness hits differently when you digest news like I've been force-fed. Might as well throw in a few microwaved starches and carbo-hydrates, fresh from freezer to plate, come in out of the rain and get my insides really kicked out.

The townie bar isn't kitschy enough to pass as ironic. When you think of lowlife bars—and the Left Coast abounds with them—you imagine Bukowski or Kerouac, misanthropes drowning sorrows in dim basements, dark coves slathered in the deepest crimsons and other murderous colors. Sliders blazes brighter than Chuck E. Cheese on meth.

When the bartender approaches, I convey I'll take a Diet Coke.

Andras and Arioch Fortman knew the site that killed my father was contaminated. Josh found documentation. I navigated the web. Nothing jumped out. Then again: how deep did I dig? Not very. My "research" was a gesture, an item to cross off a to-do list.

Freddie said to revisit Josh's emails and "double check the death certificate." Why? I got the timing of the emails wrong, and I never *saw* a death certificate—I'm not sure I'd *want* one read to me. Even if Josh found proof Fortman knew the ground was contaminated, that isn't getting him whacked by the mob. Do people use phrases like "whacked" or "the mob," except on television shows like *The Sopranos?* Josh loved that one. I never got into it. Our shared background made *Breaking Bad* the more sensible binge.

I sip my Diet Coke, watching baseball highlights on the big screens, hoping for a Yankee win or a Red Sox loss. Either will do.

Like trying to not to think of a pink elephant.

My brother deserves closure. My father, regardless of our differences, deserves justice. Debra should know. *She already does.* She's been paid—and been paid well. If she signed an NDA regarding Blackmill and Fortman, she knows the truth. My stepmom doesn't seem conflicted over the hypocrisy. My father died unjustly. He was also an abusive prick who made my mother's life hell. Can't imagine he was any more pleasant around Debra. Maybe Willa Cather got it wrong: sometimes the wicked *do* get what they deserve. I keep telling myself this is not my fight. This was decades ago. Not my circus, not my monkey.

The bartender delivers a bowl of peanuts and refills my Diet Coke, which I throw back faster than he can ask if I want to keep the tab open.

I pop a couple pills, regulating my chemical imbalance. Someone puts on Springsteen.

Some men start dying little by little, piece by piece…

"Excuse me," a woman says.

I look up.

"I thought it was you!" The woman seems happy to see me. I *might* recognize her, even if I can't put a name with the face.

"Lisa?" she says.

Now I remember. I don't need a last name.

"Mind if I sit down?"

I smile and slide over, leaving plenty of room for Lisa to take the stool beside me.

Lisa doesn't look much different than she did in high school, even if it took me a moment to reacquaint time and place. She was pretty then. She's pretty now. We had several classes together. If I remember right, we went to a dance. One of those early school dances where boys and girls stand on opposite walls, staring at shoes and giggling. I think I fell in love with her. I fell in love with a lot of pretty girls in high school. I may've waited on her doorstep one night. My heart pangs. A part of me will forever be sixteen.

She's smiling, being friendly, chatty. She knows what I am, understands my limitations. Lisa doesn't make it awkward, carrying on a regular conversation as if I were a regular guy, even if I can't contribute much beyond eye contact and facial expression. I appreciate that.

Worrying I'm smiling too much, I force a furrow, whittle my stare, try not to look so desperate, crease my brow. It's nice to catch up with an old friend and feel normal for a change.

"Holy shit," a voice says.

I look up.

This time it's a man. Buzz cut. Squinty, yellow eyes. My age. The square blocked face of an asshole. I don't know this guy.

"I thought it was you!"

Has he been eavesdropping on our conversation? Because that is how Lisa introduced herself. Then again, it's a common expression. I nod, smile. *Yes, it's me. Nice to see you too. Whoever you are.* I wait for the man to leave. I'm in the middle of a conversation with Lisa, whose company I'm enjoying. This man squeezes past, obscuring her, being rude, until she's forced to stand and excuse herself. She says it was nice seeing me again, adding she hopes we can catch up later.

"You don't remember me, do you?" the cockblocking asshole says, turning over his shoulder, snickering.

I glance past his shoulder. At a small, round table another man sits, heavier, pug-faced, expression blunted. Raising a glass, he glowers. I don't know him either. I wave to be polite.

He stands next to me, this man I've never met, invading personal space.

"Rick?" he says. He doesn't offer to shake my hand.

I don't let it hurt my feelings.

"We graduated together. Class of 1988?" He punches a fist forward, close enough to graze my ear. I don't give him the satisfaction of flinching. "Go Redcoats!" He laughs.

His friend chortles. The friend isn't fat. Just bloated. Like a guy who used to lift weights in high school but then stopped, and now that muscle has hardened into stale Bundt cake around the belly, a firm muffin top, stiff flab.

They are dressed alike, two small-town underachievers—faded blue jeans, shitkicker boots—like they've stepped out of a Wranglers commercial chucking the ol' pigskin with Brett Favre. For whatever reason, you get these types in Central Connecticut, dudes who think they're rednecks from the South, as if that were something to be proud of; the kind of guys who never read a book after high school.

I turn back to my Diet Coke and peanuts, trying to flag the check.

"I guess you didn't actually graduate *with* us though, huh?" Rick's grin disappears. "You had that … 'accident.'" He puts the word in air quotes. God, I hate that.

I wave to the bartender, point at the two men.

Next round on me. Drink up. Leave me alone. I'm settling my tab and going home.

The man, Rick, isn't ready to do that yet. He swirls a finger over my head. "Fucking junkie. Scrambled your brain like a frog in Ursula Spiegel's science class." He turns over his shoulder, to his buddy. "Jeff, you remember, right?"

"Yeah, I remember. Had to take sped classes because he forgot how to count."

"Fuck that," Rick said. "Guy can't talk."

The bartender asks what he's having.

Rick doesn't answer. Instead, he leans over, elbow on counter, mean square head in my face, staring at me but talking to Jeff. "Couldn't even say his own *name* anymore. Teacher would call on him, and he'd be all, "B-b-b-b-b-b." Rick stops. Then starts again. "B-b-b-b."

Rick sneers, snorts, and calls for Jeff, who stands up. The pair walks past me, laughing, headed for the exit. I look around the bar for Lisa. She's gone.

What the hell?

Almost fifty years old. Who acts like that?

Walking out the door, Rick and Jeff are busting a gut so hard, you'd think they saw *Stepbrothers* for the first time.

So much room for activities…

I should let it go but feel the switch trip, anger flooding, zero to sixty.

I slap a twenty on the counter, hop off the stool, and follow them outside.

Jeff has gone ahead to fetch the truck. Rick is enjoying a last cigarette by the front door.

When Rick sees me, he turns around. "Hey, it's B-b-b-b—"

I'm not the toughest guy in the world. Never pretended to be. But I told you. My old man was a boxer. I know how to throw a punch. My father taught me that at least. And like the old man, I don't suffer slights easily.

One quick left hook to the ear, hard enough to do its job. You hit an ear well, you rupture the drum. You rupture the eardrum, equilibrium evaporates. Without equilibrium, a man can't stand. Rick is bigger than I am. All things being equal, I'm sure he could kick my ass. But things aren't equal. Rick has a ruptured eardrum. When he squares up to throw a punch, he drifts sharply to the right, misses by three feet. I don't have to move. Like a kid spinning in circles until he makes himself dizzy, Rick faceplants into the brick wall, smacks his head, knocking himself on his ass. A small trickle of blood dribbles out his ear.

Jeff is in the truck, radio cranked, oblivious. The fucking Eagles. I stroll to the driver's side window, point at him, and instruct him to get out.

He can see behind me in the sideview mirror. Rick is trying to stand. Every time he gets to his feet, he stumbles around the same six feet of parking space, crashing into a new car.

Jeff shakes his head.

You don't want to get out?

Because of the rain earlier, I brought along a light jacket. I take it off, wrap my fist inside it, and punch a hole through his window.

The cops arrive soon afterward.

CHAPTER TEN

LIKE JOHNNY, I'LL WALK THE LINE

This isn't my first time in a jail cell. Although I'm pretty sure I never visited Berlin PD's refurbished accommodations. Don't think I visited the old ones, either. Most of my legal troubles took place out west in San Francisco. After I left Berlin, taxpayers voted to upgrade Town Hall, which included a new community center, senior living facility, and glitzy police department for a sleepy town's non-existent crime epidemic.

I lived in worse hotels in my twenties, single-room occupancy dumps with cockroaches so big you could converse with them over a cup of coffee, like Gregor in *The Metamorphosis*. Which stirs a funny memory. That was the last story I read to my mom. Except ... the timeline is out of order. My mother died in 2004. By then, I'd dropped out and was living in the Bay Area, hooked on meth, heroin, and anything else you'd put on the table. Yet, I distinctly recall sitting by her hospital bed, reading Kafka because I was taking a philosophy class at Central Connecticut State University. I'm getting confused again. My brain is reconfiguring history to fit with a new world order. I do not like when it does that. I feel like I am slipping through cracks, alternating realities, reinventing worlds where I am whole and restored, replacing this flawed incarnation with a functional iteration.

I wish I could chalk up these sensations to being high-as-hell, out-of-my-skull, tripping balls, like the old days when I'd shoot up narcotics until I tasted color. Early Pink Floyd tasted like cerulean.

Emily tries but misunderstands… Ahh, ooh…

A police officer appears at the bars.

"You don't remember me, do you?"

How many times am I going to be asked this tonight?

"Wayne? Berlin High…? Never mind." He rocks back on his heels, thumbs in belt loop. *I've seen this move before.* "So…" He lets out a groan that says, Oh boy this is not good. "That man you punched at the bar? Former cop. Not the nicest guy. He was an asshole in high school. He's an asshole now. He's gonna press charges. I don't know what he did to provoke you, but I'm guessing you didn't set out tonight to end up here."

Finally, a sympathetic ear.

"Listen, man, I'm sorry about your brother. Josh was a good guy. Helluva wrestler and football player, great dad. He's gonna be missed. I can't promise what the judge is gonna do, but my guess? Under duress. Your … handicap … whatever you call it. You're, um, being … differently abled."

Will you look at that? Even Berlin is getting in on the sensitivity training. Next up: stopping racism.

"Do you have anyone who can bail you out?"

I mimic a phone to my ear. The cop, Wayne, is a fast learner. He retrieves my iPhone.

I pull up Debra's contact information.

Of course, like a good mom, she's there so quick I don't have time to think of ways to break out of a holding cell.

You never know when that skill might come in handy.

———

"Oh, honey," Debra says, once she's finished the paperwork, and is walking me out of the jail to her car.

A nip of autumn air has snuck in with the early morning breeze. My stepmom says she was worried when she woke and found me gone. Although no texts have come through on my phone. I know how difficult I can be to reach. If I don't have the P2G plugged in and an adapter set up, I often don't receive notifications let alone respond.

I feel bad for making my stepmom leave her house at this hour. At least it's a short drive back.

Most of the houses along Worthington Ridge's historic district are big. Debra's is bigger than most. Perched atop the tallest hill, her palatial manor lords over suburban flats.

Walking inside, I catch the upgrades I missed before. The home, which was always large, has grown larger. New additions, including a massive kitchen, add to the splendor. The kitchen is an odd inclusion for a single, older woman who doesn't cook. Perhaps since retiring, Debra has picked up new hobbies, like baking her own bread.

It's late. I head upstairs to bed. I don't get far before my stepmom calls after me.

She's retrieved an ice pack from the freezer for my fist.

"You are your father's son," she says, forcing a grin.

I return the gesture and wait for her to leave. She doesn't. I wait for her to say more. I yawn. I don't mean to be rude.

"You get some sleep," Debra says, before turning, disappearing down the long hall.

———

I wake to a thunderstorm. The house is lightless. It is dark but morning. Ominous clouds roil and churn on the horizon. Hard rain plinks against glass, winds whooshing, water splashing off the roof. There is a clock on the bedside table. Numbers gleam red. I add fingers. Three of them.

The home feels empty. Like it did the other day when they found Josh's body.

A text dings on my phone. I translate to voice. Debra.

Hope you had a good night's rest, sweetheart. I had errands to run. Make yourself at home. I suggest you grab a pint of ice cream and watch TV. You're looking a little thin...

Thin? I'm six feet and two hundred pounds.

Then: *If you need to go into town for anything, the keys to your father's old truck are on the counter.*

I don't need to go anywhere, but it's been a while since I've seen the old man's truck. I can't remember what it looks like, to be honest. I snag the keys off the counter, and right away notice it's a fob and not an actual key, and when my dad died, that wasn't really a thing. Walking through the mudroom, I enter a massive garage. I see a truck. It's not my dad's. It's brand spanking new, or at least a recent model. Shiny, white, barely used. A large bed for tools. I shut the garage door, retreating inside to escape the relentless rain, which sounds more menacing inside the cavernous garage, rainstorm in surround sound, like an app to fall asleep to.

Opening the refrigerator, I find fresh vegetables, lunch meats, and assorted cheeses. There's a quart of milk and several juices, apple, orange, cranberry. Debra must've picked them up this morning or had them delivered. I don't recall a stocked pantry. For a moment, I feel bad for doubting Debra's integrity. After speaking with Freddie, I'd gotten all turned around.

I select roast beef, Swiss, and mustard and make a sandwich. Dark storm clouds make it difficult to deduce the exact time of day. I could easily ask my P2G, but I have nowhere to be—time doesn't matter. Three numbers say it's before ten. Close enough.

Sandwich in hand, I head back to the office, the stylish iMac desktop another odd addition for a retiree. Next to the set-up, I spy the tools of my stepmom's former trade, notary stamp and ink pad. I hope they at least gave her a gold watch at the party. I shake the mouse, stirring the computer to life. I plug my Prologue2Go into the USB port and pull up a Google browser, and have my device access "Milford Power Plant."

Unlike my perfunctory efforts last night, I get a hit on the *Hartford Courant* site. When my father was sick, I didn't read up on what killed him. That might sound awful, but I was coming off drugs, fighting my own battles, and though we *did* reconcile before he passed, I can't say we had much to say to one another, me because I literally couldn't, and my father because he was the product of a different era. My father managed to say he was proud of me for cleaning up, which was the first time my father said he was proud of me for anything.

The project that killed my dad—excavation for a retail outlet next door to the Milford Power Plant—began in the nineties. It was a massive undertaking. Last night, I glossed. This time I delve. The further I travel into cyberspace, the more I learn. Particulars I missed last night jump out. I listen, riveted to detailed accounts of gross negligence. I search for holes to poke in Freddie's story. My life will be a whole lot easier once I do.

I don't know how long I'm at the computer but three numbers turn to four. I encounter the name Blackmill Solutions. I don't hear proof linking them to Fortman, nothing concrete anyway, nor do I uncover evidence of collusion. After my dad died, there *was* an investigation, but the focus was on the power plant itself, not Fortman, Blackmill, or any other subsidiary. At the time, State House Majority Leader James Amann (Democrat out of Milford) had issued a statement that a special committee was being assembled to determine potential environmental violations by the Milford Power Plant. The article alludes to workers from an unnamed construction outfit—I assume Fortman—but again, the culprit caught in the crosshairs is the power plant, not Andy or Ari.

I hit stop. Something isn't sitting right.

Think, brother. With great power comes great responsibility…

I am far from a superhero, but last night while Freddie reiterated specifics, I couldn't help but chuckle, internally, how so many superheroes have an origin story that begins with an accident. Bruce Banner and gamma radiation. Spider-man bitten by a radioactive bug. Wolverine, a secret government experiment where he gets all his bones replaced with Adamantium. The point: to gain extraordinary powers, we must surrender something precious. (Like Thanos and the Infinity Stones.) I received healthcare and a place to live. My dad died. But what if the *real* spoils were the talents and abilities I gained from my *own* accident? When I lost … did I also win?

Besides a photographic memory, the accident instilled in me word-for-word auditory retention.

"The Feds need one more thing to push their case against Ari over the line. Guy was still a full partner with Fortman Brothers when your father got sick. Look up the story in the New Haven Register. *Your dad had a lawyer, Alice something. It's in there…"*

I refine my search, altering the timeline, adding "Alice" and *New*

Haven Register.

There it is. Blackmill Solutions. The company tested the soil. And it came back positive for trichloroethylene, which is toxic as fuck. In a related article, I also learn the Fortman Brothers recently had to pay two point four million dollars for lying to the United States government. Another violation. Seems Fortman hasn't learned any lessons. My P2G reads the specifics regarding what killed my father and his men.

Then, there at the end, a robot recites what I can't read in black and white: Blackmill Solutions is an extension of Fortman Brothers Construction. I had to search to find it, but I *did* find it.

Andy and Ari Fortman aren't merely greedy capitalists; they're killers. That's why Josh didn't want to work for them.

I start to recall conversations with my brother, where Josh talked and I listened, and now my mind, unencumbered by conventional communicative restraints, dials up those conversations, as if they've been archived on microfiche.

"I know you and Amy don't get on too well," Josh said. "She isn't like her father or uncle. They don't share shit with her. My father-in-law has money. Ari is well off. The company holds all the cash. Those two are selfish. Andy? His own kid? He wouldn't even co-sign on the mortgage to speed up the process."

Why had I suppressed that? I invented a narrative where my brother got along great with his father-in-law, augmenting facts to make reality easier to stomach.

Now that I think about it, I remember Josh telling me Andy gave them wine glasses and linens for a wedding gift. Family with that much money? Towels and cups.

Outside the rains ease up but clouds hang heavy and leave me cold.

We all have repeated phrases and patterns that soothe, offer comfort in times of distress. When we don't have our own words, we need to borrow another's. I play Pink Floyd on my iPhone.

Then I have my P2G repeat that story about the two and a half million dollars. It's mentioned in passing, a minor fine, unrelated to what killed my father. But the discovery establishes a pattern of behavior. Dialing back time, jumping around, I uncover more fines, more violations, more irrefutable evidence of Andy and Ari acting as if they're above the law.

None of this has been enough to put Fortman out of business. The construction company still ranks among the biggest in New England, and Ari has been catapulted to coffee talk in the Oval Office.

They pay the fines, bury the dead, and move on.

The sonsofbitches have the money to make *any* problem go away.

Like my dad. Like my brother.

Will I be next?

CHAPTER ELEVEN

THE BLACK PARADE

The following morning, we assemble for the big chill to say our final goodbyes. Slate skies that have been gray and gloomy since the viewing part, freeing the sun to shine majestic. Through St. Paul's stained-glass ceiling, a golden ray of cosmic light beams across the mahogany casket, a sunburst castoff from the Good Lord Himself.

Kidding. It's pissing rain. Again.

You get a lot of these summer storms this time of year, spur-of-the-moment cloudbursts, thunder booming like cannon blasts. Relentless of late. This one comes on fast and powerful, like a migraine, as we all pile into the town church where we buried our mother, our father, and now my brother. I sit in the front row with Debra, Emily, and Amy. Andy Fortman is here, Ari Fortman apparently unable to get the day off work.

Amy delivers her tear-filled eulogy. I'm not mocking the woman—I know her pain is real—but the performance feels rehearsed. Watching Emily is tougher. Losing a husband stings. A kid losing her dad cuts deeper. I can't deal with the pain, reaching in my pocket for my pills. The priest takes his place at the pulpit in his white and green robe, urging us all to open our hymnals to a hymn I cannot sing.

Released from these chains that bind me, I skip the ragged choruses, piping organs, and angel-plucked harps, free to recall better days.

My attention returns to the present with movement at the end of the aisle. Andy Fortman, who along with his brother killed my father, and maybe my brother, too, stirs, shifts in his seat, glances in my general direction.

I'm antsy, aggravated but unable to leave.

Looking to my left, I see Debra, who smiles at me. I think about the NDA she signed. Dad died. She got paid. I survive off that money. Whose hands aren't bloody? Turning, I see Amy seated at the right hand of her father. This is *her* family. How can she *not* know?

I need to follow-up. Get reports from the EPA, other vital environmental requisitions from equally powerful acronymic agencies. This requires more than surfing the web, making mental notes in-between getting distracted by hilarious cat videos. I don't know where to start. *How* to start. Not like I can pick up a phone and make a call. I need an ally. A friend. A trusted confidante willing to work alongside me, pick up the slack of verbal lines I cannot tow.

I scan the church, eyes settling on Freddie, who nods his solemn condolence, before turning away. Given his jitteriness, Freddie won't stick out his neck further. He works in the industry. Just by talking to me, he's already gone out on a limb. Any further on that branch, he runs the risk of hanging himself. He pointed me in the right direction. The rest falls on me.

I once dreamt of writing private investigator fiction, and now I must think like a detective.

What would my hero do?

First move: get our hands on Blackmill's report of the Milford Power Plant's soil. A hard copy must exist. I'll hire a lawyer of my own. As my father's son, I have rights. Of course, I'll need Debra's help to pay the legal fees. I can't shake feelings of ineptitude. I'm stepping to the plate with two strikes against me and an inability to recognize a breaking pitch.

If I can't rely on Freddie or hire a lawyer, where do I turn? I need an idealist, an ally with a personal stake; someone who still believes in right and wrong, justice, the tenants of personal responsibility; who is still young enough, fiery enough to fight for change; and who is untarnished by the cynicism that comes with age.

"I love you, Dad."

My eyes ascend the altar, landing on Em.

Our eyes meet.

———

The procession zigzags up to the cemetery off Hudson. Josh's final resting spot is the biggest plot on modest burial grounds. The Fortman Brothers want it both ways, playing dual roles of tormentor and savior.

Standing under a phalanx of black umbrellas, we lower my brother into the cold, hard ground, Andy tasked with tossing the ceremonial first shovel of earth. The soft summer rain continues to fall.

Hugging me goodbye, Emily grips my arms like a grandmother clutching the Jesus bar around Dead Man's Curve.

The after party is at Debra's, whose house is the closest, largest, and best suited to host the reception. I get the impression Amy is relieved we're not at her house.

In the kitchen, the gathering hub for such affairs, I find my widowed sister-in-law, holding court and accepting condolences, which often come in the form of cash-filled envelopes. Of all the funeral rituals, that one confounds me most. They did it for my mom, too. I do not see Em anywhere.

Few look my way; fewer still meet my eye.

I watch Andy Fortman and the men he talks to, older men I do not know. Perhaps these men work for him, men who may or may have not known my father or brother. Freddie is here, but he sequesters himself on the other side of the house. I can't say whether he is avoiding me—Debra's home is massive—but he makes no effort to seek me out. Josh's boss Paul arrives and helps Debra usher guests. Josh didn't work long for Paul, but it's clear my brother left an impression. Josh had that effect on people. The hard part over, Paul directs traffic to the feeding table. The mood has lifted, the scene less gloom and doom. There's a smorgasbord of reheated dishes in casserole pans, noodles and sauces, cheeses and meats, a section cordoned off for sweets like cookies and pies. Let the healing begin. Mirth cracks the atmosphere. Soon people are sharing funny stories, the good times. I overhear Josh's friends from high school talking about his wrestling career. A short Italian man shares a hysterical tale about a girl named "Nancy" who had a butt so tiny it fit "in the palm of [his] hand." People laugh.

Instead of laughing with them, I grow saddened. I know none of these stories. In high school, Josh and I were strangers. While he was conquering fields of battle as a dual-sport warrior, I was learning how to tune a guitar to play three chords and rock out in bars. Josh was a jock, popular. An artist, I was already an outcast. Our lives didn't intersect until after graduation, for those few, precious years we were using drugs. If I think about it hard enough, I have to admit our time together was short lived and entirely drug fueled. They were also the happiest years of my life.

I can't listen from the corner anymore, eavesdropping on stories I wish I shared.

Creeping up the stairs, I withdraw to my room and find my earbuds. Josh and I had a long-standing bet on who'd win the race to the grave. Given my brain degeneration, you'd think the smart money would be on me. Josh hated to lose.

You know it, brother.

You're going to do this now? Pop in my head, whenever you want?

It's a form of grieving. I'm sure you've covered it in all those books you've read.

If this is a memory, why do I hear *your* voice and not mine?

Oh, brother, you mean are you crazy?

I hear voices in my head all the time. They sound like *my* voice. This sounds like—

Mine?

Yeah.

And now my little brother is wondering if he's going insane?

For one, I'm four years older than you. Stop calling me that—

Three and a half years. And six inches shorter—

Five inches. And you're dead.

Speaking of which…

What do I do, Josh? Is it true? Did Andy and Ari kill our father? What about you?

I wait for a response.

Nothing.

I hear scurrying and giggling outside my room. I didn't close the door all the way. Two women sit at the top of the stairs, laughing at the lunatic acting out a conversation with himself. I slam the door shut, which makes them laugh harder.

They remain there, on the stairs, whispering. People think because I can't speak that I can't hear. Not only can I hear, but I also hear better than *you*, my remaining senses picking up the slack to compensate for what lies dormant. Even with the door closed, I hear just fine.

I don't care about gossip. This is a memorial. These two are free to grieve however they'd like, even if that involves mocking me. But when I hear, "His fucking brother," I'm drawn in.

Like an orphaned Hardy Boy, I find the empty glass from last night's water and press it to the door.

I don't recognize the voices. Why would I?

"…and remember how many times Josh would try and convince us it was because of a bicycle accident?"

"He loved him."

"He's the reason Josh got started on that shit in the first place."

"That's his brother."

"A garbage brother."

"A garbage brother is still a brother."

"I didn't see him at the church."

"He was there. Front row."

"Obviously, he wasn't saying a few words."

Giggling.

"You're terrible."

"I'm not saying anything anyone else isn't thinking. I'm glad they shipped him off to San Francisco. Can you imagine being Amy? Having to see that freak? Whinnying like a mule?"

"Stop it!"

More giggles.

"I'd see him come back, like in the store, all deaf and hee-hawing—"

"I don't think he's deaf."

"Whatever. He's a creep, a weirdo."

"At least he's cute."

More giggling.

"Make the perfect husband. Good looking *and* can't talk."

They're laughing so hard now, I resist tearing open the door. It would make them jump. Then what? I glower? Look mean? Barnyard bray my fury?

Someone calls from downstairs, and the two women head toward the voices. I reopen the door, trying to catch a glimpse. I can't put a name with the back of hair. It's better this way. Not that I'd feel the need to correct them or stand up for myself. Nameless. Faceless. Voiceless. Everyone's opinion of me in this town is the same. I'm the local joke.

I need out of the pity party I've thrown myself.

A bet is a bet, however morbid.

If Josh lost—meaning if I died first—my brother was instructed to find a place to be alone, and play "No Children" by the Mountain Goats.

Josh had a crueler selection for his passing.

I grab my iPhone. Dimming lights, I cue Frank Turner's "Song for Josh," a spot-on live performance about the premature death of a bouncer from our favorite singer/songwriter. I jam in my earbuds, crank the volume as loud as it will go, sit on the bed, and enjoy a good, long cry.

When the song ends, Frank says, "Let's hear it for Josh." The audience applauds. I dry my eyes, smooth my hair, and prepare to join the congregation of pie eaters.

Before I can leave the room, my phone buzzes.

A text message from a blocked number.

I hit translate to speech. Emily.

Sorry I didn't make the memorial. It was [garbled]… Can you meet me at the Olympia Diner? I know time is [garbled] for you. I'm here now. I'll be here all night, studying …

There is a long pause, followed by more static. The message cuts out entirely before picking back up.

I'm staying … with … a friend. My family, my uncle and grandfather [garbled]… They did something bad. I … I need to talk to you. In person. Do not talk to my mother.

This is followed by another, longer pause. I wait for more. Instead, the call ends.

I can't text a blocked number. I try anyway. A rejected ding signals "undeliverable." I have few programmed cell numbers, each under respective names. Debra, Emily, Josh. I can differentiate a "J" from "D" and "E."

I press "E" for Emily. I can't say anything, and my P2G won't translate a phone call, one of the many limitations of the device, but hearing her voice will quell my mounting anxiety.

A message greets me. It's not Emily's voice.

The number you are trying to reach is no longer in service.

CHAPTER TWELVE

BREAKFAST AT MIDNIGHT, EGGS OVER EASY, AND BLOOD ON MY HANDS

Most of the guests at Debra's have left. A few stragglers meander. The kitchen fills with echoes of clean-up, dishes stacked in a sink, plates stashed for safe keeping. I don't say goodbye to anyone, even Debra, which is rude—I should let her know her I'm leaving. I don't want her to worry. I can't risk anyone knowing where I'm going or whom I'm meeting.

Sneaking out the back, I request the Uber pick me up several houses down the block, around the bend and out of sight. First thing I do when I get in the car is tip the driver well. My inability to speak renders me impolite. Often, if a driver strikes up conversation, I'll point at my throat, which is the quickest way to convey I'm not up for talking. My Uber rider rating is two stars. Drivers think I'm rude. One review said I acted "like I was too good to talk [to him]."

The tip makes this driver happy. *Too* happy. Because now he won't shut up about what a "nice, nice man" I am. Maybe I tipped him a grand. I punch in "1s" and "0s," digits I can recognize. 100011110101. Maybe in the end, it will turn out I've been an insecure android this entire time, artificial intelligence with an inferiority complex.

The Uber drops me off at the Olympia Diner.

In my high school mystery series, I often depicted my amateur PI conducting business at the Olympia Diner. Like the *Lincoln Lawyer*. Except instead of the backseat of a luxury automobile, my hero held his meetings in the back booth of a greasy spoon. In later versions, I'd transplant the diner to various states across the country. New Hampshire. Minnesota. Upstate New York. Tweak the name. Change the town. I was always writing about the Olympia Diner. The late-night dinette on the Berlin Turnpike is a regional staple with a rich, storied history. They make coffee-table books about it. (You can find them on Amazon.)

The rain has let up, evening air cool, crisp, invigorating. I feel wired, running hot. I pat pockets for pills, which are color coded so I don't take the wrong ones. I require several a day; a timer perpetually buzzes reminding me when it's time to take another.

The timer buzzes. I take another.

Without Freddie, my niece's message wouldn't have registered the same. Emily's text sounded frantic, concerning on its own. Drug abuse is hereditary. I might be worried Emily was popping Adderall.

I was fortunate not to have kids. I can't imagine how parents navigate that minefield, the "Do as I say, not as I did" platitudes that must ring especially hollow during teenage years. What did Josh tell Emily about his drug use? The girl is almost eighteen. She knows what drugs are. Kids sniff through bullshit faster than anyone.

Walking across the restaurant parking lot, I feel a wave of nostalgia cascade. How many high school nights did Jim, Jack, Rich, Ron, and I end up here after a movie or concert? Many of those guys were at Sliders the other night, I saw a few later at the viewing, a couple the church, one the cemetery, none at the reception. No one said as much as "hello."

I have bigger challenges confronting me than a bad reputation. A young woman who lost her dad needs my help bringing down one of the state's most powerful families—*her* family—mine too, if only through marriage. I'd love nothing more than to ignore this. Turning away isn't an option. When Emily confirmed Freddie's revelation, I had no choice. Once is an accident. Twice is a pattern yet to be discovered. The narrative rolling around my skull, which until a few days ago I'd have called preposterous, now seems however improbable a certainty: the Fortmans had my brother killed to prevent the press from revisiting Blackmill's connection to their construction business. Their impudence regarding the Milford Power Plant infuriates. Andy and Ari believe they are above the law. No one is, and if I can find a way to make enough noise, I can help pound that final nail in Ari Fortman's political coffin.

I push through the front door, its ringing bell delivering a rabbit punch to the hippocampus and ventral striatum, the sections of the brain that retain our oldest, fondest memories.

Dinnertime isn't a popular hour for the restaurant—the Olympia Diner isn't a fine dining establishment. Most of its traffic comes later, college kids trying to sop up a drunk with a midnight meal. I don't expect it to be crowded. The Olympia Diner, with its glowing pink neon, 1950's aesthetic, is famous for all-day breakfasts after closing time.

A pair of hearty truckers straddle stools at the kitchenette counter, backs to the door, plumber cracks on display.

Checking up and down the aisle, I find no one else here. I'm thinking maybe my niece is taking a cat nap, curled up in a corner booth—that used to be our spot, me and the guys, back in the day.

Thankfully, Emily didn't inherit my brother's humungous size, taking after her mother. Still, Emily should be visible. She's not.

She isn't here. She wasn't at Debra's. She's not at the diner. Prepared for all possible contingencies, I brought along my P2G. After hooking it up, I fire off an email, waiting for a response. The only cell number I have for Emily doesn't work. I have no other way to get in touch with her. She warned me not to confront her mother, which I have no interest in doing. Emily said she'd be here studying. All night. I check the clock. Fortunately, it is an old-fashioned one with hands, not digital. I am a visual learner. A tick past halfway, I deduce it is seven p.m. Maybe she stepped outside for a break? How would I have missed her in the parking lot?

I spot a waitress. Not as young or alluring as I recall. Then again, we all get old. I pull out my iPhone and scroll till I find a picture of Emily, pointing at the photograph. I gesture around the dinette, conveying the question I need answered. Maybe it's because I'm holding an assistive device. Maybe I just look helpless. Whatever the reason, the waitress catches on.

"You're looking for her?" the waitress says, growing excited when I nod. "You're wondering if she was here!"

Like a goddamn game of charades, I place one finger on my nose, pointing another at her. The waitress beams. Play stupid games to win stupid prizes.

The waitress' face ebbs from satisfied to pained. *Something is wrong.* "Yes, she was here." She points at the clock. "A man came and got her. About forty-five minutes ago."

What *man?* Forty-five minutes ago? Forty-five minutes ago I was receiving her text.

"She left with him. But…"

But what?

"Didn't look like her boyfriend. He was older. Like a dad." The waitress stands, arms akimbo. "She *really* didn't want to go with him."

I throw up my hands, as if to say, "Then why did you let her leave?!"

The waitress doesn't dignify my outrage. Or perhaps my silent routine doesn't warrant a response beyond a shrug.

"I was wrong though," the waitress says, tapping the picture on my phone. "She gathered her stuff and even smiled. That's when I realized."

Realized what?

"How much they looked alike. Of course, he was bigger. *A lot* bigger." She shakes her head, a red, frizzy tangle, like Flo from that old TV show, not the insurance commercial. The one with Mel's Diner. I can't recall the name, my head spinning. She raises her hand to match this man's gargantuan proportions. "Must've been six and a half feet tall."

While I'm computing what this means, the waitress uses the down time to clean a spot on the countertop.

I need more information—speeding her along with a wound-up wrist. *Then what?*

"Then they left." The waitress smiles. "Your friend is very generous. Left twenty dollars for a coffee and slice of pie."

I wait for more, face flushed.

After I stomp my foot, she tenderly touches my arm. "Don't worry, honey," she says, "I've seen enough to know."

Know what?!

"It *was* her dad. Even overheard her call him 'Daddy' on the way out."

Dad?

Josh?

Kiss my grits.

CHAPTER THIRTEEN

IT WASN'T ME, IT WAS THE ONE-ARMED MAN

A swath of rain returns as I wait on another Uber. I am sick of wasting time and money on ride shares. Should rent a damn car. (Yes, I know how to drive.) Standing around, I have too much time on my hands, wondering where Emily is—and *whom* she is with. Despite the waitress' claims, Emily hasn't left with her dad. Josh is her dad, and Josh is dead.

She called him Daddy.

Why would the waitress lie?

If the Fortmans can scrub the web—is it a stretch to think they can fabricate an overdose? How much to grease a coroner's palms, bribe a police chief, forge a death certificate—a death certificate Freddie advised me to double check?

Why would Andy and Ari want me to think Josh was dead if he wasn't? Why would my brother stage his death? This is nuts. I'm not thinking straight. That's all my head does: recycle crazy, crooked thoughts.

But…

What if that *was* Josh? What if that was what Emily had to tell me? My brother didn't OD. He and Em are on the run. Because they've uncovered the Fortmans' nefarious sins and evil plans. I can't say *what* those plans are. I know what everyone knows: Ari Fortman, a major player on the global stage, finds himself caught in the crosshairs of a criminal investigation, and is forced to take drastic action…

Cut. Scene. Print.

The scenario is too fantastic. But I can't stop writing the script. In my head.

Josh told Emily it wasn't safe to wait, too risky. Maybe Fortman mercenaries spotted them, me. Maybe they figured out that wasn't Josh's body they buried. Who is the puppet? Who is the master?

If I *were* writing this story, that's a nice turn. Brother fakes his own death, goes underground, and teams up with his old partner in crime. Two wrongs to make it right. Stretches the tenets of credibility, sure. You only need readers to suspend disbelief long enough to dig in the hook. If readers like a story enough, they'll buy in, come along for the ride. Some of the best books have the craziest turns. Hannibal Lector wears a scalped human face for a mask. Andy Dufresne spends twenty years tunneling a hole at night. Tyler Durden ends up being Jack's broken heart.

What do you think? Want to take a ride? Hop in!

By the Olympia's entranceway, a vintage cigarette machine poses by the stairs. You can put in quarters, jerk a knob, and get a pack. I make change for a twenty, drop in many (many) quarters, and snare a box of Camels.

Outside, I light up with the complimentary matches, as I run through all the outlandish threads and madcap storylines. At first, I was elated Amy opted for a closed casket. Now I'm kicking myself for not popping the lid and sneaking a peak. What proof do I have Josh is really dead? I never saw the body. I can't read a death certificate. Yeah, it's crazy. But is it any crazier than having an uncle-in-law working for the president of the United States, colluding with foreign governments, attempting to rig elections to install a dictatorship? Ari Fortman was at my brother's wedding eating shrimp. Now he's giving press conferences from the White House lawn.

I've been listening to too many mystery novels and true-crime podcasts. Can't read. Can't write. Can't speak. I'm going to uncover a sinister worldwide plot?

I'm cracking.

Do you know how frustrating it is to have a thought—a cogent, tangible thought—as clear as a Caribbean beach after a tropic storm, these words you hear in your brain, right on the tip of your tongue—but when you go to speak, nothing comes out?

It will drive you insane.

Out of options, I must confront Amy.

The Uber drops me off at the house on Christian Lane. This is not a conversation I'm looking forward to having, especially so soon after we buried her husband. Only what if we didn't? That's the real question: how much does Amy know? Some? Part? All? Josh loves her, and she loves him. But Amy *is* a Fortman. Where do her loyalties lie? My head spins, I can't think straight, my very person split in two. I feel like I used to before I lost the ability to speak, how I'd sputter and stutter, tripping over my tongue, hung up on a single letter, like a record stuck in its grove, forever skipping.

I haul out my Prologue2Go, which I will need to communicate with my sister-in-law. Thankfully, the sky has wrung itself dry.

The Uber pulls away, bringing Amy to the door, glass of wine palmed.

"What are you doing here?" she asks.

Play it cool. If she doesn't know, her hating us is the least of our worries. And if she does know? We either have an ally, or … we are stepping into a trap.

Walking closer, I extract my Prologue2Go, holding it up for her to see. Amy recognizes the device and sighs. The P2G does not inspire rapid results.

I twist and dial knobs, before settling on the correct color-coded button.

Can we talk?

I wait for her to say, "Oh, isn't that adorable! You have a little Speak and Spell! Next thing you know you'll be counting on your fingers like a big boy!" I brace for the insult.

Only it never comes. For the first time since I've known my brother's wife, Amy doesn't look like she hates me. If I didn't know better, I'd swear her eyes brim with compassion, understanding, empathy. Could mean many things. At face value, the day of a burial, she's hurting. No matter how little Amy and I see eye to eye, we both lost a loved one. I must allow for that possibility as well. Whichever way this latest Schrödinger experiment goes, whether we open the box to find Josh dead or alive, the moment must be killing her too.

Amy walks in the house, leaving the door open for me to follow.

The home, which I recall as immaculate, clutters with dirty laundry and unwashed dishes, the hopelessness of not caring.

I'm not a conspiracy guy. Emily said she was staying with a friend. Maybe she meant a *boyfriend.* Though that means my seventeen-year-old niece is calling her boyfriend, a man my brother's age, "Daddy." Cringe, as the kids say. I must consider this reality too, however twisted. When I was writing stories, that was the first rule I learned when dealing with darkness: you must be willing to go where others fear to tread.

When all the other senses fail, you lean on your instincts.

What are my instincts telling me now? I can't hear an answer above the voices inside my skull begging me to turn around, run away, and not look back; this will not end well.

"I'm not in the mood to talk," Amy says. "It's been a difficult day. Isn't it time you go home?"

I scan the P2G, searching for the best preset response. I can't find one. *Trust me, I don't want to be here either, lady* isn't an option.

I walk to a framed photograph of the happy family. Amy, Josh, my niece. I point at Emily, shrug, look to the ceiling, show my palms, hitch my shoulders, desperate for Amy to infer what I'm asking. *Where is my niece?*

"Emily?"

I nod emphatically.

Amy shakes her head, groans. I've hit a sore subject. Her reaction would be the same, regardless of whether the cat is alive or dead.

I press a new button: *Want to grab dinner?*

Amy looks at me like I'm a two-headed goat at the traveling freak show. Unable to see beyond the P2G's limitations, she's forced to consider if I've just asked a recent widow, one who doesn't like me, if she's hungry. Again, I point at Emily's picture on the wall, then to me, then back to her. I mime eating. Fork to mouth. I'm trying to convey Emily asked me to meet for dinner. It's a great deal to cram in and transmit with limited resources. My Pictionary clues fall short.

"I don't know what to tell you. Emily's ... not here."

I hold an imaginary phone to my ear, pointing at the picture, passing along the invisible phone. I want her to call Emily. From *her* phone.

"Call her? I've been trying." Amy folds her arms. "All day. She won't pick up."

Won't pick up? When I called, the phone was out of service…

She's lying.

Amy heads into the kitchen, pulls a carafe of white wine from the refrigerator and refills her glass, which was already half full. My sister-in-law then heads to the liquor cabinet, fetching a top shelf bottle of mezcal.

Presenting the label, she sets it on the counter for the offering. "Josh said you were a fan."

Amy *knows* I don't drink. I've been off drugs and alcohol for thirteen years. Never mind the fact that mixing medications with something as strong as mezcal wasn't a good idea when I *was* using. But, yes, Josh had it right: if I have an alcohol weakness, it is mezcal, one of the purest, most distilled liquors. If done correctly, a full glass is under seventy calories. Healthier than soda. It's seldom done correctly.

"I know you're on the wagon." Amy shakes her head. "It's not like you're clean and sober with all those pills they got you on. If anyone deserves a drink today, it's you." She oozes warmth. "You buried a brother this afternoon."

Did I, Amy?

Amy pulls the cork, nudges the bottle along. I can smell the smoky aroma from several feet away. Unlike tequila, which is derived from one kind of agave, artisanal mezcal utilizes over three hundred species of the plant to harvest and carefully select, requiring maturation, an exquisite process that can last as long as forty years. *Espadín. Tepextane. Barril. Medrecuixe.* We're not even digging into mineral content and soil components. Making quality mezcal is an artform. Like I say, if I have a preference…

Amy walks away, abandoning the mezcal to tempt, like this is a Somerset Maugham novel. I slip the razor's edge, following her into their spatial living room.

Anytime I've been to their house, the action revolved around the kitchen. The space invites company. They have this marble island bar, with tall stools covered by comfortable cushions. Passing the island and stools, I spot Josh's usual seat, evident by the sizable indent of his fat ass.

Watch it, brother...

It looks recently sat in.

Sadness hangs over the home. I know that sounds obvious. A man—a husband, father, brother—is dead. Or ... a woman has discovered her father and uncle are capable of murder, and the man she loves has been forced into hiding. I can't get a handle on my sister-in-law's emotions, usually a strength of mine. Reading people is a tool I need to survive. I'm quite good at it. Amy's expressions vacillate at warp speed, from vitriol to nightingale, like a feral cat sprinting to another room. I'm at a loss.

Familial crime syndicate. Lethal liaison to the president of the United States. Dead husband. Daughter picking the worst time to flake on coffee or best opportunity to fly the coop. All are simultaneously unlikely and equally plausible.

Whatever caused Emily to pack up and rush off involved a fight with her mom. I was warned against talking to Amy. Perhaps I ought to have listened to my younger, wiser niece...

I catch up to Amy in the living room, tap her shoulder, point out the window in the direction of the Berlin Turnpike. I mime driving, spinning an invisible wheel frantic, ramping up the urgency, gesturing at a photograph of Emily on the wall, and then throwing my arm around an invisible person, before raising my hand high. I am attempting to ask *who* the friend was. *Let's start with how tall...* My charade prompts only manage to infuriate Amy more.

"I don't know what you want me to say—I know it's hard for you!

But I'm … I don't have the patience right now. I can't understand what you're asking me!"

I hold up a finger, scrolling through my iPhone, till I find the text Emily sent me. I'm not sure I can trust Amy. I am also running out of time.

I hit the link.

Nothing but a line of scribbled text. No hyperlink.

Amy peers over. "I don't know what you want to show me, but since you can't read, I'll tell you what it says: 'This link has expired.'"

Emily sent a time-sensitive link. *In ten seconds, this message will self-destruct…*

Then I do the thing I hate most about my dysarthria. I grow frustrated, straining, trying to push out syllables and sounds. As if through force of will, I will be able to summon the words that have alluded me for years.

Which leaves me braying like a mutant horse, face beating red. The harder I try, the worse it gets. I flap my arms and clomp by heels and can't stop shaking.

Amy comes over and does something I would never expect. She hugs me. Few people touch me—I don't let them. But she hugs me, like a real sister, taking my hands in hers, before pulling me close. I don't stop her. "Shhh," she says. "I know. I mean I don't know." She throws back her head, but not in a vicious or vindictive way. "It must be so frustrating not to be able to say what you… You can't even draw a picture." She exhales and leads me to the couch. "I know how much you love Josh…"

Love. Present tense, not past. Intentional?

Before we can sit, the phone rings. Landline. The call comes from two locations, behind us in the kitchen, and echoing a moment later from another line upstairs.

"Stay here," Amy says, making for the upper level and the phone farthest away.

Above me, I hear a phone snatched from its cradle. Inching closer to the well, I listen to hushed tones of panicked speech. I crane my head up the well.

I hear, "Yes, he's here ... I'll try ... he's upset."

I think this is what I hear. It's hard to be sure over the whir of air whooshing through vents, the electrical drone of multiple appliances and other sonic devices, the ringing in my ears brought on by the sudden migraine. I'm on the bottom rung, patting pockets for pills, when I hear a door creak open upstairs.

The noise does not come from where Amy stands.

Their house is big. Not Beverly Hills big, but big enough to tell the movement comes from another room, on the opposite side, the far end of the house. Then: louder noises from outside, engines rolling into the driveway. Counting is hard, but I can tell it's more than one vehicle.

I run from well to window. Three black sedans. The first man who steps out doesn't surprise me.

Andy Fortman is her father. Wouldn't be the strangest thing for Dad to show up. Why the entourage? Why are they holstering handguns, tracing the property to establish perimeter?

I soon have my answer.

There he is, emerging from the last dark-tinted vehicle. The man who left this town; the man who now operates on a much grander scale; the big shot who shouldn't be concerned with this podunk place.

Ari Fortman.

Peeping through blinds, I watch the brothers talking, staring at the house and pointing at the drawn shades where I hide.

If Ari helped kill and cover up the death of my father, I shouldn't be surprised he'd try the same with my brother.

And I matter less than both.

CHAPTER FOURTEEN

ON THE RUN

I'm not waiting to meet the United States Secret Service, and I sure as hell don't have time to sit around for ride share.

Tearing through the living room, I push aside lamps and chairs, smacking into the flat screen, so hard I rip it from the studs, television crashing to the hardwood floor. Boom. Smash. Shattered. Through the back door, I leap off the stairs, darting into the surrounding woods. Despite recent gentrification, Berlin still enjoys heavy forestation, woods thick with alcoves and places to hide.

Maybe I hear Amy calling my name. Maybe I hear men shouting to find me. Maybe I am losing my goddamn mind.

I am in good shape. In addition to walking the Institute's paths daily, hiking its surrounding hills, I often jog. One year, the Institute brought some of us to Bay to Breakers, which is a quarter marathon race in San Francisco. I finished second, losing to a much younger counselor who'd been All-American on his college track team. I have the medal framed.

Shrouded by deep, dark wood, I run, hop, and skip across the rippling creeks that divides the center of town, behind the old Farm Shop and out-of-business Country Farms, happy memories of my youth demolished to pave way for bigger, better, and more convenient chains. Whether my brother is alive doesn't change my mission: I must make sure Emily is okay. If that *was* my bother back at the diner, he knows I'll follow through and find both. And if it wasn't? I need to locate Em more than ever.

Unable to separate fact from fiction, I take out my iPhone and P2G and throw them in the water. I can't risk being tracked. I don't know how fast the government can triangulate a cell signal. I don't have time to find a hot spot, hook up my P2G, and carry on a conversation by translating text to speech.

Where are we running to?

The first person I think of is Freddie. He was Josh's oldest friend and business partner. A business partner he ripped off. I've known Freddie my whole life. He's a good man. But *anyone* would be pissed over that. How much can I trust him?

Next, I consider Paul, whose card is in my pocket. Josh's new partner still believes in my brother. He likes me. But what do I know about him? Freddie and Paul live in opposite directions, and even if I were willing to roll the dice and trust one of them, each is too goddamn far.

As I slink up the muddy banks, crawling from the muck, backlit by the glow of Berlin's tiny town center, I prepare for black sedans with federal plates to come whipping around the corner, semi-automatics aiming for my knees. I am out of time. There is only one person I *know* I can trust. My mom. Stepmom. She's old, doesn't need the aggravation, and I have no clue what she can do for me other than offer shelter from the storm. Debra has always had my back.

I'm under a mile—best guess—from her house. If Debra didn't care about my well-being, she'd have stopped paying hospital bills a long time ago, evicting me homeless on the streets of San Francisco.

I like Freddie. Paul is a fan. I'll put my life in Debra's hands.

Crossing Farmington Avenue, I sidestep bright headlights and blaring horns, jumping another creek, kicking my sprint into high gear as

I weave between backyards, some familiar, some renovated. I climb the hill of the old armory, scaling Worthington Ridge, head down, pumping my arms and running hard as I can.

By the time I reach Debra's, I feel like a kid again, returning home after one of those epic, backyard football games in the snow and cold that stretched limb and wrenched ligament. My muscles burn. I can barely breathe. I'm hurting, but in the best possible way, the kind that reminds me I'm still alive.

Pushing through the front door, I hold a finger to my lips. Debra, who has been watching television, cranes and stares.

"What is it?" she asks.

I lock the door, pull the blinds, and find a chair to sink into.

Debra comes to my side, as I drop my head in my hands. Despite the warm night and overactivity, I'm cold, sweating buckets, hyperventilating and shivering. My body floods with chills. I feel like I might be sick.

My stepmom rushes to the sink, fills a tall glass with tap, and returns to set it beside me on the table.

"Drink that," she says. "You'll feel better."

I chug the water and feel better. Running a mile as fast as I can through the swamps of Berlin, I'm a quivering, muddy mess. My thighs ache and temples pound.

"Where is your P2G?" Debra asks, knowing it's the quickest way to get answers.

I don't have answers for her. What I have are questions. A never-ending series of them. I want to know about my father's death and what the Fortmans knew and when they knew it. I want to know if she's heard from Emily. I want to know if I'm crazy for wondering whether Josh is still alive.

Most of all, I want to know if Blackmill and Fortman bought her silence.

Even if I could speak, write, or draw, I wouldn't have the time to ask.

The police sirens catch up with the lights splashing off the walls. Authorities arrive, squad cars skidding in the driveway. Berlin's finest bust through the door and instruct me to put my hands in the air. A brief, irrational thought flashes in my head.

Reach behind your back, like you're making for a gun. Let them do what you don't have the balls to do, what you've never had the courage to do, and end this wretched, silent hell.

Before I can talk myself into—or out of—it, Wayne, the cop from the other night, runs in front of the others.

"Put down your guns!"

The only thing that stands between me and death is a guy I may or may not have had geography class with thirty years ago.

You can piece together how the rest plays out. Procedure. Protocol. En route to be processed. I'm placed under arrest for bursting into my brother's house and tearing their television from the wall, scaring Amy. Even though *some* of that is true, I have no way of explaining what I heard or saw. Neither Amy, nor Andy, nor Ari are here.

The police read me my rights as Debra demands they put away the handcuffs.

"Property damage?" she hollers. "I'll write a check right now!"

The cops hold her back. It's former classmate Wayne who explains this is for my own good.

Deputies lead me outside into a waiting circus. You don't get many high-speed police chases in Berlin. The local press, what limited options there are, have been alerted.

Officers cordon off a path, contain the frenetic scene out front. Cameras flash. Reporters ask for a statement. None of this is explicable. All I have is Debra, who knows whatever happened back at Amy's house, I didn't mean to scare anyone. She'll bail me out and help explain at the precinct. Except I'm not put in the back of a cop car. I'm delivered into a waiting ambulance, where I am restrained, tied down, strapped in like a madman. I'm thrashing, flailing, silently screaming.

One of the EMTs takes pity, threading a line and loading up a syringe.

"Relax," he says. "This should take the edge off."

The edge is taken off all right.

Icy opiates slowly fill my veins, and I am gone.

PART TWO

THE BALLAD OF DWIGHT FRY

CHAPTER FIFTEEN

SEE MY LONELY LIFE EXPLODE

"Welcome back," I hear a woman's voice say.

My eyes are slow to readjust to the dim lighting. I no longer enjoy the slow, cold, icy flow of opiates in my bloodstream. It still feels like I am moving through mud, stuck in sludge. I haven't done hard drugs in a long time. I didn't blow my sobriety back at Amy's, regardless of how tempting that bottle of premium mezcal glistened on the marble countertop. EMTs shot me up with pharmaceutical-grade morphine. It's not a relapse if it's doctor approved. We ex-addicts call that a "freelapse."

Whatever high I enjoyed is long gone. Amy's feels like a million years ago, my head thick as the storm clouds burbling outside these windows covered with grates and bars. It isn't just the reinforced glass adding to this sense of imprisonment. In the immediate distance, mountains, capped with snowy peaks, tower and loom. Frozen waves of iced sheets suspend over craggy sheafs and foreboding cliffs. A steady, heavy snow falls.

Since when does it snow in August in Connecticut?

This isn't August, and we aren't in Connecticut.

Each movement renders me a fly stuck in maple syrup, as if I've been awakened from a forty-seven-year coma.

From my uncomfortable chair, I stare at the woman, who sits behind a large desk. She is the doctor, the one in charge. More than the white lab coat, the aura she projects and her impeccable posture give it away. Auburn hair, stern if attractive face. She's younger than I am but clearly more accomplished. I've *seen* this woman before. We are in her office. The wall behind her showcases personal portraits in between the collection of certificates, awards, commendations, and diplomas. Of course, I can't read any of these. The formatting tells me what they are *meant* to be. Except the "writing" doesn't resemble letters or words. My misinterpretations adhere to a pattern. That pattern may be indecipherable and incomprehensible, but they take *some* form. Meaning, I can tell they *are* letters, *are* words. I just can't read them. This time, I see scribbles, hastily drawn lines, a toddler mimicking writing. Am I getting worse?

"You don't remember me?" the doctor says, briefly saddened, before perking up behind her desk. "That's okay. No worries. We have to do this sometimes." She smiles warmly. "My name is Dr. Flynn."

I detect a slight Midwestern accent. I want to laugh but no sound would come out. *That's* where I've seen her before. She looks like a popular author who wrote a bestseller about a missing girl.

"I know," she says, still smiling. "I share the name of an author you enjoy reading."

She means listening to. I can't read. An author I enjoy *listening* to.

"We've made so much progress," Dr. Flynn says. "Please don't let this setback deter you."

She waits. As if I am supposed to join in, add to the conversation. She must know I am unable. Yet, I can't shake the feeling I am being goaded.

"What month do you last remember?" Dr. Flynn asks. And when I stare blankly, as I am wont to do: "I am going to list the months. When

I hit the right one, let me know."

She doesn't get far, starting with August. I raise my hand.

"Three months," she mutters, scratching a note onto a pad, before manufacturing optimism. "That's okay. This isn't uncommon. Two steps forward, one back." She holds up a finger. "I don't want to alarm you. I will explain everything. Do not worry." She leans toward me, urging me to remain calm, like I'm a temperamental child prone to pitching fits. "You fear you are getting worse, yes?" The doctor pulls back, prims her mouth, tilts her head at a supportive angle. "Not true. You're not getting worse." She points that same finger, enthused. "You're getting better."

I don't need the barred windows to deduce I am in a psychiatric facility. The geography screams East Coast. Maybe not Connecticut but still east. Higher up. I'm guessing Vermont, New Hampshire? The question plaguing me most—how long I've been here—has been answered. Three months.

November? Explains the snow. Assuming we are high enough in the mountains…

There is a calendar on the wall. I can tell it's a calendar because of its design and layout, soothing pastural motif adorning the top half, Bingo squares on the bottom. Like with the commendations on the wall, I am stymied by more than an inability to count or read. These aren't my usual scrambled numbers. Everything is a scribble. It's as though someone has gone through the trouble to mimic what they *think* I see.

I point at the calendar, hoping the doctor will decipher my question, namely: what today's date is.

"Today is Wednesday," Dr. Flynn says without hesitation. "Wednesday, November first."

Three months? I recall none of it. She isn't lying. It's snowing outside. Why would a doctor lie anyway? Other than I may have stumbled upon a horrific coverup perpetuated by one of Connecticut's crookedest companies?

I won't hazard a guess. All I know for sure? Like Billy Pilgrim, I have become unstuck in time. What have I been doing? And *where* am I?

"You are in the New York State Asylum for Lunatics," Dr. Flynn responds, answering this question I am thinking.

I wait for a smile. None comes. No one calls a mental ward that anymore. An asylum for lunatics? In the 1800s, maybe. Not now.

The doctor extracts a stack of pages from her desk drawer, a half a dozen or so, which she shuffles, reorganizes, patting into a perfect square, laying down the neat bundle, before sliding the entire presentation across her blotter, in front of me.

I don't move. She nudged the pages closer.

What does the doctor want me to look at? My medical report? Case history? Doctors don't share your patient files with you. I've been in enough rehabilitation centers, dual diagnosis clinics, and psychiatric wards to know that. Doctor's charts come in manilla folders. Always manilla. Oh, and I can't read, which she damn well knows.

Glancing down, I still anticipate a medical report of some kind, with diagnoses and dates of admission—formatting that will betray clinical formality, which will satiate my curiosity. That is not what is there. When I look this time, I *don't* see scribbles. I see words. Real words. I can't read them. But I can tell they are words. Blocks of text that form prose.

I recoil from the pages, and the doctor snatches back the stack, slides it around, and begins reading.

PART ONE

THE BEGINNING

ONE MORE CUP OF COFFEE BEFORE YOU GO

Today, Josh would put flowers on their mother's grave.

Jobs seldom delivered him this close to Bennington, Vermont, the small town where his mother Toni was born and now buried. Josh kept meaning to visit. At the end of each grueling day, he found new reasons not to. Sciatica flaring. Daylight fading. Depth charts to log, AA meetings to make. Bullshit excuses. Josh didn't visit Toni's tombstone because it would hurt too much. Especially sober. He didn't want to deal with the emotions it would dredge up—about his dead mother, his dead father, his big brother, who though technically alive was still stuck in a hospital three thousand miles away with little hope of getting out...

Dr. Flynn stops there. "Do you recognize that?"

I do. But *what the actual fuck?* It's not possible. It is a story I've been writing. *In my head.*

Dr. Flynn points at the door, then to her computer. "It's your work. But you already know that, don't you?"

No, I do not! It isn't possible. *No one can read your thoughts!* For a moment, I consider the possibility that, somehow, through my Prologue2Go, I've managed to translate ideas to the page. Except ... I threw my P2G and phone into the sludgy criks behind my brother's house.

My brother...

My mouth falls slackjawed.

The doctor points at her door. "You come in here every night and write." She smirks. "The first time, you actually picked the lock. You don't remember that though, do you?"

I shake my head no.

"You have a photographic memory."

I know that.

"You saw my keys." The doctor stops. "You memorized every groove, every indent, ding and ridge, and in the bathroom, using a spoon from the cafeteria, you carved a key out of hand soap." She laughs. "Your friend Frank, who makes furniture downstairs in the workshop—that's for our … more progressed … patients. He helped harden and glaze the key." Dr. Flynn peers toward her office door. "This is an old institution."

I spy the traditional keyhole, which resembles the outline of a woman in a dress, a logo you see on a restroom door. *Picking locks?* I must look worried, panicked.

"You're not in trouble. Frank got a scolding but in the end we—the other members of your treatment team and I—wanted to see where you were going with this." She points at the ceiling, where a small red light blinks. "We have you on tape. Want to see the footage?"

I'm not sure we do.

"We're all desperate to help you get past your mental roadblocks. You weren't trying to escape—" The doctor stops. "There's nothing wrong with you. You can speak *and* write."

Side-eyed, I glance back out that window, where beyond thick metal bars heavy snow continues to fall. Winds howl in blizzard conditions. We are high in the mountains. I am dressed in a hospital gown with flimsy booties. Even if I could pry open the bars like Big Chief, where would I go? I'd freeze to death before I took my first step.

Dr. Flynn shakes her head. Not with admonishment but admiration. "A key out of soap! That's some Alcatraz-level ingenuity." A soft laugh. Hard to pinpoint the underlying emotion, the doctor's countenance threading the thin line between impressed and cautious, proud but leery.

"We started to leave the door unlocked," she says, winking. "What was the point?" She bends to her side, retrieving a larger stack of papers, dropping them on the desk. Not quite the size of a manuscript… "You've written this in under two months. From these pages we've made tremendous strides."

My throat feels on fire. Words threaten to push through. I *feel* them, syllables and vowels on the cusp of escape. I haven't encountered this sensation since I got to the Institute. Over a decade ago.

"You," Dr. Flynn says, pointing at me. "*You* wrote this. You *can* write. You can read. Most important of all … you *can* speak."

I don't know what to say to that. She drums her fingers off the book—this book I've supposedly crafted in my copious free time. I am not going to read it. I don't want to read it. I *can't* read it. I don't get the chance to touch a single page before the doctor snatches and stashes the bundle in a desk drawer, turning a lock, which I don't think I'm meant to pick.

A gust of wind throws snow against the window, hard enough that I flinch.

"I'll give you the CliffsNotes." She winks. "It's how we've been able to help you. From the clues *you've* planted." She points at my locked-up, purported work. "Now in this story—and it is *quite* a story. Made-up, fantastical, wildly imaginative."

Hard stop. Point hammered home. Nothing I believe is real.

"It's about an older brother who harbors profound guilt over his younger brother's drug addiction and alcoholism. Heartbreaking. In the story, this older brother recounts how his parents died young, detailing his own struggles with drugs, alcohol, and homelessness. But it has a happy ending. For our hero. He cleans up! Sadly, his brother cannot do the same. Because this older brother cannot forgive himself, he saddles himself with an affliction, a condition that doesn't allow him to communicate." She catches my eye. "Sound familiar?"

Where's the part where Josh dies?

"I'm sorry to say," Dr. Flynn continues, "your story isn't entirely fantasy. Sadly, much of what you've written *did* happen. Your mother and father passed away many years ago. You have a stepmother, with whom you are very close."

I know! It's my fucking life.

My head hurts, temples throb, signaling the impending thundering migraine. Then it hits, like an earthquake on bedrock. Boom! Blood rushes to my brain, overpowering my skull to the brink of aneurism. The pain is so severe, I fear I'll go blind.

The doctor passes along a cup of water with a pair of pills.

I hesitate.

"The migraines are back, aren't they? I can see it in your eyes. Not everything you imagine is fabricated. That is your medicine. Take it. You'll feel better."

I am in a mental institution learning my entire life has been a lie. I am not drawing a hard line at accepting pills from strangers. I throw back the caps and grind the bitter narcotic. I know painkillers when I taste them. These don't taste like the oxy I used to eat, chew on, suck feverishly to extract effects as fast as possible.

She said my parents are dead. What about Josh? Please, tell me Josh is still alive. I can feel his presence.

I pantomime from me, to her, jumping up, holding a hand high, then back to me.

"Your brother?"

I nod.

"You want to know if he's alive?"

I nod with increasing intensity.

"Just ask."

I open my mouth, straining to scream. No words will come.

The doctor is a sadist, delighted by my inability to speak, refusing to offer solace until I perform tricks like a circus monkey.

Dr. Flynn points at the manuscript. "You tell me."

I wait for the punchline.

"There is nothing wrong with you," Dr. Flynn says, definitively, facts beyond reproach. Water wet, sun hot. "You do not have aphasia or …" She peers down, toward my alleged writings, stowed for safe keeping, secured under lock and key. "Dysarthria. You *do* have a certifiable malady." The doctor waits. "You've been diagnosed with 'confabulation.' Do you know that that is?"

I shake my head.

"It's not easily defined. Confabulation is a term coined by Karl Bonhoeffer, a German psychiatrist." Dr. Flynn again stops, waits. It feels strategic, these pauses. "In your … book … you talk about 'gaps in time.' That is one hallmark of the disorder. It affects memory. It's our belief that you shoulder such debilitating guilt over your brother—" She holds up a hand before I can object.

This is a lie. The Fortman Brothers have sent me here to make me believe I am crazy…

"Have you asked yourself the obvious question yet?"

Obvious? What on God's green earth is obvious about any of this?

"If you couldn't read or write," Dr. Flynn says. "How else would you have typed all this? How would you have relayed this information to the reader?" The doctor gestures at her desk drawer. "It's all there, in black and white. If you aren't writing this, who is?"

I don't have an answer for that.

"You'd like to speak with your brother, wouldn't you?" She shakes her head, sad, slow, pitiful. Nothing about her query indicates he's dead. Nothing verifies he's alive, either. "Of course," the doctor says. "But first…"

I feel as if I've been given a test. And failed.

"I'm sure you're aware," the doctor continues, in a bureaucratic, didactic tone, "we have protocol. We can't *allow* a patient visitors—can't confirm they are here…" With each phrase, her voice escalates, reaching a crescendo on that final word.

My heart drops.

"I mean, not without their signed consent." The doctor grins, whips out a piece of paper, sliding along a pen. "If you sign this confidentiality release…"

I don't have to read it. I don't need to be able to write. I can grasp a pen. I snatch and scratch. X marks the spot. It doesn't look like my name. She doesn't seem to care. *CYA. Consider your ass covered, Doc.*

Dr. Flynn snags back the paper, pleased.

"We can continue our session later." The doctor stands. "Right now. I think there is someone who would like to see you very much."

The doctor saunters across her office, turns the knob, and the door creaks open.

CHAPTER SIXTEEN

THERE'S NOTHING TO WRITING. YOU SIT AT THE TYPEWRITER AND BLEED

Debra covers her mouth as tears well and fill her big, dewy eyes. The joy is undeniable. My stepmom throws her arms around me, holding me tight, like a drowning woman clinging to a buoy.

"I knew you'd come back to us," she whispers in my ear.

My initial frustration that my brother wasn't waiting on the other side of that door gives way to a smile I can't stop. I've been living a nightmare. How much time have I lost? This book Dr. Flynn has shared proves I am not hopeless. I am still confused, abnormally so, but a picture is growing clearer. I keep talking about wanting to *be* a writer. I *am* a writer.

"We called her the moment we noticed the change," Dr. Flynn says.

"Since Josh's funeral," Debra says, letting go. "I've been so worried. You seemed to be regressing, and then that night you showed up at my house, all sweaty and the police came screeching in, the fistfights, breaking Amy's TV, the hallucinations…" Debra leans in again for one last hug.

My brother *is* dead. I, however, am very much alive.

Things are getting clearer, but clearer doesn't translate to crystal. I still have questions…

When do I get out of here?

Like she's reaching in my head, the doctor plucks, dusts off my query, holding it up, an invisible index card to examine. "We still have much work to do."

Debra takes me by the shoulders, squares my line of sight. "Don't give up now."

I point outside. I want to leave with her. Now.

"Oh, honey," Debra says. "This is where you need to be for the time being. That man you punched in the bar—do you remember that?"

I remember. These past three months lay out of reach, but everything until that point resides fresh in my mind. Ari, Andy, Josh. Blackmill and Fortman. What I *need* is to separate artistic liberty from my warped interpretation, cast aside the superfluous, leaving behind only the concrete, tangible, irrefutable. The truth.

"He's pressing charges," Debra says. "I'm working with a lawyer to get the case dismissed. It's going to take time. Meanwhile, you being in here helps us. Legally."

No one needs to explain why. In a mental hospital, I am untouchable. Like a rehab, it's a haven, safehouse, a sanctuary. The long arm of the law cannot breach the sanctity of anonymity.

"But also," the doctor is quick to interject, "your stay with us is paramount in terms of your treatment."

"Yes," Debra agrees. "Getting you better is all that matters."

The doctor lists courses of action. With my writing breakthrough, I will return to groups and one-on-one sessions, mainly art therapy. Most of all, Dr. Flynn wants me to finish writing the book I've started. She *needs* me to continue, she says, and it doesn't matter, if I am skeptical. *She* believes in me. And that makes me think of a song I wrote a long time ago. At least I think I wrote it.

I know a junkie who believes in me, and I … I believe in you…

You wrote that for me, brother…

"…and I have the utmost faith this is the start of a wonderful new chapter," Dr. Flynn concludes.

I *feel* the words the doctor tells me. I sense a response *is* there, *inside* me, and I swear I am on the precipice of its rolling off my tongue, except … my brain wants to power down. I grow sluggish, mouth thick. I gum out my tongue, a beefy, swollen slab of muscle belonging to an engorged cow, lapping cud. My eyes blink involuntarily, and though I don't want to, I begin to grunt, swaying side to side, tapping my feet, flapping my arms. I can't stop.

"What's happening to him?" Debra asks, eyes fearful.

"A side effect of the medication," Dr. Flynn says. She does not appear concerned. Maybe that is her job, to project non-plussed, cool, collected. The doctor picks up her phone, mandates instructions to staff. It's a code, colored in red or blue or white. I don't know. I'm losing my bearings. The skies outside are icy and black, and now that icy black has breached the perimeter, snaking inside these windows and walls, vining down cracks, roots wrapping around my ankles. I open my mouth to scream but no sound comes out. My lips and jaw keep expanding, wider and wider, until I swallow the entire room, eat the world, devour a universe, and nothing remains.

———

I open my eyes to nighttime. Tiny pellets pummel the tin roof and glass. I am in a bed. Earlier, snow fell. What hits the roof now is not snow. It is freezing rain, hail, sleet, hard stones. This room is frigid.

My mouth feels normal again. I am not flapping my arms like a deranged emu, my throat no longer clogged with masticated meat. I expect that when I try to move my hands, I will be restrained. I look down but do not find wrists in restraints. I am shocked to move freely, swinging my bare feet to the cold floor. I am in a hospital bed. This is a psychiatric hospital. The room is sterile and free of overly sharp objects. I have an end table with rounded, padded corners. Glued to the table sits a lamp, which I switch on. A private room. The storm ceases to rage.

The light is dim, a low watt bulb projecting as much power as a child's dull nightlight. There is a window. It is barred, crisscrossed, hatched and reinforced. I can tell the facility is old. Upgraded but old. A few modern touches bring an ancient architectural design into the twenty-first century. A light plate. Sockets and adapters with USB ports. Cameras blink red in corners.

I still wear a standard hospital gown, tied in the back, bare-assed in the breeze. Someone has removed my footwear. I find my booties by my feet. I slip them on and stand at the window. Mounting snow drifts. High capped mountains and surrounding rocky, inhospitable terrain contain me within these natural geographic walls. Even if the windows were not barred, the glass is reinforced. I'm not getting out through a window.

Making for my door, I expect to find it locked.

It's not.

Checking up and down the hall, I encounter a standard if more modern hospital ward, light fixtures in miniature cages. There is an old-time charm to the design. I remind myself that any facility still using outdated terms like "lunatic" and "asylum" wasn't built this century. Even so, the casualness and lack of security surprises me. Unlocked doors. Unguarded hallways. Safe passage.

They want us exploring.

To my left, double doors. These are locked. There's only one path I'm meant to take. It's not a long hall. Moonlight guides my way. A solitary door awaits at the end. I recognize it from earlier, though I have no conscious recall, having experienced it from the inside, when orderlies dragged me out, sedated and incoherent, to bed.

I have done this before.

I turn the knob and find myself back in Dr. Flynn's office.

We started to leave the door unlocked…

She wants us in here.

I wait for my brother's voice, the one conversing with me as if he were still alive. He's been directing my mission.

No voice comes.

On Dr. Flynn's desk sits the computer. I check the camera in the corner. No light blinks.

Sitting at her desk, I shake the mouse and the screen lights up. I poise my fingers above keys, open myself to the magic that is supposed to flow through me.

She showed me a story, right? Read words—*my* words—back to me.

The screen is blank. A cursor dances. The keyboard sits in front of me. I recall the quick brown fox jumping over the lazy sleeping dog from typing classes in high school. When I put my fingers to keys, I am confident that is what I've typed. I don't lack dexterity to press a button. Whatever is on the screen, it is not a quick brown fox jumping jackshit but an abomination of the holy written word.

Gobbledygook. Nonsense. A madman's lament. However…

What I've typed does not resemble the scribbles on the wall, the words making up the doctor's awards, doctorates, and degrees. Those commendations are scribbles; what I see on the computer screen resembles what I'm used to. It's incomprehensible but there is cohesion.

Am I getting better or worse? I see letters on the screen—I know they *are* letters—some part of my brain still works. Why doesn't the writing on the doctor's wall match up? The writing there doesn't read *like* scribbles; they *are* scribbles. I can't help but suspect a practical joke. I am beyond salvation. No amount of duct tape, solder, or chicken wire can hold together the slop. My mind has turned to mush, breaking down, like soft bread left too long in warm water.

I press my fingers to keys, apply more pressure, as if this will make a difference.

No words come. There will be no miracle. No magic. No one is getting resurrected tonight.

I search for the familiar icon of the internet. Give me a chance, see if I can find a text-to-speech option. There is none. Forget text-to-speech, I find no icon. For anything. Just a blank screensaver. Trees, mountain, rock. No files. No applications. Nothing.

I hear a noise in the hall, a door opening, and I power down the computer. Which is pointless. It was left on. I don't have time to delete whatever nonsense I typed. Moreover, the doctor wanted this, didn't she? I duck behind the desk, as if this subterfuge will camouflage.

The knob slowly turns.

I brace for a security guard or an orderly. What will they inject me with this time?

The door falls open.

It is not a guard or an orderly.

Standing there is an ordinary man in civilian clothes. He's older. Maybe late sixties, early seventies? Scruffy beard, weathered visage. He's not small, retaining heft from younger days. Sturdy, formidable. But also worn down and weary. Like Mike Ehrmantraut from *Breaking Bad*, same sloe, languid eyes and too-old-for-this-shit disposition.

"What are you doing in here?" he asks.

I can't answer. This man must know that.

"Come on," he says. "Get out of there before they catch you."

If I had my P2G, I might be able to convey that the doctor explicitly told me to come here. At night. To write.

To write? Ha! You can't write.

The man knows this too, coming to my side, ushering me out into the hall, which more closely resembles a residential home with each passing minute.

The man walks me back to my room.

"Get some sleep," he says.

I look at him confused. He is not impatient with me or angry.

"Not again," he says, resigned, lachrymose. "It's me?"

I don't know any *me?*

The old man sighs. It's kind, fatherly.

"It's okay, buddy. I'm your friend." He thumbs over his shoulder. "I live on a different floor." He waits for the acknowledgement I can't give him. "We're friends," he repeats. "You had another episode." He doesn't say this like a statement. He doesn't ask it like a question either. "Sleep," he commands. "I'll be back in the morning. We have breakfast together every morning. We're friends."

I know. We're friends. You keep telling me that! Except I don't know who you are.

"This will all be clearer after a good night's rest."

I don't know why I should trust this man but I think I do. I'm also exhausted and have nothing to do besides sleep. If this old man says he's my friend, he'd be the only one I have.

This is how I meet Frank.

CHAPTER SEVENTEEN

FRANK HUNG HIS WILD YEARS ON A NAIL HE DROVE THROUGH HIS WIFE'S FOREHEAD

Frank is at my door at sunrise. Although I am taking the sun rising on hearsay, since outside still blusters and gales. I'm left to wonder if I dreamt the moonlight last night. The grove of evergreens and pines do not evoke Upstate New York, a region I visited often with my mother and brother when we were young, since we have extended family up there. Or did. Like almost everyone else in my life, they too are dead.

"Ready for breakfast?" Frank asks.

The New York State Asylum for Lunatics comes as advertised. The people surrounding us *are* batshit. Some throw pudding or applesauce at the wall, smearing fingerprints. Most sit and stare out windows. A few screech and punch the side of their own heads. The asylum smells like a zoo.

We enter a dayroom. Off in the corner, a very large man sits in a wheelchair. His head is severely misshapen with a huge dent as though he's been beaten by a baseball bat.

"That's Benny," Frank says. "He's your friend too. You like to sit with him and stare at the big, black crows."

I break off and make for Benny, craning to look at his face. Even though he is in a vegetative state, I catch his eyes and see a part of him remains aware, awake, alive.

Frank takes my elbow, steering me away from Benny, toward the smell of food.

Inside the cafeteria, we stand in line. Some people can get their own food. Some require it delivered to them on rolling carts.

Sitting at the table, just the two of us, I accept I *do* know Frank. Because he understands my mannerisms, the means and methods by which I communicate. We are simpatico. When I first meet someone—or even if I've known them for years—it can be difficult to convey my intentions. Frank catches on right away, which tells me I've spent time in his company. He anticipates what I am about to say and can interpret my wordless messages.

"When you were in the office last night," Frank says, scooping a soupy spoonful. "Were you trying to access the internet again?"

How does he know?

"When you can't write," he says, slurping, "that's what you try to do."

I'm not sure what we are being served for breakfast. Bloated raisins bob in a watery, milky pool. I assume oatmeal.

So I can write?

"Yes," Frank says, inside my head. "You can write. Some nights it doesn't happen, and that's when you start scouring, in search of the internet." Frank points up at the cameras surrounding us. "They don't like that."

We eat in silence.

Then he whispers, barely moving his mouth, "That's what you have me for."

Frank is an ally. He knows about Ari Fortman, my theories, which I've managed to share over these past few months, while mired in this confabulated state. Frank tells me they let me use "some e-reader thing-y" to communicate, which is how he knows. He says they took it away when I began writing, to push me not to rely on it. "It" must be another Prologue2Go or some similar assistive device. I motion, pushing invisible buttons on a naked table. Whatever it was, I want it back.

"Not gonna happen," Frank says. "They want you to be independent." He stops, cranes, left, right, finger to lips. "Don't worry. I know all about the Fortmans and Blackmill. You have to trust me."

Frank, with senior patient privileges, goes on to explain how he has been able to flesh out and confirm my hypotheses. He functions as my eyes and ears of this institution. His recounting of what I uncovered before I got unstuck in time and lost three whole months also proves I'm not totally bonkers.

How many days do we do this? My forgetting I know him? He must be sick of rehashing.

"It's okay," Frank says, still not moving his mouth much. "I'm used to our morning briefings. This past week or so, you've been coming back to life. It's been dicey. Blotchy. You've returned though. Now we can finish what we've set out to do."

Frank then recaps what we—he and I—have learned about the Fortman Brothers. I'm not imagining it. Frank confirms what Freddie confided in me, about Blackmill Solutions conducting the testing for Fortman. I really want my "e-reader thing-y" because I have so many questions. Frank holds up a hand. I think he's being needlessly cautious.

Then an orderly materializes from the ether, looming behind our table.

"Hey, Bill," Frank says. "How's it going?"

"It's going." Bill stands firm. "What you boys talking about?"

Frank laughs, "Good one, Bill."

"Just remember, Frank. We let you eat up here together because we're trying to *help* him. Not fill his head with delusions."

"Of course," Frank says, waiting until Bill walks away and his back is to us, before wriggling his eyebrows, as if to say, *Told you so.*

After breakfast, we retreat to the smoker's cage, where Frank gives me one of his Camel cigarettes.

Communication without words, as I've alluded to once, twice, or a billion times, is not easy. But Frank and I have found a way to converse with one another. Even without my P2G. Call it birds of a feather, great minds, or two doomed sailors on the same sinking ship.

One look in my eye conveys the question I want to ask him.

"Why am I in here?" Frank shifts his gaze. "I killed someone." He catches my stare. I don't sense Frank is lying. He displays none of the pantomimes that betray falsehoods or mistruths. Then he adds, "My wife."

Is he sharing this to intimidate me? Asking a man why he's locked up is normal. Homicide is hardcore.

"…butcher knife," Frank continues. I've missed a chunk of his story. He mimes stabbing a blade into his own brain. "Caught her cheating. Saw red." He looks away, at the falling snow. "That's the story, anyway."

Frank doesn't clear up that statement, leaving me to infer. Guilty, innocent, framed, all or none of the above?

Like we're playing a game of two truths and a lie, I believe the adulterous rage and murder. The lie is why he's in here.

"Ari Fortman sent you to this place to die, y'know?"

I'm not sure what I do or don't know. I drag on my cigarette, pondering.

Frank checks with the orderly who isn't paying attention. "We stick to the plan. Okay?"

I nod, though I don't know what the plan is.

Frank checks his make-believe watch. "Better hurry. You're gonna be late for your session with the doctor."

CHAPTER EIGHTEEN

DOCTOR, MY EYES

Turns out, it isn't all gloom and doom in the asylum. I'm not telling you it's like the old Club Med rehabs I used to frequent, with tennis courts and meals catered by the Marriott, back when my addiction was at its most suburban and privileged, but there *is* a rehabilitative component to my incarceration. There are counselors, therapists, and mental health practitioners who treat patients like actual human beings and want to see us get better.

I experience this now as an orderly delivers me to a new doctor's office.

My new doctor is named Kubica.

Apparently, Dr. Kubica and I meet daily. We've been doing this since I've been here. Three months. As usual I am forced to infer, interpret, conclude. Nothing is spelled out for me or apparent, and I can't exactly *ask* questions, can I? Like using shadows slipping from walls to tell time, I search out clues to provide an accurate reflection. There are no mirrors in the asylum. For obvious reasons.

Dr. Kubica discusses our work together, which recounts the remarkable progress I've made. I have yet to see any of this progress, save for some pages Dr. Flynn shared, pages that, yes, contained my words even if I have no recollection of having written them, making for one hell of a magic trick. I let my mind go where intuition delivers it, down a deep, dark well impossible to escape. This is what makes the Fortmans' plan so brilliant: I *should* be hospitalized. Not for being insane—I'm no more insane than you—but *on paper?* I should never be allowed outside a hospital. The one thing that has kept me a free man? Financial solvency, courtesy of my stepmom. Until she gets me out of here I must behave, maintain my cheery outlook, and be grateful for what I *do* have: food, warmth, clothing, and shelter. I'm safe— safe from the police, safe from Andy and Ari. Inside these walls, I am untouchable. Maybe the Fortmans aren't so smart after all.

Dr. Kubica doesn't care about my version of reality. I learn early on not to broach the subject of injustice or wrongful imprisonment. Like Tommy Lee Jones in *The Fugitive*: she doesn't care. Similarly, my gestures of poking at imaginary buttons—my silent pleas for the return of a communication device—go ignored.

Her job is to get me talking again. Without mechanical assistance. I am a baby being dropped in water. I will swim. Or I will drown.

Initially, this confuses me since speaking proves counterintuitive to any malicious agenda. If I were to speak, I could explain how I don't belong here or, at the very least, get a message to the outside. I increasingly worry about Emily and Debra. If I am right and my being here is tied to the Fortmans'—and specifically Ari's— plans, no one I care for is safe.

Of course, this relies on my interpretation and summation, and I think we've established I'm not a reliable narrator.

What condition do I suffer from? Where I come from, my dysarthria is advanced. A part of aphasia, the disease is degenerative. At the Bay Area Institute for People with Traumatic Brain Injury, they say I've passed the point of no return. I can't be cured, symptoms only managed, leaving me one step removed from comfort measures invoked. But if I am to believe Dr. Flynn—and now Dr. Kubica—I am a victim of confabulation. Big difference. One is futile until fatal. The other offers ... hope. Confabulation is a fancy way of saying I confuse easily. Which I do.

Dr. Kubica says she sees I've suffered a setback.

"I don't want you to worry," she says. "Two steps forward, one back. You know that."

Do I? Right now, I don't feel as though I know much of anything.

Dr. Kubica informs me she is a speech pathologist. Judging by her matter-of-fact tone and lack of emotional display, I assume we've had this conversation before. Naturally, I am suspicious of progress.

Yet, the start of that book in Dr. Flynn's office... The words I wrote...

Today's activities begin with ones better suited for clumsy tots than grown-ass adults. Blocks. Thick magic markers. Point at the cat. Draw a shape, any shape. A deflated balloon? A deformed cow's udder? Good boy!

It doesn't take long for me to impress upon the doctor that I find this process demeaning.

"I know it's frustrating," Dr. Kubica says. She sounds tired of having to repeat the same words of encouragement. "I need you to trust me."

Despite previous prognoses and diagnoses, Dr. Kubica remains steadfast in her assessment that I can be mended. She says the Institute has been lying to me. She says some hospitals don't care about fixing patients, and are happy to collect the monthly rent check. I feel bad thinking the Institute has been bilking my poor stepmom, who doesn't know better. Perhaps, it's an honest mistake. Dr. Kubica says dysarthria and confabulation can present similar symptoms. Lucky for me, Dr. Kubica is one of the foremost experts in the field. *Do I trust her?* I think

I do. Like Frank, I take solace in her company.

"Keep trying," Dr. Kubica says, wrapping her hand around mine. Together, we hold a fat magic marker. "Close your eyes, breathe, find your center."

Doing so reminds me of mindfulness classes at the Institute. I've never known the East Coast to be so hippy-dippy. But I admit it soothes.

Dr. Kubica explains these warm-up exercises are no different than an athlete performing calisthenics before practicing. We are stretching out the gray matter. Work it out. Don't stop. Push. Above all: *believe*.

I am also lazy. Or rather I can see the writing on the wall. There's a joke in here somewhere. And, like the Boss says, it's on me.

Dr. Kubica won't let me quit. She says she's treating my situation as a personal challenge.

By mid-morning, I'm starting to buy into her can-do attitude.

Dr. Kubica hands me a coloring book. She wants me to stay within lines a mile wide. I fist a magic marker, angry at being infantilized. It is not easy, but soon, I am completing the task, and in doing so I gain confidence. I am remembering. Is it possible for me to find a way back to who I once was?

Over the years, doctors, even ones convinced of my dysarthria, contradicted themselves. Yes, I have a degenerative condition. MRIs and CAT scans also show a working brain. Outside of that small shadow inside my skull, my internal wiring remains intact. Meaning: there is no *reason* I can't speak.

Dysarthria is a word. Like aphasia. Like cancer. Like death. Like confabulation. Bad words no one wants to hear. I accept that I've gotten complacent over time. Even when I *could* speak, I wasn't a huge fan of conversation, people not high on my list of things to do.

This is a roundabout way of saying that during my one-on-ones with Dr. Kubica, I embrace the fight left in me.

I will speak.

Before we call it a day—and it's been a grueling, albeit productive, session—the doctor takes my hands, like a mother to a child, though she can't be any older than I.

"Tell me," she says, rubbing her thumb over the back of my knuckles, "Do you still worry about the bad men coming for you?"

———

On the smoking porch, I am animated, worked up. Frank, my friend, urges me to calm down.

Dr. Kubica's parting quip about "the bad men," i.e., the Fortmans, reaffirms my worst fears. How does Dr. Kubica know about the Fortmans?

Unless I told her.

"Yes," Frank explains, calmly, rationally. "You shared your fears of the Fortmans with Dr. Kubica."

How? I can't speak! I can't write!

Frank, like a loving older brother, reaches out and takes me by the shoulders. "I told you already. They let you use a tablet. At first. You're better now. How else would I know to be looking into this for you?"

Frank casts suspicious eyes over the smoking porch. When he's satisfied we are ignored, he reaches for his back pocket.

Frank's snagged a copy of today's paper. He announces today's date: Monday, November sixth, two-thousand seventeen. He shows me the front page: Arioch "Ari" Fortman, the man responsible for killing my father—and maybe my brother—stands next to the president.

The president. As in of the United States.

"These are dangerous men you want to go after," Frank says, tapping Ari's pixilated face. "I love you, buddy. We need to be smart about this. Even if you weren't locked up in a mental hospital—and you are—even if you could communicate like a regular person—and you can't—what's your plan? How do you plan to bring down Connecticut's mob?" Frank drags a slow finger over the photograph. Ari to the president, the president to Ari, before tracing a circle around the perimeter to the men in black, armed security detail at a press conference.

I try to speak, straining, eyes bulging, arms flapping. I know I look like an imbecile; I don't care.

"Calm down," Frank says, looking over my shoulder to make sure an orderly isn't watching. "*I know Ari Fortman is a bad man*," he says. "I know he hurt you. I'm trying to help you move on with your life. Maybe it's time to let this go."

Later that evening, lying in my bed, I think about what Frank said.

Let this go…

And do what? Nothing? It's out there—hard intel proves the Fortman Brothers were aware that job site was toxic. I won't rest—I *can't* rest—until everyone knows. I cling to this certainty. Because the rest of my world is so *uncertain*. Outside of Frank, Dr. Kubica, and a catatonic lunk in a wheelchair named Benny, I can't trust anyone in the hospital. After that first day, I never see Dr. Flynn again. With each passing day, I am able to answer more questions.

Except the one tormenting me most.

How did Dr. Flynn get the start of my book if I didn't write it?

Racking my brain, mulling every possible scenario, I come up empty.

Dr. Flynn's story was preposterous. A key made of soap and glazed? Yet, Frank confirmed it. I have zero recall of whittling a bar of soap, or of breaking into an office, and I know I can't write because every time I try, I manage nothing but chicken scratch, my "writing" less legible than a drunken doctor's script. I fare no better typing, banging on keys with fists like a monkey hammering out advanced symbols and uncrackable passcodes. I have no means to share what I'm thinking.

How do I let *that* go?

Dr. Flynn read *my* story, *my* words.

She stole the words from our head…

Impossible. There is a logical explanation for everything. It's called science. I'm not wearing a tin foil hat. I consider all scenarios; nothing is too outlandish. Best I can surmise: during these three months—a chunk of time I can't account for—while I remained mired within a fugue state, granted access to a P2G or similar assistive device—I somehow managed to get my subconscious to transfer thoughts to the page. Except a Prologue2Go can only do so much. There is no app or tech for telepathy. The words Dr. Flynn repeated were verbatim, word for word, which extends far beyond the preset phrases available via a P2G. Sure, it's possible the New York State Asylum for Lunatics has more advanced technology. If so, where is it? Why can't I use it? Especially now that I am, as doctors maintain, "so close"? For a man who once fantasized of being a writer, Occam's razor, in this case, feels like a gaping plot hole.

I tell myself some questions can't be answered. At least not when you want them answered. I remind myself it will all make sense in the end. It always does.

With each return to Dr. Kubica's office, I must confront, battle, and fight against this skepticism. Dr. Kubica is very good at her job. She doesn't let me give in, won't let me give up, quit or surrender. Her enthusiasm and confidence in me is infectious. I find myself increasingly determined. Dr. Kubica wants me to speak. I want answers about the Fortmans. I will use those two goals, which are not mutually exclusive, to get what I want. It won't be easy. The center must give.

The blood-dimmed tide rises…

As a non-verbal communicator, you feel pressure in your skull, which builds relentlessly, as you roll your boulder like Sisyphus. And I understand evoking Sisyphus to illustrate redundancy is tantamount to a freshman girl taking introduction to poetry and writing about Persephone, but that doesn't make the analogy any less apropos.

With each newspaper Frank shares, I vow, pledge, promise to try harder—*do* better. I owe it to Freddie and Emily. Both have something to lose and were brave enough to trust me. Freddie *has* a family. This *is* Em's family. Me? I have nothing. No one will miss me when I'm gone. I'll throw myself on that grenade to save others because why the fuck not?

The only thing stopping me is me.

In my head, the montage of a *Rocky* movie plays. I envision myself pummeling slabs of frozen beef, cracking ribs, bloodying knuckles. I pound a glassful of raw eggs and take to the streets, lumbering lopsided, dormant, underused muscles burning, aching, until I ascend the long stairs and hopak in Converse sneakers.

Dr. Kubica sees the fire in my eyes, and uses my ardor as fuel.

"I believe in you," she says.

No one's ever believed in me. Maybe my mom before she died. She used to think I was special. My brother did too. At least for a while. Mrs. Virostek in high school. For so long now, though, I've been surviving, existing, treading water, wallowing to whittle away time. I've gotten complacent, letting others do my speaking for me. I've had nothing to fight for. That isn't true anymore.

The only skill I possess is tenacity. I can bang my head against a wall longer than you. I will need to tap into that indefatigable spirit, harness it for energy. I *know* I have it in me. I've lost my voice. I must find it again.

I try. I really do. I open my throat wide, stretching and straining vocal cords. I give it everything I got. What comes out of my mouth projects little more than a grumpy mouse's angstiest squeak.

"Don't give up!" Dr. Kubica implores.

How do you convince neurons and synapses to reconfigure? Fire up a dead engine with a spent battery to restart a lifeless lump? Especially when it's been idle for so long?

"I can see you're thinking," Dr. Kubica says.

Yes, I am thinking! Frank read to me from today's paper. Ari Fortman, former special counsel to the president of the United States, grows more powerful by the day. The president may have moved on but Ari is still a force to be reckoned with. The situation has grown dire! He must be exposed to the masses for the slimeball he is. The fate of the free world may very well depend on it. That isn't hyperbole. Ari Fortman is a murderer with his finger on the button. Nuclear war. Global annihilation. Why can't anyone else see it? If not me, then who?

Behind Dr. Kubica, out the window, I catch the snow fall. We are deep into winter. I am not crazy.

"Let's try this," Dr. Kubica says, calmly. "Mimic this sound. Try … 'ha-ha.'"

I can't help but laugh. Internally. My mind flashes on an obscure definition few know.

A **ha-ha** (French: *hâ-hâ* or *saut de loup*), also known as a **sunk fence, blind fence, ditch and fence, deer wall,** or **foss,** is a recessed landscape design element that creates a vertical barrier (particularly on one side) while preserving an uninterrupted view of the landscape from the other side.

What better word to try and emulate? What sound better captures the hell I am in, this silent void of my skull, outward views obstructed, constrained by a situation that is anything but funny? For years, I've existed solely within a six-inch space between my ears. My imagination has turned out to be both a wonderful servant and a vengeful master.

I am also intrigued by the specificity of her challenge. Though Dr. Kubica has no way of knowing this, back when I was in college, I'd enrolled in a creative writing course, which was taught by a professor named King. At the time, he told us he was working on a novel. I was a kid, slowly falling to pieces. I didn't care about anyone else's book. I cared about the one *I'd* someday write.

Well, I'd be damned, if years later, while scrolling through Audible, I didn't stumble across Professor King's book: *The Ha-Ha.*

It's about a brain damaged man who cannot speak.

This isn't a coincidence.

I am laughing. In my head. As usual, the sound remains confined, ricocheting around my cranium like a blaster shot fired inside the trash compactor of a space soap opera.

Except today.

Today, a sound comes out.

No, not a sound.

A word. A real goddamn word.

"Ha … ha," I say.

CHAPTER NINETEEN

RETURN OF THE COUNT OF MONTE CRISTO

"Hey, buddy," Frank says as we smoke cigarettes, watching snow fall through the crosshatched squares of our cage. It's very cold. I'm bundled in donated sweaters. No one bothers to check on us anymore. "I hear those meetings with the doc have been coming along swell."

I don't know how Frank would know this, but it's hard not to smile. It just took that one word to break the spell. I'm not rapping or speed reading. But I *am* talking again. I still have miles to go. Every journey begins with a single step.

I've been inside the asylum now over three months, the last two weeks being the most productive. Today is Monday, November thirteenth. I've worked hard to regain what I lost in the accident. I didn't believe it was possible. Even when I convinced myself I could do it, there was a defeatist part of me that refused to buy in. But I've done it. I really have.

"Tell me," Frank says, "How are you today?"

"G-g-g—" I stammer, fighting against getting flustered, frustrated, wanting to give up.

"You got this, buddy. Take your time."

I steady my breathing, focus, draw upon all my strength, the core of which centers on positivity and gratitude. Which is imperative, Dr. Kubica insists. In the beginning, I was focused only on revenge, paying back the hurt I owed. What they'd done to my father. What they'd done to my brother. Like hitting a golf ball (yes, I play the sport—I was quite good when I was younger; I'd tell you what I shoot in a round, but you'd never believe me), the farther you want to the ball to go, the easier you have to swing. It's counterintuitive.

Relax.

"Come on," Frank says, grinning. "Don't be rude. I asked you a question. How are you doing?"

"G-g-good."

"Look at you, buddy. Turning back into your old self."

Since Frank doesn't live on this floor, I don't see him as often as I'd like. But he's as responsible for my resurgence as Dr. Kubica. They took opposite approaches. The doctor harnessed hope and optimism; Frank used my naturally rebellious streak to spark and motivate.

I don't want to get ahead of myself or break my arm patting myself on the back. It's hard not to bask, though. Like riding a bicycle for the first time, catching a baseball from your old man, or finally learning how to tie your own shoes. The sensation is overpowering. I can't help it. I feel the tears mounting. One of my biggest fears: crying in front of others.

Stupid, I know. At the Institute, they call that "toxic masculinity." When I grew up it was called being a man, crying a sign of weakness. You can post all the PSAs or inspirational memes you want, when you're a boy and you cry in front of your dad and he's standing there, towering over you, calling you a "mama's boy" and chastising you to "stop being such a pussy" or calling you a "faggot," it's harder to shake. You internalize the shame, and it festers.

"I'm proud of you, buddy," Frank says.

I can accept an insult much easier than I can withstand a compliment. Tell me I'm a piece of shit, garbage, useless, a bum. Blame me for my brother's drug problem, which is what led him to Amy and that goddamn family. Fine. No problem. Tell me I'm worthwhile and deserving of being loved, and I fall apart. Anger is an energy. That's all sadness is, right? Anger turned inward. Wishing to spare others, you learn to hate yourself.

And now I'm sobbing. Frank is uncomfortable. Nothing makes a grown man as uncomfortable as another grown man crying. Yet, I can't stop. Frank motions for me to keep it down, then he grabs me, and I should recoil, have instinctual fear, given this pathetic, childlike state I've reverted to, but I don't. I melt. He holds me, and I let him. He holds me and lets me cry for a long, long time.

When I've calmed down, Frank waves me along with his head, toward a corner of the cage, safe from prying eyes. He pulls out the day's newspaper—I assume it's today's paper.

It's not.

It's letters. Handwritten letters. I can't read them. But I know who they are from.

Emily.

"Hey, buddy," Frank says, "Want me to read one?"

I do. But seeing my niece's instantly identifiable script jolts me back to the present, begging an equally pressing question: How does—*why does*—Frank have them?

Frank anticipates this. "Buddy," he says. "You know they've made me, like, your special friend in here. A guardian. I look out for you." He catches my eye. "I've looked out for you, haven't I?"

Yes, you have.

"Say it."

"Y-y-y-yes. Y-y-you. H-h-have."

"There you go, buddy. Deep breaths. The staff knows you can't read. Yet. We didn't want to overwhelm you. I've been waiting for the right time. Don't be mad, okay?"

I'm not *mad*, per se, but I've been worried sick—

Frank puts his hand on my shoulder. "This feels like the right time."

He starts reading, and any lingering feelings of anger slip away, as he fills me in on Emily's life at White Mountain University. I don't know what I was expecting when I finally heard from my niece. Panic. Concern. A situation that demanded my immediate assistance. What I get instead are normal letters one could expect from a seventeen-year-old college student. The classes she's taking. A boy she likes. How much she misses her parents, which strikes me as odd. She includes both. Why shouldn't she? It's just that one is dead. *She never mentions Josh's death.* I know these letters are from her because she talks about stuff only Emily would know, like those regrettable, goofy, matching daisy tattoos Josh and I got, particulars of our youth, the in jokes, tone. It's Emily.

Where have these letters been? I catch Frank's eyes, and the expression he returns conveys conflict, as if allegiances are being tested.

A non-verbal processor, I've grown adept at reading people's truthfulness. There are pantomimes that betray duplicity. Frank *isn't* lying. He also is not being entirely forthright, and I can't figure out for the life of me what he'd have to withhold.

In our conversations, Frank has made it clear how much he hates Ari Fortman. I know Frank cares about me and has my best interest at heart. That's the first skill you pick up when you're like me: the ability to sniff out bullshit. Nothing Frank says is a lie. Pieces are missing.

Frank reads more letters. There are several. Everything in Em's life is pleasant. I don't know if he's skimming or skipping sections. It *sounds* like he's reading everything, and why wouldn't he? Frank, Emily, and I are all on the same side.

Aren't we?

CHAPTER TWENTY

THE WAITING PLACE

Complacency is a slippery slope. Especially when you have to carry that stone—a stone whose sole purpose is to drag you down. Sisyphus, be damned.

I've painted these three plus months in the New York State Asylum for Lunatics in the most accurate light I can. It hasn't been all sunshine and rainbows, but it hasn't been the worst thing to happen to me either. I am coming back to life. Those parts of me deadened and numbed from the accident have been allowed to regenerate, new nerve endings sprouting, granting permission to *feel* again—the good, the bad, and all those beautiful mishaps in between.

The one downside? Since that first day with Dr. Flynn, Debra hasn't been in touch. I opt for a "no news is good news" approach. I miss my stepmom. I need to accentuate the positive. Frank reminds me so much of Josh, in his size, his kindness, and the silent burden he shoulders. Regaining my abilities, I *feel* younger, like I'm turning back the hands of time. I'm getting better with my numbers. I try not to let the lack of communication from Debra get me down. Three months isn't *that* long. I have faith she is doing everything within her power to get me out.

My days consist of a strict schedule, a routine to which I rigidly adhere. Some might resent having their day so dogmatically mapped out. Not me. Left to my own devices, it's been well established, my results tend to suck.

So, it's up at seven, followed by breakfast, coffee, and morning cigarette. Then it's morning check-in, morning group, one-on-one with Dr. Kubica, lunch, afternoon check-in, afternoon group, and so it goes. I spend my free time in the smoking cage with Frank, who seems to have a new letter from Emily every day. Frank also shares the daily news with me. Ari is often in the headlines. The president is *always* doing or saying something crazy. You have to hand it to the guy. If nothing else, he's entertaining.

All in all? Weird as it might sound, it's not a bad life. I have a roof over my head. My belly stays full. Frank shares his cigarettes with me. This won't last forever. Debra is working out a plea as we speak.

It's just … where's the urgency? The fire that was driving me, this need to protect Emily—has been extinguished. I accept that my mania—my confabulation—contributed to my mental instability, which fueled outlandish scenarios. Benefiting from hindsight, I can see how it happened. Ari Fortman *is* a duplicitous, slimy, Washington lobbyist—and Blackmill/Fortman *did* know the ground that killed my dad was poisoned. But that is capitalism, the price of doing business in a free market economy. Call it collateral damage. Fines were paid, lawsuits settled, everyone shook hands and moved on. Everyone that is, except Josh and me. I'm still trying. As for my brother? He was shackled by his addictions, unable or -willing to let it go. The personal injustice committed against him—our father leaving everything to others—it was too much for the big guy. That final cut pushed him over the edge.

I've surrendered delusions my brother is still alive. I also acknowledge, on a deeper level, I *refuse* to let him die. I carry on conversations with him, where we joke and laugh about the good times, and he asks me questions, and I'll answer aloud. No one looks at you funny in a mental institution when they see you talking to yourself. Surrounded by grounded turkeys attempting to defy gravity and catatonic lumps with dented heads, these one-way conversations read perfectly natural.

That's why complacency plays the long game.

Remember the Dr. Suess book, *Oh, the Places You'll Go?* A favorite for newborns and recent grads. There is one section in that book that haunts me.

You might be wondering why I'm evoking literary analysis on a children's book, especially when I will never see the inside of a university. Unless I'm visiting Emily, that is. It's because Dr. Kubica, in her attempts to get me to read, has gifted me a stack of children's books. We are starting at ground zero. I don't believe these books come via hospital funds. Meaning Dr. Kubica bought them herself. It feels like she's taken a special interest in my case.

If I'm not mistaken, I gave *Oh, the Places You'll Go* to Emily when she was born. And I will likely send another copy when she graduates college. Revisiting the book, I find its impact—and that one passage in particular—hasn't softened with age.

THE WAITING PLACE

Waiting for a train to go or a bus to come,

or a plane to go or the mail to come,

or the rain to go or the phone to ring,

or the snow to snow…

Everyone is just waiting.

Though I can't read, I have that passage memorized. When I recite it for Dr. Kubica, she'll clap. I feel silly but proud. The woman is a doctor with years of training and expertise. I doubt she confuses my parroted ruse with bona fide reading. Still, it *is* a form of reading, this rote memorization, helping me reconnect faulty circuits, and we can't let perfection be the enemy of progress.

Why then am I so disquieted?

Josh is dead. Emily is okay. I can get on with my life.

And yet …

That passage won't leave me alone.

Everyone is just waiting.

I'm trying to explain how this connection gets made, which will propel where we go from here. Because it happens fast. I would love more organic propulsion, the Justice Department officially indicting Ari Fortman for his crimes, some other life-or-death impetus. I don't want you to feel like I'm cheating or this turn isn't earned. It's the totality of dreary days, the summation of a hard life lived harder than you can imagine, the droning repetition that I both appreciate and am beginning to resent, the time I feel slipping through my hands…

That's how it hits me, like one of my migraines. Fast, mean, relentless.

Why did they want the laptop?

I could've mailed it. Authorities didn't want me to mail it. They wanted me to hand deliver it. It was *that* important. Which brings me back to my conversation with Freddie outside the Erickson & Hansen Funeral Home, where he implored me to revisit those final communications with my brother. My brain, for all its faults, stores and catalogues info like a champ. I dial up Freddie's exact words:

If Josh did find something last minute? He'd relay that information to you. He trusted you more than anyone in this world…

My laptop belonged to the Institute. I used it for homework, and to communicate with my brother, nothing else. We'd email, FaceTime, text. Josh and I were closer than most, and our exchanges could get deeply personal. Family dynamics and dysfunction, our father and the affliction of his violence. But his final emails? Benign. Extra ordinary. Freddie said Josh uncovered a secret. Why wouldn't he tell me? Doesn't make sense, add up, compute. It's completely antithetical to our relationship.

And then I understand.

Because Josh *did* tell me. I didn't pick up on the clues.

Josh would've known our electronic communication would be dissected by the best and brightest minds—Ari has the United States government at his disposal. My brother couldn't risk sharing anything overt, couldn't spell it out. He'd have to be subtle, coy. My photographic recall allows me to revisit those final emails, everything he talked about, like a film projected on a screen. I study, examine, dissect, word for word. Nothing jumps out. He mostly talked about … our mother.

On the surface, that isn't too weird. A source of never-ending guilt, the hell we put the poor woman through. I remember at the end Josh and I separately sneaking into her hospice, stealing fistfuls of her morphine, and when one would catch the other, we'd act appalled. *How could you? To your own mother?*

That is what addiction does. It splits you in two. There is the you that is *you*, and then there is the *other* you. Which is which and who is who, a point of view.

We all live in cages. Don't act like you're any different. Your cage might be a cubicle or a factory or a tin can you drive around in delivering important documents. But it's a cage, nevertheless. What's the difference between a prisoner serving a life sentence and a nine-to-fiver stuck in a dead-end, soul-sucking job that siphons all their time? Who among us is free? We're all just rats on a wheel. Yes, I've mastered the profoundly obvious. That's what I do, how I whittle away the time. Like carving keys out of soap and hardening them in a furnace. Fire burns. Soap melts. And Josh was delivering flowers.

To our mother's grave.

No one else would catch that. Josh buried more than flowers.

He left a message for me. I can *feel* it. We are tethered by brotherly bonds that death cannot sever.

This is when I decide I must break out of the New York State Asylum for Lunatics.

And I know how I will do it.

CHAPTER TWENTY-ONE

THE DEVIL IS IN THE DETAILS Pt. III

"You sure you're ready?" Frank asks.

Not the response I'm expecting. Which would've been, "You're out of your mind!" Or "No way! Impossible!" That's when I know it can be done. I sense Frank has been waiting for me to ask—as well as the conflict raging inside him, like when Luke tries coaxing his dad to abandon the Dark Side.

Am I ready?

I wouldn't have asked otherwise.

"Out there, you'll be drawing attention to yourself. Stay here, buddy. It's not so terrible in this zoo, is it?" Frank tries to laugh it off. His expression wanes sincere, and it hurts, knowing someone loves and cares about me that much. "I don't want anything bad to happen to you. You're the first friend I've made in a long time."

That's nice to hear. I feel the same. And, no, it's not awful in the asylum. Some days it's downright pleasant. Frank is right: I'm safe here. The authority's insistence of getting their hands on the laptop, the need to deliver it in person—Josh's clandestine missives—could be a coincidence.

Except, if I learned one thing listening to audio books on private eyes and true crime? In the world of investigation, there's no such thing.

The question isn't whether I'm ready or if it's possible.

I know what can be done, but I can't do it alone.

The question is will Frank help?

It was during one of our smoking cage conversations, shortly after we became friends. Inhaling butts in the icy air, the subject of escape came up, hypothetically. Mindless chatter to kill the time. Humor me.

"If I wanted out of this place?" Frank had said, blowing slow rings. "Easy peasy Japanesey."

From our suspended cage, he'd pointed below, into the blanket of white covering the lower floors. As a long-term patient, Frank works down there, making furniture for the asylum, which they sell for profit, paying prisoners pennies on the dollar, keeping idle hands busy.

"Once a month, the third Thursday."

I stared.

"That's when they ship out the furniture we make. Some of those boxes contain dining room sets, chairs and tables." Frank had shrugged, sucking on a nub. "I wanted out? That's how I'd do it. Crate myself inside." He nodded into the mist. "Trucks start making local deposits within a couple hours. Might be a bit cramped. Plenty of air to breathe." Frank sailed his hand over the snow-covered horizon. "After that, you're home free…"

That was the entire conversation on the subject, a tossed-off few sentences sandwiched between Frank's insistence the 1978 Yankees would beat the more vaunted '98 team and ruminations on his favorite author, Richard Brautigan.

"And then what?" Frank asks.

We're back to the present, sharing the same spot in our cage. I could let another ten years pass, and we'd still be in this same spot. I won't allow myself to become another casualty of The Waiting Place.

Josh left me a message from beyond the grave, and I need to see what that message is.

I point at my chest. *Let me worry about that.*

"You want my help? You have to say it. You're going to need to talk out there."

He's right. I can't get lazy, falling back into old patterns. Sometimes it's easier to act out than it is to speak out.

"I … w-w-w-will … b-be … o-kay."

Frank rolls his eyes, shakes his head, employs a dozen other dismissive movements designed to get me to change my mind. It's unnecessary. He could just say no. Secretly, I think he *wants* me to make a run for it. Frank is old. Maybe once upon a time, he, too, entertained notions of breaking out of this place. At his age, it's not a realistic option anymore. He can live vicariously through me. I don't know his motivations. But if I were, say, writing a character, that's what I'd do. I'd have an older prisoner, one who takes a shine to a younger inmate, recognizes in him a kindred spirit. They'd share a common enemy, say, the Fortmans. Pupil to student. Mentor to protégé. Like poetry, it rhymes. The son becomes the father, and the father becomes the son.

Even as Frank is pretending to talk me out of it, I can sense his excitement building.

"What will you do out there?"

I don't tell Frank about the flowers or mention my mom's grave—he wouldn't understand. Josh's cipher was intended for me and no one else. Instead, I repeat what I've said so many times. It is my party line, my official stance, creed and slogan.

"N-nail th-the b-bas-t-t-tards to th-the w-wall."

"You're gonna bring down Ari Fortman." Frank's eyes light up, brighter than I've seen. Two high-watt bulbs embedded in deep-set sockets. Because Frank hates the Fortmans—and Ari in particular—as much as I do. Sometimes I think he hates them *more*. Ari is an easy man to hate, even if you don't know him personally. Just look at his smug, oversized head in the papers or on your television screen. Guys like Ari Fortman are a reminder that declarations of independence are a farce; that it's a rigged card game, and if you've been playing by the rules all along, you're a sucker.

"But how?" Frank asks, this time more urgent.

"L-let m-me w-worry ab-b-b-bout th-that." I hold firm. I won't hang anything concrete on him. Not because I don't trust Frank—I trust him with my life—I won't put Frank in harm's way.

Like I say, he can say no. I'll find another way. I could wait for Debra to come through, a prospect that feels less likely by the day. Maybe I cut a hole through chicken wire and risk frostbite, hypothermia, blackened toes and amputation. One way or another I'm getting out of here. I'd rather die than let Ari and Andy win.

I said long ago the only way anyone leaves this place is in a box.

CHAPTER TWENTY-TWO

THE NEW YORK ASYLUM FOR LUNATICS REDEMPTION

The furniture ships out Thursday afternoon. Third Thursday. Every third Thursday of the month. That's what Frank says. We wait. Which isn't as easy as it sounds.

Like Tom Petty (and Dr. Suess) tells us, that's the hardest part. Waiting. With emancipation on the horizon, days pass slower than ever. Watching paint dry, grass grow, kettles taking too long to boil. I use the extra time to shore up my communication skills, putting in extra effort with Dr. Kubica. I know she had bigger plans for me, but I can't tell her we've run out of time. I've learned enough to ask for limited directions—where is the nearest food or bathroom. I still can't read, but certain letters pop out more than they used to. I can spot "E" and "X" easier than "Q" or "Z," which won't be a Scrabble game-changer but should help me navigate highways. I try to keep my mood upbeat, stress-free, joking and kidding when appropriate. That's how I've been as a patient. It hasn't been an act. Working with Dr. Kubica has been beneficial and enjoyable. Counting remains beyond my reach; complex mathematics elude my skillset. Even before the accident, I seldom needed quadrangles or a hypotenuse. I can visualize geometric shapes; I don't need to label them.

Of course, no plan can go off without a hitch. There must be obstacles presented, hurdles placed in our hero's way. Otherwise, why not have the warden unlock the door and allow me to walk me out?

The first problem: the furniture ships during my afternoon session with Dr. Kubica. These sessions highlight days. I like the doctor. There is a part of me—a significant part—that wants to tip her off because I am twenty-three percent certain she'd help. Maybe she'd try to talk me out of it, get me to abandon revenge in favor of improving my ABCs. Continuing my treatment doesn't quench my thirst for justice.

Over breakfast, I am running through various ailments that can sideline a patient for an afternoon, when a counselor informs me that Dr. Kubica won't be in today. She's not feeling well.

I have not seen Frank for three days. As soon as the counselor leaves, Frank enters the cafeteria, skipping the line, and taking a seat across from me. He doesn't have a tray or any food.

I attempt eye contact, but Frank won't look at me. When I touch his arm, trying to learn why he's upset, all he says is, "I'm sick of oatmeal."

Which prompts a chorus of wild cheers and raucous wails from the neighboring table. To be fair, Frank could've said he hates ducks and gotten the same reaction. The men on this ward (save ol' Benny) are itching to start a riot. If you've never experienced institutional living, you might not understand. Not wanting to go somewhere isn't the same as being told you *can't* go somewhere. The asylum is tinder in search of a match.

Out on the smoking porch, Frank interprets Dr. Kubica's absence differently than I do. For me, it's a sign. I've long followed them, relied on them, a belief rooted in everything happens for a reason, even if we can't understand those reasons at the time. Sometimes it takes thirteen years. Finally, my life is making sense. I'm also in a good mood, perhaps *too* good, which grates on Frank, who has adopted my dour disposition.

Weird, how people swap roles.

"I don't know what you keep smiling for," Frank says. "But I'd appreciate it if you'd knock it off. You're grinning like a goddang hophead."

I look away. I don't want to agitate him further. I write off his surliness as waking up on the wrong side of the bed. Or maybe something is in the air. There are countless maxims and adages to excuse a bad mood.

The ward is often rowdy. Today, it's worse. Inmates bounce off walls, batty. It's like a barnyard before a storm—goats, cattle, and hogs anticipating the encroaching bomb cyclone. Gums flap. Caterwauls unleash. Through the cage's window, I spot ol' Benny, with his giant, misshapen, bent head, slumped in his chair, and I think if there were a time where he might say a few words, today would be it. The mood is that surreal. I'm waiting for a vegetable to jump up, tap-dance, and sing showtunes.

In therapy, we call this transference, projecting our emotions onto others. I understand what's going on. I'm getting out of here. Frank is not. That must sting. Yes, he could come with me. I invited him. He's scared. He's right to be scared. When officials are alerted of an escape, all roads will be sealed off, in and out. APB broadcasted. All-points bulletin. Be on the lookout. Escaped mental patient. Proceed with caution. I've watched movies. That's why hiding in the furniture crate is such an integral part of the plan. I need to get beyond town limits, past checkpoints and perimeters. By the time authorities are looking for me, I must be long gone.

The hands of the clock drag. I attempt to act nonplussed. Any time we're alone, Frank seems pissed off. For the first time since meeting him, I avoid Frank. We have a plan in place, and if when the time comes, I get to the door and Frank hasn't kept his word? Well, that's that. I'll find another way. Losing a friend will sting too. But whatever it takes I am getting out of this place.

With Dr. Kubica unavailable, I have hours at my disposal, which I spend lying on my bed, staring at the ceiling, trying to still my busy mind. I've never been good at that. It doesn't take long for *any* thought to circle back to the monumental task confronting me. I search for holes to identify, plug, fix, caulk, spackle, but only succeed in locating more potential pitfalls.

First and foremost: why is this so easy?

It's not, though, is it? Not really. I've ingratiated myself to the right person. Frank, with his senior privileges, functions as the insane asylum's version of a prison trusty, a middleman who's earned the respect of staff, and thus is granted more freedom. I know counselors and doctors are thrilled with Frank for the way he's taken me under his wing, how he's helped nurse this broken bird back to health. They are always congratulating him. I often see Frank alone with staff. They joke and laugh, as if he were an employee too. *You need to release me into the wild, Frank. It's time for me to soar.*

I wonder where Dr. Flynn is. I never see her after that first day. Her office now belongs to another doctor, a man. He is tall, slim, and grave. I don't know whether Dr. Flynn has been moved to another unit, promoted, or fired. Given the intensity of our first interaction—at least the first I recall—I'd anticipated seeing much more of her. She'd positioned herself as a prominent player. It's like she's been written out of the story. I tell myself I am looking for trouble where there is none. Today, I am leaving. Am I too giddy to spot the obvious danger, the signpost flashing up ahead, the one that warns against meeting devils you don't know?

The next time I see Frank, I change my mind: he's not worried I'll get caught.

He is worried I won't.

"And then what?" Frank pleads with me after lunch, where we sit in the smoking cage. The cigarette feels like a last one before the firing line.

"I n-n-nail t-t-he b-b-b—"

"Bastards to the wall. Yes. I know." Frank's mannerisms, the hostility, jerky hands and rapid speech, belie a man sick of subterfuge and secrecy. I can't tell him about what I plan to do because I don't *know* what I plan to do. I have one destination in mind—my mother's grave. What happens if I get there and don't find anything? I have no back-up contingency. I am not thinking well. They've prescribed me an obscene amount of medication, which I've needed to ween myself off of. At the med counter, I pretend to swallow half a dozen pills, tabs, and capsules, spitting them out once I round the corner and find a bathroom. I've been doing a good job. I think. I don't know what these drugs are, their half-lives, or if I can expect to experience withdrawal. Lately, I've been getting these little lightning storms crackling in my skull. Not too bad. Every so often, though: zap! I'll grow dizzy, imbalanced, afraid I'll fall. I share none of this with Frank.

"I-I'll b-b-be f-f-fine."

This is the only answer I offer. The statement, memorized and easy to repeat, is meant to quell Frank's fears. If I'm cut down by a sniper twelve feet beyond prison walls? Where's the great loss? Outside of my niece, no one will miss me. I know that sounds depressing. To me, the sensation is liberating. Win, lose, draw: I will be done with The Waiting Place.

"The Fortmans are bad people," Frank says. He says it with such intensity, you'd think they'd murdered *his* father and brother. "Whitey Bulger has nothing on those two. Especially Ari. I'd love nothing more than to see that asshole get what's coming…"

His words trail off, lost to the wailing winter winds.

I'd accuse Frank of hyperbole. If I didn't find the New England gangster analogy so spot on. Both are bad dudes. The big difference: Bulger spent years working as an undercover informant for the government. Ari Fortman doesn't need to hide or cut any backroom deal. Every day Frank shows me a picture of the prick operating out in the open. Front page of the papers, gladhanding with the elite, posing for photo ops despite legal woes. The greatest trick the devil ever pulled wasn't that he didn't exist; it's that with the right profit margin no one gives a shit.

I'm not sure how I'll get to Bennington. What will I do once I kick open that box, hop off the truck, and land in snow? I don't know. Hope for a soft landing? Hitch a ride to Vermont? Steal a car? I've done it before. I have no identification. I understand in many ways, this is a suicide mission. I accept my prospects are dim. I don't expect to take down the Fortman Brothers. Like Rocky, I know I can't win. I just want to go the distance. Give it my all, stay on my feet and survive the final bell. I must try for my brother's sake. It's the least I can do. He sent me a secret message, "X marks the spot." I need to uncover what he planted and make sure Emily is okay. See her with my own two eyes. After that? I don't want to die. I'm not looking forward to it. I also don't much mind if I do. I know that sounds morbid. I'm not sad. I'm neither pessimist nor optimist. People who know me would claim the former. I'd argue the latter. I've lived in a brick building for a quarter of my life, a man-child unable to hold a pen correctly, and I've woken every day and managed to do my best. I'm almost fifty years old. My only friend is a man I met a few months ago, and one I recall a third of that. I have a stepmom. I also accept that Debra is at a stage where, if we're being honest, my … removal … would be met with relief. She'd never admit it. I know she loves me. But every day I breathe costs her money. I'm a drain.

I could wait. Perhaps, her efforts will pay off. I'll get summoned to the principal's office. Receive a hall pass. Techer's note. Told I'm free to go. If so, what has this episode cost me in the end? A few months of my life. In exchange? I've regained the ability to speak. I've come out ahead. I also don't believe a goddamn word of that.

"There's no talking to you," Frank says. I don't know how much of the conversation I missed.

When Frank accepts he can't talk me out of it—I am going to do this with or without his help—and without his help he knows I have *no* chance—my friend begins to come around. We stop quibbling. He finds me a change of clothes, jeans, tee, flannel, and jacket that fit my six-foot, two-hundred-pound frame. They feel so warm and familiar, I'd swear they've been tailored for me.

While a patient at the asylum, I've let my beard grow hobo scraggly. In my goodbye bag, Frank packs a razor, tiny canister of shaving cream, and an envelope. When I peek inside, I don't need to count the twenties to know I will have options.

There is a note as well, a simple directive. Like playing Wheel of Fortunate, I'll take a "B," "E," add in a space, throw in a "C" and "R," and another "E," and I'll solve the puzzle.

Be Careful.

And now I'm reading too.

At one o'clock, as planned, I sneak down the unit's far corridor, past the kitchen and supply room, rounding the corner, entering blackness. Feeling my way, I find the normally locked basement door left ajar.

Frank chose this exit point because it's a blind spot for the cameras. I slip through the crack, and slink down the old, creaky stairs.

Down the long hall, men stack boxes, hammering crates, chattering. A weak light, like a spelunker's dying headlamp, fades as they walk away. As per Frank's explicit instructions, I make my way to the large crate, the one nearest the loader and stuffed with a dinette set. I crawl inside, creeping back to the deepest recesses of this innermost cave, huddling into a ball. I turn from the light, so that even the whites of my eyes stay hidden; and I pray to those things I claim not to believe in.

I steady my breathing, find that meditative center, stilling my environs. I might even fall asleep.

Then: the pounding of a nail, a final wall erected, and I am sealed within. Time passes. I can't say how much. Closer to an hour than a cluster of minutes. The box is hoisted to a chorus of foul-mouthed men, oblivious to the human cargo inside. With a thud, I am loaded into the back of a trailer. Hatch. Snap. Lock. A smack on the side sends me off.

An engine growls. Gears shift, wheels roll over dirt, gravel, ice, snow, and now I am on a road. I smell fresh air for the first time in ages. It smells like antiseptic and the sea. No alarm bells ring. No hound dogs yap in hot pursuit. I hear no bullhorns or sirens. Like I was never here.

The drive doesn't take long. It's short enough that I don't have time to consider whether to bust out of the box but long enough that when the vehicle stops, I know we are nowhere near the asylum.

I listen for the sounds of traffic. A gas or weigh station, perhaps. It doesn't feel like we've driven on the highway. I hear nothing but vast country silence.

Even when the gate lifts, and I hear the heavy steps climb aboard—even when the crowbar pries out the nails and I see Frank standing there—I don't understand.

"Why didn't you listen to me?" Frank says.

It isn't until he pulls up the gun, orders me out into the middle of the cold woods, and tells me to get on my knees that it hits me: I'm not as smart as I think.

CHAPTER TWENTY-THREE

A MURDER OF CROWS

"Why didn't you listen?" Frank repeats, his sloe eyes agitated.

We are standing among a copse of trees, which adds to the gold-fish bowl aesthetic. Walls of evergreen and granite, the hard stone my father and brother used to drill, split, and blast, rise high into the gray sky. Bedrock, Earth's foundation. No one within earshot. When Frank levels the barrel, aims the muzzle, slips his fingers inside the trigger guard, applies the slightest pressure and blows my fucking brains out, the cannon blast that results will be swallowed by the holler and dense forestation of these natural formations.

"All you had to do was stay put," Frank says, and even now he sounds like a man trying to convince himself there's a way out. There is. But for only one of us.

It's like our roles are reversed. Frank holds out hope. For my part, I am resigned. Perhaps even relieved. With his free hand, Frank clutches a brown, paper bag, which he tosses at my feet.

A deer encroaches, skittish and uncertain, as if it might be food.

"Shoo," he shouts. The deer wanders but doesn't move far. "Open it."

Still on my knees, I peek inside and find my wallet and identification.

"You'll need those for the coroner to identify the body." The revolver squarely on me, Frank's hand trembles. I don't get the impression this is his first time with a gun. His nervousness stems from trepidation, apprehension, remorse, guilt, the emotions that have bogged me down for years, kept me inactive, sloth-like, incapacitated at times. I recognize the symptoms. That's what those emotions do. They hinder; they do not motivate.

He doesn't want to pull that trigger.

We stand seven, eight feet part, best guest. I'm getting better with my numbers. If I fell face first, I'd land short of his boots. We are in a perfect circle of white, surrounded by grazing deer. Big, black birds perch on bare, broken branches, a murder of crows, and all around us snow. I've lived this scene so many times. The bleakness. The surrender. The near euphoria that signals the end is nigh. And I wouldn't being thinking of words like "nigh" if not for Nick Cave and that girl who really, really liked me, and how that one night, all fucked up, she sang me "The Ship Song" on her grandmother's piano before taking me to bed, but I was too fucked up to get it up. She said, "You're a real rock star," and I said, "Oh, no, you go too far." I'm a thief, a fraud, an official appreciator of the talent of others, my life a collage of song snippets and obscure pop culture trivia. I am the speaker in Tobias Wolf's "Bullet in the Brain." Nothing is real, everything absurd, the dream within the dream.

"Can you stop doing that for once?!" Frank is shaking the gun at me. "Stop drifting off to la-la land! Man, are you *ever* in the moment?"

That makes me laugh, and my juddering makes Frank angry. He wants me to show fear, to beg, to barter, as if sticking around this place offers intrinsic rewards. I've been trying to die for years now. That's what the drugs were. That's why I was content to stack blocks in a brick building, waiting for cells to break down, pissing out pieces of what I used to be. I've been killing myself in the most lackadaisical fashion possible. Suicide for the lazy. It's hysterical, if you think about it. I mean, you can't think about it *too* hard. But if you think about it *just* enough… Comedy. Tragedy plus time. All I do is misread situations and mess things up. Why should today be any different?

I take in the expanse of white, the subtle shades, which offers contrast. Doing so makes me think of when I got to San Francisco and how I joined a big band and replaced a lead singer who went on to front one of the biggest rock 'n' roll bands in the world—I could tell you the name of the band but you wouldn't believe me—while I dragged down the remaining members with my megalomania, crippling heroin addiction, and questionable vocal talents. I used to be able to sing. By that point, I didn't want to sing, didn't care about staying in tune, had no interest in supplying a pleasant listening experience for the audience. I wanted to stand high, lord above all, and scream at those beneath me, inflict them with my anger, ire, and jealousy. I wasn't jealous of that other guy's band, the singer I replaced. I didn't care that they were getting played on KFOG and dude was banging women *way* out of his league with his phony dreadlocks. I was good looking. I didn't hurt for women. I was jealous of everyone with a working brain—and not because of the fracture that continued to divide my cerebral cortex like split rock. Long before the accident, I knew I was different from these people who could think clearly and speak well, who didn't stutter or feel inadequate. All I felt was pain, all the time. How can you explain personal pain? A teenager's brain trapped inside a twenty-three-year-old man? Twenty-three turns forty-seven real quick. No one cares about a forty-seven-year-old malcontent. We could chart my origin story, go back to the beginning, and you'd have to know I would end up here.

A large deer with antlers, I guess that makes it a buck, clears a spot beside Frank with its horns, scratching for food.

"Will you fucking say something?"

What would you like me to say, Frank? Even that buck isn't scared of you? Deer are notoriously skittish. Yet, no fear. Or do you want to hear that life isn't fair? Bad guys don't get punished? Good guys don't always win? I can't say that. There is no good or bad or right or wrong. Everyone is the hero of their own story. You want me to fight back? Pitch a fit like a brat throwing a tantrum over not getting the specific cookie he wants? I already had this realization, Frank. Years ago, when I stopped doing drugs. They dragged me to sobriety kicking and screaming because no one understood how much pain I was in. It wasn't until much later, I realized everyone hurt the same way. Sure, your pain is unique. Just like everyone else's. Like that R.E.M. song we used to make fun of because it was so earnest and sentimental, but that's the thing with sincerity: it's easy to mock. The more damaged you are, the quicker you turn everything into a joke. You're not fooling anyone with that mask you wear. Acting like it's a big goof to soften the blow. A wink and a nudge. So you get all these joke bands where everything is a gas, jumping jack flash, endless tracks about erectile dysfunction in the key of D.

Ha ha.

It's easy to make fun of everything when you don't stand for anything.

"If you don't say something," Frank says, seething. "I swear to Christ, I will shoot you in the stomach and let you bleed out. I'll fuckin' do it. Don't test me, buddy."

I watch the flurries float and flutter. Bucks, doe, and fawn stamp imprints in the snow, prancing around covered oaks, in these fields of white that bury small, dead flowers. Until now, I'm not sure I ever noticed the contrast of white on white. If I'd tried, put in some effort,

I think I could've fronted a successful band. I have a natural ear for melody.

Frank lowers his gun. "Say something!" He's pleading with me to give him reasons not to shoot me. But I knew he wasn't shooting me five minutes ago.

"I … have … to go."

Frank howls a laugh. It echoes, races, carries, and rattles across the valley floor, up the jagged, ragged mountain sheafs, clapping back on us in this giant fishbowl.

Two lost souls swimming…

Everything is a song lyric if you try hard enough.

"You just had to stay there *a little while longer.*" Frank brings up the gun, levels it, keeps it trained on me.

Frank isn't going to shoot me. Well, I'm eighty-four percent certain he isn't going to shoot me. I could get off my knees, which are freezing by the way, rush him, call his bluff. Instead, I remain rooted to the earth, fight-or-flight leaning toward the latter, so maybe those odds aren't as favorable as I'd like to believe.

"You know why I'm in the asylum?"

"Y-you k-kil-l-led y-your w-w-wife."

"Yeah. I did. And that puts you in prison, buddy. Except I worked for a very powerful family. A very powerful family that pulled strings. Got me McMurphied and placed in a nut ward, which is no picnic, but it beats fighting off rape in prison showers. And all it cost me was a favor. A favor I'd have to wait twenty years to pay back."

It's easy to put two and two together. Like I said, I'm getting better with my numbers.

"The Fortman Brothers?" Frank says. When I don't confirm, he unnecessarily adds the word, "Construction?"

I nod. Which is easier than saying, "No shit."

"That's why they sent you there." Frank shakes the gun. "We had to make it *one* more day. You signed the papers. The girl." Frank looks toward the heavens. "The girl," he says again, slower, softer, sadder. "But the furniture ships when the furniture ships."

I don't care about timetables. I'm thinking about my niece.

I readjust my odds to a coin flip. No, he doesn't *want* to shoot me, but at this juncture it might be the path of least resistance.

"They called in a favor," Frank says. "When Ari Fortman calls in a favor, you pay it. It's either you or me. I still have a family out there. I have a son and daughter. I can't even tell you how old they are. I can tell you they hate me. For good reason. I'm going to die inside that asylum. But Ari Fortman? I don't do this? They'll go after my kids. My only legacy. It's you. Or it's me."

If I could respond quick enough, I'd love to offer my take on the situation, start a discourse beyond "we are all going to die" platitudes. This idea of being trapped in cycles of dysfunctional debt fascinates. We owe hurt. Or we are *owed* hurt. Perpetual, painful reciprocity. No one is innocent. The wheel won't stop spinning until we break the cycle.

"I'm not the only one involved," Frank says. "Why do you think it was so easy for you to leave? Why didn't Dr. Kubica show up today? You just walked out of a mental hospital—"

"I-i-n-n a b-box."

"Did you think escaping a lock-down psychiatric facility would be that easy? Do you know why today is so important?"

Frank doesn't give me a chance to respond.

"I like you, buddy," Frank says.

"I l-like you t-too."

And the strange thing is we both mean it.

"But, son, you're in over your head." Frank's face contorts, confliction ripping at the seams. "Meeting you," he says. "Watching you fix your brain and talk again, it was like God was giving me a second chance. I'm old enough to be your dad. And maybe that's fucked up, me putting this on you. But I never got to be one, y'know? I helped you, didn't I, buddy?"

"Yes." Without hesitation.

"I helped you, right?" Frank says. "I was good to you, wasn't I?"

For a while at least. I nod. Frank bobs his head, scratches his scraggy chin with the muzzle. "But blood…" Frank's arm stiffens, gun once-more squared. "Truth is, you're not going to make it. You want to know why I helped you? It wasn't this. You have to believe me. For a few moments there, I believed—honest and true—you could pull this off. Get to the Fortmans. You know *something*. You don't want to tell me because you want to protect me, the urgency to leave coming on so fast." Frank points with his free hand, up the road. "When we left, I intended to take you to the highway. You saw all that money I gave you?"

"Th-th-thanks."

"I don't want a thank you!" Frank says through gritted teeth, which seldom happens in real life. In books, people talk through clenched jaws, which is not physically possible. It's done to show a character is angry. I know Frank is angry. So he speaks through gritted teeth. "I wanted you to bring the bastards down!" Frank waves the gun over his person. "Look at me! I'm old, broken, beaten. You? You're healing growing stronger. There's still fire in your eyes. *You* can do this!"

I shrug. I don't have a say here. This is the coin toss. Either I live or Frank does. I'm not the one doing the flipping.

I lock eyes with a doe. Such sad, mournful eyes. Her buck places itself between us, as if I'm the danger.

"I *hate* Ari Fortman. More than the merciless god that put me here. I did what I did. For that, I will burn. I don't deserve forgiveness. Ari didn't put me in that asylum to help me out. He put me there to use, an asset, a bargaining chip. That's what Ari does. Why do you think he's thriving with those snakes in D.C.? You heard all this crap about him going to prison. Prison for Ari Fortman? Ha! They might make a dog-and-pony show out of it, put him in some cushy, low security Federal pen. A few months. He'll be pardoned in a year. It's a game, buddy! It's all a game! And it's stacked. Against you. Against me. Everything is in favor of the Fortmans of this world. *They* are why your father died, your brother, and now if I don't do this—the only goddamn good thing I've done with my wretched life—my children's memory will be wasted too."

I'm swapping those odds, putting my chances of walking away from this at seventeen percent.

Frank doesn't cock the hammer. You don't need to cock a hammer to fire a gun. It's a movie trick to show a villain is serious. I know Frank is serious. I also know he's hurting. I wish I could throw my arms around him, hold him the way he did me in the smoking cage.

"The first thing you do, buddy," he says. "Slide off the safety."

I watch as he makes a production of it.

"If Ari and his brother don't die, they will make you suffer. Anyone left you care about? That stepmother who's taken care of you, who's like a real mother to you? She gone. And that niece? Yeah, Emily."

Hearing Frank say Emily's name, I feel the fight in me stir. Like a boxer knocked down in the twelfth, the air sucked out of him, I search deep for a second wind, rising from my knees. It's about time I took a stand where I belong.

"She'll be next," Frank says. "You think because she's Andy's grandkid that matters? Ari wants to hurt you more. There's no love in that man's heart. He's a machine, a single-purpose bulldozer. Gain power, roll over, pulverize anyone standing in his way. Andy too. They're sadists, sociopaths. I'm sure Andy and Ari liked your father fine. Your brother too. When he became a threat, did they hesitate? They will make your life a never-ending hell. This is a mercy killing."

The big, black birds perched on bare, birch branches sit still.

It all goes silent.

The Earth.

The oaks.

The hills.

Even the snow stops, large crystalline flakes suspended mid-air.

The last thing I hear before bullet pierces brain is the frantic sounds of galloping, graceful limbs and flapping wings fleeing skeletal trees, soaring into the distance.

PART THREE

RECKONING

CHAPTER TWENTY-FOUR

NOTHING FEELS BETTER THAN BLOOD ON BLOOD

When I feel nothing, I look down, pat my body, surprised to find it intact. No blood. I think Frank's fired a warning shot or maybe killed a deer.

I'm mistaken.

For a moment, Frank's body remains impossibly upright. The hole that's been blown through the back of his head has opened a portal. I swear I can see straight through to the other side, where my brother stands. The gunshot hasn't killed Frank. Not right away. He still appears alert. The moment is almost imperceptible, but in that fraction of a millisecond, before all life leaves Frank's body and eyes, a small, sad smile carves on his face and his lips move, as if he's trying to speak. I'd like to believe he's wishing me luck.

Then Frank falls forward, plank stiff, face first, white snow stained blood red, spreading like strawberry syrup. Of all the odd associations, that's the first one that comes to mind: my hometown's yearly fair. The Berlin Fair was a cultural event, three celebratory days cordoned off by stacks of hay in the pouring rain. Even now I can smell it, the farm animals, sheep, pigs, horses, the deep-fried, fatty foods, and … shit. French fries, giant powdered donuts, animal droppings. The big draw was the culinary treats. The town landed a long way from Soho. In Berlin, fried dough is considered exotic. The grounds also stank like funky dung. I remember Josh and I would be so excited to get snow cones. Even if it rained—and it always rained during the Berlin Fair. Didn't matter which weekend they held the event, which month. September, October, whenever. That's what Frank's blasted head reminds me of, lying there in the snow: sticky strawberry syrup poured over clear ice shavings.

Then it's just the two of us.

Me and my very much still alive brother, Josh.

Josh is holding a gun, which smokes. It's pretty cool to witness, the wisps of heated steam rising from the muzzle into slate skies. Maybe Dad was right, and he *is* the manlier of the two. I've never fired a gun. My brother might as well be Charlie Bronson, the way he stands with his smoking gun over the fresh kill. His revolver is identical to the one Frank had pulled on me. I can't give it a name.

I should be surprised. I'm not. A part of me refused to let Josh die. A part of me clung to the belief that one day I'd open my eyes and my baby brother would be there. I never lost faith. When my mother used to drag me to church, there was this one biblical reading that stuck, like The Waiting Place, how if man had faith the size of a mustard seed, he could command a mountain to throw itself into the sea. I don't know if my faith is as big as a mustard seed. I do know it's powerful enough to resurrect the dead.

"How did you know—?"

"Tracked." Josh points at Frank's truck as he holsters his firearm behind his back like a bad ass in a movie. I don't recall my brother's owning a gun, let alone shooting anything. Dad might've taken him hunting. I wouldn't have been invited. My father ignored me most of my life. "Those hauling trucks have a GPS," Josh says. "All freighters use them. I had one in my truck. Can't buy a goddamn truck these days without it. Boss man always wants to know where his drivers are."

Josh towers above, like I remember him, larger than life, six foot six, three hundred pounds, cynical, surly, a sparkle in his eye. The warmth never leaves his face. We both have resting asshole face, culled from years when our father used to make fun of us if we smiled. Anytime our mom smiled, he'd tell her to "knock it off" because it made her "look stupid." Josh scowls. But he can't hide who is he, not from me.

I see beyond the mask. I remember my baby brother from when we were kids. He didn't always look so angry and irascible. His eyes used to crinkle with kindness, cheeks cherubic. Out of the two of us, my baby brother inherited our mother's enviable, more likable disposition. I was afflicted with our father's violence, rage, and willingness to act on it from the start. It was only later Josh gave into the hatred and sorrow too, let that blackness fill his heart.

It's not a competition. In most ways, like many sons, Josh and I are replicas of our father. Two sides of the same delightful coin. We look like him. We act like him. We harbor his wrath and vindictive spirit.

I always suspected, Josh or I would kill somebody one day, our tempers and inability to control them getting the best of us.

I would've bet on me.

I stare at the dead body, bathed in blood, coming to terms with the tough decisions we all must make.

Like you said, Frank … it was you or me.

Tear-filled, I run to my brother and wrap my arms around him, shaking.

"The crying, shaking hug." Josh laughs. His laughs envelopes his entire person. The crying, shaking hug is our private joke from the time Josh found me walking along the side of the road after I skipped out of another rehab, when he rescued me with half a bundle of heroin and fresh pack of rigs.

I don't want to let go, afraid that if I don't keep my arms wrapped around him, he'll vanish, disappear forever. I can't lose him again. Without my brother, I'm so non-existent, Marty McFly's already lost half a leg.

Questions flood my mind, but I'm too scared to stop holding him. I've missed his smell, the grease and grime, the orange pumice soap, even that pungent, ungodly stench from his stinky shoes.

Josh peels my hands. "We'll have plenty of time to catch up on the ride."

He doesn't need to tell me where we're going.

It's been a long time since I've visited Mom.

I wish we could give Frank a proper burial. Dig a ditch, utter a few words. We don't have that luxury. The ground is frozen solid. A car might drive by any moment. This snow-covered stretch of road is remote and remains unplowed, but it's accessible. I am still an escaped mental patient from a psychiatric hospital. I don't know who was in on it, who helped Frank get me out of there so the Fortmans could execute me—Dr. Flynn, Dr. Kubica, the board of directors, every looney tune patient? Everyone remains a suspect. Except poor bald catatonic Benny in his wheelchair. Sooner than later, I will be discovered missing. The manhunt will be on.

The truck has a latch, a tailgate lock, which is easy to disengage. I snatch the keys from the ignition. We drag the carcass, a thick streak of red trailing behind the blasted head, a fresh coat of paint slathered on a naked canvas. I unhitch the back, load Frank in the boxcar with the furniture, and seal him inside. It's less than a creature of God deserves, but it's the best I can do. I bless myself with the stations of the cross. At least he won't be eaten by wild animals.

I replace the padlock but it won't snap in place. I kick fresh powder over the bloodstains, concealing the crime scene best I can. It's a sloppy job that won't hold up upon closer inspection.

Josh has removed the GPS from Frank's truck. Working in gravel pits and quarries, he knows more about trucks and their gizmos than I do. I wouldn't know where to look.

"I'll drive," Josh says, climbing in the front seat of Frank's truck.

I don't see any other vehicle. I don't question how Josh got here. I tell myself he must've parked deep in the holler to stay stealth. The answer suffices, is enough to get me in that cab with him.

Of course, he's driving. My baby brother has taken charge of the mission. It's the only way to get us home. I can't think straight.

My questions can wait until we are on the highway.

Soon, Josh has us blended in with the traffic on I-90. We're just another inconspicuous truck commuting among a glut of them. I turn to him. He's already lit a cigarette. I motion for one.

He slides out a Camel, holding off passing it along. "These things will kill you." He laughs so hard, I swear the cab shakes. "I thought you quit. Why would you pick up this filthy habit again?"

"Nothing else to do in there," I say, lighting up.

My brother keeps his eyes peeled, checking the side- and rearview. I mirror his motions. No one follows. A light snow falls, or it's ground cover swirling, icy remnants kicked back into the atmosphere, the sky weaving a tapestry of silver, white, and gray. The roads are still slick from earlier storms.

"I'm glad you figured out the clues," he says. "Sorry, I couldn't spell it out."

"Took me a while."

"Three months in the loony bin. I can't imagine."

"No worse than some of the rehabs I was in."

"That's why they wanted your laptop," Josh says. "To scour, find out what I knew, what I told you, which is why I had to be sneaky." Josh beams. He's got a great smile. When he's happy and unburdened, he radiates joy. Death has been good for him. "I knew you'd get it."

"The flowers," I say.

My brother looks over. He seems far younger than I remember, almost kid-like, smooth shaven, which he hasn't been for years. I'm witnessing Josh Benjamin Button before my eyes. "I've missed you," he says.

He's talking about more than the last time I saw him. He means those wild drug days, that crazy time in San Francisco, twenty-whatever years ago, because once I cleaned up and he didn't, it was never the same between us. Wasn't possible. Not when one of you pulls his act together and the other keeps running. An invisible wall is erected. When we were both using, though? Man, it was a helluva ride, and we were tight. Like the Boss says, nothing feels better than blood on blood. I know we have a mission to complete, but I wish I could stop time. The moment feels perfect. Smoking cigarettes and laughing with my brother. This is Heaven. I want to place it in my forever box, seal it up tight, stow it away for safe keeping, take it out whenever I get lonely, which I know will be coming soon.

"Trust me," Josh says, refocusing my whimsy. "They're doing a deep dive on that laptop you gave the police."

"Let them. I only used it to communicate with you."

"That's what they're looking at."

"Who's 'they'?"

"Cops. Andy, Ari. Hartford detectives. The Feds. Authorities. All the same. There's them. And there's us. Eventually, they'll piece together the clues. We don't have a lot of time."

"When did you figure it out?" I ask.

"When did I know my father-in-law and Ari were trying to kill me?"

"For starters…"

"For starters…" he says. "I know as much as you do." Josh cracks his window, flicks his burning butt. "I stopped off for gas one morning. The cashier put something in the coffee. Every day, same gas station, same time. Predictable patterns. That's how they got me. If we are to pull this off, you'll need to be *unpredictable*."

Patterns become patterns because of repetition. Repetition defines predictable. Disrupt regularity, you interrupt expectation and circumvent the future, altering fate.

"When I realized they'd spiked the coffee, I threw it out. But it told me I was onto something." Josh lights another Camel. "I'd been looking into some heavy shit. Family tree project for Em. On the web. They must've been monitoring my activity." He side-eyes me, as if uncertain how much to divulge out loud. *Why? It's just the two of us, right?*

Or maybe I misread the look and I'm supposed to fill in the blanks. Yes, that's what I'm supposed to do. I need to put it out there. I need to speak for him. Once I do, it officially becomes part of the story.

"Freddie," I say.

"Freddie was telling the truth." Josh jabs the glowing cherry tip at me, getting fired up. "Blackmill Solutions is part of Fortman Brothers. How you like that bullshit?"

"They knew the soil that killed Dad was contaminated."

"Yes." That look again. "Then they opened up their fat checkbook and bought everyone off. Anyone taking the money had to sign an NDA."

Josh is not telling me anything I don't already know. He can only tell me what I already know.

"And now that Ari is splashed across front pages everywhere," he continues. "A major player on the national stage, he can't let the public find out."

The winter wonderland whizzes by. The frozen world outside these windows blur and obfuscate. It's difficult to get your bearings facing such instability. We leave the high ground and hit a new highway, where traffic slows to a crawl. With the calm, I begin to collect these random scraps and loose threads, rearranging them to try and form a clearer picture, find meaning, make sense.

"Sit tight, brother. I know you confuse easily. This will all make sense soon."

Time is playing games with me. I'm unstuck, free floating. I can't wrap my brain around any of this. These questions burn, burrow, take root. More than the Fortmans, I want to know about him, about *Josh*.

"Where have you been?" I ask. "Does Amy know? What's it's like, dying? Did you see Mom?"

"You know as much as I do," Josh says once more, irritated having to repeat himself. "Pay attention. We don't have long now."

Both hands on the wheel, Josh doesn't bother glancing over. "I can only reword it so many ways, brother. You're the writer. We're in the middle of it, man. This shit is unfolding in real time. How long have you been locked up, two states over and several hours away, awaiting what? Word on an assault case?"

I must admit, when he puts it that way, the punishment smacks of cruel and unusual.

"They shipped you off. Because they needed you out of the picture. They have plans—big plans. Takes time to pull off. Blackmill, Fortman." He stops. "Emily."

"Emily."

"My daughter is all that matters anymore."

I don't have a response. I mine the darkest depths. Even I can't fathom such evil.

"What? You think because she's Andy's granddaughter, Ari gives a shit? Andy and Ari are *brothers*." Josh flashes a glance.

A brother is as close as you get to another you. I'm sure having children is similar, I wouldn't know, but the power dynamic is skewed, relationship unbalanced; authority doesn't afford equality. The cycle—birth, growth, re-birth—requires instruction, tutelage, compliance. But a brother? That's you split in two.

I said these things to *Frank*, not Josh. How is Josh repeating what I said when he wasn't around? I know the answer of course. I fold my hands in prayer. *Please don't take him away from me again.*

"That's a lot of faith for a guy who claims not to believe." Josh laughs. Each time I hear his laughter, a fire rekindles inside me, one that had been in danger of being snuffed for good. Josh is starting to fade. I can't hear his voice as clearly, can't picture him as vividly.

We don't have long now…

"The accident," I say. "What's wrong with me, Josh? What if I can't write—"

"Ha! If you couldn't write you'd die. It's your whole world, your art. You *need* it to live. You can threaten to quit, give up, spend all your time whacking a ball around a country club. You, brother, are an artist. It's how you make sense of your world. What else are you going to do? Work a regular job?" He cracks himself up over that one. "You're not cut out for the life I lived." Josh peers at my soft hands. "Manual labor? The gravel pits me and Neil worked? Would've eaten you alive. Be thankful for that."

He's not wrong. I am thankful. I couldn't hold down a day job even when I was able to communicate. I only know how to do one thing:

create worlds. All my self-worth and -identity comes from it, this symbiotic relationship between life and art; one fosters the other. I feed off it.

The rest? Where I've been? How much time I missed this go-round? I know something bad happened, something after the accident, an event so impactful and devastating that I began to lose my ability to function. I am not well.

"That's when you started to slip," Josh says. "Your condition growing worse, when you realized you couldn't save me. You withdrew. It started with the stuttering. You couldn't get words out. Remember that doctor you had—"

"I've had a lot of doctors—"

"That therapist. The one who told you, over and over, who tried to hammer it through that thick skull of yours to stop punishing yourself. He asked, 'Do you think this is what your brother would want?'"

I turn from him to keep from crying.

"And you said, no." Josh faces me, looking ever younger still. "And you were right. No, I don't want that for you—to see you spend your life punishing yourself? I'm gone. My life was my life. The choices I made were my own. I ended up where I did because I was a grown-ass adult who made some dumb-ass decisions. None of that is on you. *I* may be gone. You're still here."

I feel like Kylo Ren Force-ghosting Harrison Ford to absolve his sins. That's some next level megalomania.

I'd point out the gaping plot hole, except I must employ a similar device if I am to salvage a happy ending. I'm sick of sad endings. I'm tired of goodbyes.

"I don't want you to die!" I'm screaming it. I hear it, so loud. In my head. Makes my ears damn near pop, the shrill cadence and piercing tone. I'm also climbing a steep mountain road.

"I don't leave this world when I die," he says. "I leave this world when you die…"

I look down at the burning ember, scorching second decree burns between my fingers. I inhale the sickening stench of singed flesh. I've exited in Bennington, Vermont, turning up the old dirt road toward the cemetery where our mother rests in eternal peace.

"You remember writing that?" Josh asks.

"I d-d-didn't w-write it. Sp-sp-rings-s-steen d-did. F-f-f-for th-th-the B-b-b-big M-m-m-an. And I c-c-c-can't w-w-write."

"Didn't you retain anything from all that education? You're the one who told me. A first-person narrative can be written—on the page—or the words can be a person's thoughts. It's all the same. We're in *your* head right now. I gotta go, brother. And you gotta let me go. You won't be alone. I'll see you in your dreams." Josh glances over with a final smirk. "One last crying, shaking hug for the road?"

When I reach for him, nothing's there, and I'm left with smoke I'm trying too hard to hold.

I sit alone again as darkness descends, winter's tolling bell dragging the sun below the surface. I'm parked in front of an iron-wrought, rusted gate. Soon, I will get out, search for a planter of flowers, and dig in the hard, cold ground until I discover the truth.

I also accept whatever Josh has left for me to find won't be easy to stomach.

The hard, cold truth never is.

CHAPTER TWENTY-FIVE

YOU'LL BE A SONG I PUT IN A LETTER

The cemetery is unlit. It's late, dark. I don't imagine this small space with its tiny tombstones gets many visitors during primetime. When our mother died, neither Josh nor I had the money for an elaborate show, but we could've done better than this. In the end, it wasn't our decision to make. Mom was a simple woman. Her only request: to be buried her next to her mother, our grandma Helen, in their hometown of Bennington, Vermont. I understand that desire to return home. When I go, I will be buried next to Josh. We all return to where it began in the end.

Checking Frank's glove compartment, I find a flashlight, which doesn't turn on until I smack it twice. Still, it fights to fade. Then I punch it a third time.

It is cold and windy. The cemetery blusters, the valley cloistered and gloomy. I haven't visited my mom's gravesite in ages, but I know where I'm going, muscle memory kicking in. I follow the guiding light, which deposits me in front of the humble marker. *Here Rests … Loving Mother and Daughter …* all those meaningless words you pay someone to etch into marble, striving to stick the landing, knowing you'll stumble and come up short.

I shiver in the frigid air, hands in pockets, still grappling for words and failing.

I don't care how old you get. A boy never stops needing his mother.

There are flowers, all dead. *This* is my clue? I never knew Josh to be such a Stones' fan. We have the matching tattoos of flowers, daisies, because of that little indie film we saw in San Francisco in the '90s. I'm reaching. He said he was leaving flowers on our mother's grave. I see flowers. Old, withered stalks with decomposed heads. I can't tell what kind they originally were. Snow slants harder.

I drop to my knees, scratching at the frozen dirt, tearing fingertips bloody. I should go back to the truck, find a shovel, a steel pail, a goddamn screwdriver, but I want to hurt, I long to ache as my skin rips, tears, bleeds. A fingernail splits. I don't stop digging. I keep scraping, clawing, my fingers talons. I am impervious to pain, even as the wounds and throbbing worsens. Immortal, I will never die. I will work my fingers to the bone.

I dig and dig and dig.

Nothing.

I head back to the truck, rifling for a tool, a neanderthal in search of any sharp object.

The longer I look at the headstone's planter bed, the more I wonder if I am the first person to do this. This could be why the flowers are dead.

Someone got here first.

They've been ripped by the roots. It *was* a clue. Josh *told me* he was going to visit Mom's grave for a reason.

He also said it while you hallucinated your brother was still alive.

No, he would've corrected me. I'm not crazy.

It was in the story you wrote.

This *story*. This … plot.

Spreading the head, I light up the fields. Josh didn't bring me here for nothing. Beneath the heavy eaves of drooping evergreens, I find it.

I'm not just looking for flowers. I'm searching for *daisies*, a variety our mother held no special affinity for. They are not easy to spot, white camouflaged by white.

When Josh visited me in San Francisco back in the '90s, we watched a film Jack Kerouac and Allen Ginsberg had written. The short black-and-white movie played at an arthouse, the Roxie Theater on 16th and Valencia, next door to Truly Mediterranean, this hole-in-the-wall with the best shawarma, Iron Man eat your heart out. David Amram, who visited my college, composed the score. There was a tattoo parlor next door. Wasted, Josh and I got a matching set.

The name of the film? *Pull My Daisy.*

I pull up my pant leg, ill-advised in the freezing cold. Icy daggers pierce exposed, bare, pink flesh. I need to see it, make sure I haven't invented a convenient reality to solve the case. There it is, on my calf, the small, cheap-looking tattoo, faded and bleeding outside the lines.

"Pull My Daisy," as in when I'm dead.

God, Josh and I thought that was so funny. Those are the best tattoos. The ones you find hysterical for fifteen minutes until you sober up and say, "What the fuck?" Then we got high again and laughed our asses off.

The detail about delivering flowers wasn't a throwaway line. This was never an allusion to a Rolling Stones song. Josh and I didn't bond over the Stones. We preferred the Hold Steady, who opened for them. I could use some Adderall about now.

At the daises Josh planted, I note the strategic placement: close enough for me to see but not so evident they'd be spotted by our enemies.

The daisies aren't in a great shape. The flower tolerates cool weather, and can survive a temperate winter. Their premature death—it's been three months since Josh planted them—helps our cause. If I didn't know what I was looking for, I might not have found them.

Then again, I'm following the map we laid out, together, Josh and I, across spiritual planes.

Driving a big boot into trowel, I penetrate the hard soil, breaking ground.

I stab and scratch, burrow. After several minutes, I fear I am mistaken, once again having invented convenient details to suit my vision. Then my spear strikes paydirt.

A small, metal box.

Like a kid at Christmas, I extract it from the earth, flipping open the lid to discover what's been hidden inside.

A small package, wrapped in plastic, double secured by electrical tape. It takes forever to unravel.

A USB stick.

I don't stop at the USB stick. There is more, buried deeper. I drive farther into the frozen. The ground is a rock. I'd need one of those drilling and splitting machines to get this deep...

Something *is* there. I trace an outline with the trowel, until a larger shape emerges. Bigger, boxier, squarer. There's a handle. I toss aside my tool. Without gloves, I am shredding fingers to the knuckle. I grip, pull, yank, tug, jerk, until I can shake loose the bulky configuration from its cryogenic chamber.

Now out of the ground, the chunk of metal I clutch means nothing to me. I have no idea what am looking at. It's like a canister. With a handle on its side, the black, dinged tube is the size of a water bottle, sharpened to a corkscrewed point.

A drill bit.

Sometimes, when I'd fly back east, I'd tag along with Josh to jobs sites before we got high. I'd sit in the truck while Josh worked, urging him to hurry up by banging and groaning, antics lost to the thundering of hydraulics of steel chewing rock and stone, spitting out crust and shale.

Why would Josh bury these two items separately? Suddenly, my ribs are drawn to the object, and I have my answer. A magnetic drill bit. By the way my coat pocket affixes like superglue, I see we are dealing with a very powerful magnet.

What am I supposed to do with this?

Except not get it near a computer…

Now you're getting it, brother.

I need to find a computer to plug in this USB stick and learn what's on it.

I flee in search of an internet café. Whatever is on this USB stick, Josh went to great lengths to protect it. He also took equal measures to ensure that after I learn what's on it, I am to erase all evidence, leaving no trace.

I'm headed east, in the vague direction of White Mountain University, Emily's college. I should be grateful I don't have my phone. I'm not giving them another way to track me. GPS would be nice, though. Finding my niece's exact address will require additional effort but at least I'm moving in the right direction. With each passing mile, I distance myself from the carnage I've left behind.

At the base of the mountains, I enter a small town called Ashton, and stop at a 7-11 to buy a pair of headphones, the plug-in kind. I convey to the clerk I'm looking for an internet café. He points me down the street to a coffeeshop called the Happy Bean.

Happy to find them still open, I order a coffee, which I pay for in cash, and take my bean in front of a computer. The café is modestly crowded, given the late hour. Most everyone on their individual devices, ignoring each another. Josh will have installed a text to speech option. I won't have much time.

Patterns, brother. Disrupt patterns. Destroy, reorganize.

At the computer, I freeze. This is a stupid idea. As soon as I plug in that USB stick, I'll be leaving behind a digital fingerprint. I'll need a credit card to log on—internet access isn't free—which means stamping intel on an electronic archive. You can delete all the private browsers you want; your porn search history is never secret. I can't be sure erasing data extends to Mastercard headquarters.

I don't need Wi-Fi—I need access to a computer that is not password protected.

We need access to a computer that cannot be traced back to us.

New plan.

The café has a phone book, the old-fashioned kind with Yellow Pages, which is rare these days. It's attached with a steel rope to the desk. I open the directory. As if I'll suddenly be able to read because earlier today, I squeaked a few syllables. I need downtown, a shopping plaza with stores. Big, chain stores, somewhere with a lot of traffic. Sometimes the safest place to be in a riot is in the street.

Walking toward the counter, I catch the angry barista's attention, and point at the book. I'm hoping the fiery young woman will misconstrue my stammering as teeth-chattering cold and not rudeness.

She doesn't, and a look of disgust overtakes her expression. My inability to ask what I want colors her distain. She motions out the window, the closest I'm getting to directions. Before I leave, I point at the paper bags behind the counter. I haven't ordered food and have no reason for one. She groans, passing me one. I hold up three fingers, and don't leave until I have three paper bags, one for each new grave they'll need to dig if I end up being right.

CHAPTER TWENTY-SIX

LIVE FREE OR DIE

Leaving the small town of Ashton, I drive a couple miles—I assume it's a couple miles—it's ten minutes—I assume it's ten minutes because I sing "American Pie" in my head. By the time I reach the three men I admire most, I am entering a newer, busier suburban hood. There is a plaza near an onramp. This one has a restaurant and retail outlets. The restaurant sells seafood. The giant smiling lobster gives it away. There is also a Best Buy.

I walk in like I belong, USB stuffed in one pocket, magnetic drill bit, triple bagged, in my fist. I don't get three feet inside the store before a helpful greeter stops me.

"You'll need to check that," he says, pointing at my paper bag.

I hate playing the handicap card. It's humiliating. It's also the quickest path to get what I want.

Bringing out the headphones, I point at my ears. The ineffectual squeals from my mouth do not resemble words. Which is my intention. I am disabled. I point at the electronics section. I feel like John Hurt with a potato sack over his head screaming I'm not an animal. I need what's in this bag to test prospective computers. The customer is always right.

"Of course, sir."

I smile a thank you, making for the demo section with the Macs. I use a Mac at the Institute. I'm about to plug in the USB stick, when another tiny man in a little vest approaches.

"Can I help you, sir?"

I play the same card that has gotten me this far, pointing at the computer screen, broadcasting my feebleness in a high-pitched, nasally whine.

Until he too grows uncomfortable and leaves me alone. This is how I navigate life's inconveniences and difficulties: maximizing another's unease until they go away. I'm not proud of it.

Josh will have converted files with easy text-to-speech access, giant button in plain sight. I say this to myself over and over. If there isn't a text-to-speech option, if he'd been in a hurry or thought I'd have my P2G with me, I don't know what I'll do.

Within this world I've created, my brother fulfils a vital role, no different than any other player I choose to keep around. Every character must serve a purpose or they get cut. *Of course*, there's a big red text-to-speech button.

I plug in the headphones, the old-school kind that covers your entire ear, hitting play.

The first document the robot reads is our father's will. I already know what it says. Amended as he lay dying in a hospital bed, Neil rewrote it to leave everything (save the Harleys) to Debra, including lawsuit funds and considerable savings to be dispersed at her discretion. Nothing has changed. As I've mentioned, ad nauseum, my stepmother keeps me alive. And she helped Josh too, if not as much as he'd like. In her defense, Debra was put in an unenviable position, parceling out payments piecemeal, my brother always in danger of relapse. The will is legit. It was filed with the probate court in Moodus, Connecticut. You can read it too. It's a public document.

Then the robot stops reading the will, and a second recording plays. This is the part where Blackmill Solutions enters the equation with their admission the ground was toxic. A later section confirms Blackmill's ties to Fortman, which, to *me*, is tantamount to a confession Andy and Ari are guilty. Of course, it's penned in the legalese that obfuscates culpability in a court of law.

Beyond the window, scenery whips by, cars, trucks, buses. I keep my eyes peeled for blazing police lights. I construct fantastic scenarios. The angry barista reported a suspicious man grunting too much in her coffeeshop; the greeter at Best Buy suspects I might have a bomb in my bag. I'm not thinking well. There's a reason I was in that hospital.

Focus, brother.

I'm not sure what holds up in court. At the very least, the admission of guilt reinforces why the Fortmans were so generous with their money, even if the information isn't earth-shattering or hot of the presses—its inclusion doesn't aid Ari's cause.

Listening to the rest, the droning of copyright law should put me to sleep—the robot recites data and facts passionless, staccato, dull—but fight-or-flight adrenaline keeps me alert. I'm also wondering if I've slipped from time again because it's still light out and this is winter. Did I pull over and sleep?

Those are parking lot lamps.

For thirteen years, I've been fed pills. I don't have any pills now. I'm unsure if my thoughts are getting clearer or cloudier.

Focus, brother. Listen…

I am listening! Ari and Andy did nothing wrong. Or they did but no one cares! Here's a few million dollars out of the goodness of our capitalist hearts. Don't ever talk about it. While this may be the first time *I've* heard it spelled so plainly, I can't say whether the Fortmans would feel the need to murder to keep it secret. Yes, Ari's in hot water down in Washington, and if someone—say, my brother—was planning to push the Blackmill angle with news media outlets, it *could* make Ari's life worse. But how much worse? The man is facing charges of colluding with foreign governments. I can't believe assembling easy-to-follow flow charts of ditch digger deaths shifts paradigms in the grand scheme of eco-political climates. Public records and non-disclosure agreements can gum up the works of a publication. Just ask Dick Cheney about his wife's lesbian pornographic novel that will never see the light of day. Still, it's not the smoking gun I'm looking for.

Out the window, a car pulls in the lot. It parks next to Frank's—now my—truck, which I am keeping an eye on. I don't know why I get an uneasy feeling. The roads into this small New Hampshire town land a long way from the bustling metropolis. Even if I've found the one plaza with modern amenities, we are nowhere near New York City. It's a big lot with plenty of well-lit, ample parking. Why are they sitting next to *my* truck?

I press the volume higher to distract me from the car—and whoever sits inside. It's not a crime to park next to another man's vehicle in a commercial lot. The car, a dark sedan—*why are all the nefarious cars dark sedans?*—feels like it's come for me.

Stay on task, brother.

The settlement amount, which I already knew was large, is even larger than I imagined. The money awarded Debra adds zeroes, plural. Josh said he didn't trust Debra. I lauded her generosity, but this clause contains an addendum, which stipulates a *specific* percentage of the money *must* be spent on my brother and me—from medical and dental care, to housing and transportation, even vacations. Per diems, daily amounts, yearly percentages, factoring in interest rates, with cost-of-living increases. These are hard and fast numbers. My stepmom could disperse funds as she saw fit, but she *had* to disperse them. We are talking millions. Six point eight, to be specific. Three point four. Each.

I listen to the reading of a *lifetime* annuity, spitting out mammoth monthly sums. I'm sure Debra has been keeping track. I don't know how much the Institute costs or the seed money needed to bankroll a new company—not to mention bailing out the owner when he abuses drugs. Then again, Debra never repaid Freddie, did she? And when Josh started working for Paul, he was back on salary. Paul owns JP Construction. My brother had no stake.

That's not the issue. It's that payment is stipulated. In legal black and white. Debra had to spend *millions* on us. Did she?

I start to wonder what if Frank was right. Did Debra pay to keep me locked up and out of the way? With insurance, my care out west still grants my stepmother a hefty profit margin. Debra also didn't want me near my brother. Together, we *were* trouble. I'm a walking vegetable. I'm not hiring a lawyer to double check figures. Now that Josh is dead, his money is off the books. Right?

Then a passage grabs my attention, causes me to slam on the brakes, hit rewind and play it again.

In the event of death, any and all remaining monies shall be dispersed, in their entirety, to, between, or among the deceased's offspring on his or her eighteenth birthday.

I'm never getting married or having kids. With Josh gone that money doesn't go to Amy, and it can't remain with Debra. This is the reason for Josh's urgency. On the day she turns eighteen, Emily will inherit a windfall.

That day is tomorrow.

CHAPTER TWENTY-SEVEN

COLLEGE REUNION

My dream job would've been to be a consultant on *Breaking Bad*, like
Jerry Stahl, author of the recovery masterpiece *Permanent Midnight*,
pointing out all those small addict details Hollywood never gets right.
(Note to Vince Gilligan: pure crystal meth burns clear, not black.)
From a writerly perspective, I appreciate how *Breaking Bad* showcases
a pertinent storytelling device. Every protagonist needs a superpower.
Take Walter White, for instance. When Walt gets in a jam, what does
he rely on? Chemistry. We *all* have such powers, not just superheroes
or movie characters. My brother Josh's superpower was drilling and
splitting. To bore through hard outer shells, my brother used an assort-
ment of drill bits. When he needed me to erase a computer's memory,
he accessed the right tool for the job: a drill bit with a magnet powerful
enough to scramble a mainframe. Josh stole the idea from *Breaking Bad*,
but Gilligan stole it from one of the *Die Hard* movies, and those film-
makers stole it from somewhere else. Nothing is original. Good artists
borrow. The great ones steal.

I'm not able to leave the magnet behind long before a clerk spots it
and calls me back to retrieve my forgotten item. I hope it worked.

When I walk out of the Best Buy and into the parking lot, I look for the car that had been parked beside the truck. That spot is now empty. I can't be far from Emily's college—New Hampshire, like most of New England, only extends so far. I've never visited White Mountain University. I don't know much about the school except what Josh told me: it's a good one for creative writing. My niece shares off-campus housing with friends. I can't recall an address off the top of my head. I can't memorize phone numbers, either. Last time I rang Emily, her cell, one of the few numbers I had programmed, was out of service anyway. I could've sent an email inside the store, but that would've required more technology and time than I had. Whenever Josh and I would FaceTime, he only wanted to talk about his daughter and her accomplishments. What good dad wouldn't? Talking about Emily also allowed my brother to ignore heavier, more existential topics, like our drug addiction and dead parents. Josh wasn't being disingenuous— Emily was his entire world.

Now that world is being threatened, and I'm the only one left to save it.

The lines of the road are dark. Trees encroach, speared upslope, rising higher, long, spiny branches strangling the weak light of the moon.

The bright beams materialize from nowhere, as the car races up behind me. Great. Now I have some fool riding my bumper. That's my first thought—a jerkwad tailgater. That's how focused I am. I don't realize this is the *same* dark sedan from Best Buy until it's almost clipping my rear end, its headlights extra blinding.

The car eases up, falls back, before speeding, racing towards my tailgate like it intends to ram me off the road. Part of my brain, the rationale, reasonable one not looking for trouble, clings to the belief that whoever is behind the wheel is just in a hurry. We're on a narrow two-lane with little room to pass. I'm a cautious driver. I'm lying to myself. I just opened a file I wasn't meant to see. How do *they* know? Who are *they*? What will they do with us when they catch us? No clue. But this car is riding my ass and I'm getting pissed. I mull hitting my brakes, a stunt my father would pull anytime someone got too close. The old man would slam on his brakes and God help the sonofabitch if he got out of his car. I consider pulling over, seeing if whoever will pass. I'm not willing to wager my life.

Through the harsh, smacking headlights, I try to get a head count on how many people are in the car. I am confident of at least two—I can combine one and one. The tall trees loom larger, swinging and bowing in the harsher winds of the valley.

I imagine I hear a gunshot fired, aimed for my tires. Taking the corner too quickly, I slam on the brakes, sliding on the slick road. The car zips past, nicking my bumper, spinning out of control, skidding ass backwards across the ice, shooting down the street before careening into a ditch. When my truck comes to a stop, the other vehicle is about a football field away. The car's front hood is kinked and popped open, and stream billows from its engine.

The fender bender has me turned around as well, headlights facing in the opposite direction. Pedal to metal, I return the way I came, searching for a big green sign, one with an "E" and/or "X," a means to get out of this place.

Driving away, I calm down. You don't play life-or-death games against someone who doesn't care about whether they live or die. I'd love heroic closure, to solve this puzzle and honor my brother's legacy. But the sooner I'm dead, the sooner I see him.

Coming over a hill, I catch the right I missed the first time, which takes me out of the cuts. If I had a phone, maybe I dial roadside assistance, get them to check on the poor bastards I drove into a ditch for tailgating. What if it was just a dude and his date running late? I don't want anyone freezing to death because of my hysteria. But then I'd need to stay on the line so a tow truck could trace the call and pinpoint a location. I decide to let God sort it out.

The trip to White Mountain takes longer than expected. I stop at filling stations and mime for attendants, who supply directions. I stick to the major Interstates whenever possible, skipping quicker, more direct—and confusing—routes.

When I get to White Mountain, the first thing I do is find a Starbucks. I'm running low on fuel, and gas station coffee sucks. I point at the menu, and after the barista sees me stuff a generous tip, I inquire about the college. He tells me how close I am. Two rights and a left. I smile. Our conversation takes place with an economy of words; I feel my verbal bullets running low, vocabulary slipping back to monosyllabic grunts.

For a moment, I am okay. Or as okay as any escaped mental patient behind the wheel of a stolen vehicle can be. Anxiety still riddles. I'm being hunted by local and state police. Probably the Feds, too. Given Ari Fortman's ties to Russian organized crime, we can't dismiss the possibility the United States government has gotten in on the action. I'd like to chalk that last one up to delusions of grandeur. I'm a forty-seven-year-old disabled man who uses his fingers to count. Rationalization does little to calm jittery nerves.

The night bruises deep purple and traumatic. Flurries drift through headlights. Stiff winds knock snow off mountain faces. I try not to let my brain drag me into bleak, hopeless corners, shunning thoughts about how this could all be a waste of time. Emily is likely home for Thanksgiving. With tomorrow's birthday, she's a millionaire. If not home, she could be living it up. Unless she's being hunted down. *Is she even aware of the high stakes?*

The Starbucks employee's directions weren't complicated. One street this way, one street that, a couple turns and here we are.

The White Mountain campus sprawls. A giant clock tower with old-fashioned hands stands at its center. After eight o'clock, most classes are over.

It's been a while since I've been on a college campus. I try convincing myself I don't stand out. Unlike my brother, I aged well. I'm forty-seven, but a young forty-seven. The Institute has a gym, which I hit daily. I can't keep my chest puffed for long.

Who am I fooling? I am an old man surrounded by young students—young, impressionable, attractive students who have their whole lives ahead of them. If I was ten years younger and half the man I thought I'd be, maybe I manufacture a little swagger. For whatever reason, it's only girls walking around the quad. The university is co-ed. Maybe it's ladies' night.

I tell myself no one watches me, but I *feel* their eyes. Given the holiday break and late hour, White Mountain isn't bustling. Still, several students mill and meander, more than I'd expect.

And there's no way to say this next part without sounding creepy. The girls walking around are twenty-one, -two tops. Not much older than Emily. I may be twice their age, but I'm still a man, and it's hard not to be awed by their beauty.

Self-awareness is neither inherently good nor bad. I can be aware that, yes, I am old enough to be some of these girls' fathers while still noticing how attractive they are. Slinking around White Mountain U, I am surrounded by cute girls in North Face jackets with fluffy pink mittens wrapped around their own Starbucks, because no self-respecting college cafeteria forgoes franchising a Starbucks.

Listening to them giggle, talk, and laugh, I get a lump in my throat. It sounds egotistical but I'm not unattractive. In another life, I might merit a second glance. Tonight's math problem is addition minus attraction. My chance to be normal has come and gone. My self-consciousness projects a warning sign, like that weirdo neighbor you avoid making eye contact with lest you get stuck suffering updates on his worm farm.

White Mountain is a small, exclusive, private university, but still too big to hope I can pick a random student who knows my niece. I have to try. When two girls walk past, I wave to catch their attention, like the world's hippest grandpa. The pair stop to be polite.

I attempt to ask if they know an "Emily," but no words come.

At Best Buy I played up my inability to speak, a means to an end. But I spoke with Frank, and by the time Josh and I met up, I was speaking in complete sentences. Of course, Josh was never there, was he? I imagined a full-fledged conversation. In my head. Like I am doing now.

This leaves the girls confounded, as anyone would be. Then I do that thing I hate so much when I'm flustered. I stammer and stutter, sputtering like a dying, old motor. I start flapping my arms.

The girls giggle. They don't do it to be mean. You must view it from their point of view. Strange man approaches, and instead of asking questions like where he can find parking or Founder's Hall, they're forced to suffer a madman's rendition of Old MacDonald's Farm.

The pair makes funny faces at each other, before breaking out in laughter. The girls peel off, leaning heads on each other's shoulder; laughter grows louder as they walk off into the distance. In a lifetime defined by humiliation, this latest embarrassment bedazzles a jester's thorny crown.

There's a fountain. It's not running of course. It's the dead of winter on White Mountain. Pipes freeze. The seats have been swept clear of snow. I sit down. Now that I'm alone, I try again. Just one word. For my ears only. Any word will do. Bird. Cat. Dog. Any sound. I'll take "Ha ha." Nothing.

What do I do now, Josh?

"Hey!" a girl says. "I know you."

I peer up.

"You're Emily's uncle, right?" She turns over her shoulder, pointing into the night. "She has pictures of you in her room. This is *so* weird."

A couple thousand students, yeah, it's weird, but not like lightning striking twice or winning the lottery weird.

"I'm Lily," she says.

I smile. If she knows Emily, she knows I'm a non-verbal communicator. I convey I want to find my niece but don't know where she lives. This might seem like asking a lot, but I am adept at using my hands and facial expressions.

Lily's face twists in a way that renders me uneasy. "Were you supposed to meet her?"

I offer a non-committal wince. I resist the temptation to stab my own chest. *Me. Friend.*

"I just saw her…" Lily trails off. "Do you know an older guy? Like you. What was his name?"

There's a lot of older guys like me. I can't think why any would be up here bothering Emily. At least no good reasons. Lily brings her hand low to demonstrate a short person.

"He said he was her dad's business partner…"

Paul?

"Freddie!" Lily exclaims. "Emily called him Freddie." Her face squirrels up. "Do you know him?"

I nod, which appears to be put Lily at ease.

"Em and I were coming back from the library. And this guy shows up in a truck…" Lily stops, biting her lip, her discomfort returning. "He sorta…"

What?

"Took her away."

CHAPTER TWENTY-EIGHT

COLLATORAL DAMAGE

I know Freddie is pissed at my dead brother for all the money he stole. He has every right to be—Josh has—had a drug problem, and he took advantage of their friendship. If Josh were here, I know he'd say he's sorry. But he's not. I can do it for him. It's not the same. Having been in my brother's shoes, I sank low. When you're an addict, you don't stop digging just because you hit rock bottom. The last people I stole from were friends. It was a source of pride. At the end, though? I stole from my own mother. At that point, you're not expecting to be around long enough to apologize; and it's easier to beg for forgiveness than it is to ask for permission.

Still, taking Emily? To settle a score? That doesn't sound like the Freddie I know. The girl I spoke with, Lily, implied Emily seemed hesitant to go. Or am I reading too much into the situation? Freddie watched the girl grow up. Then again, Emily isn't that same girl any-more, is she? Come a few hours, she is a woman worth seven figures.

Which leaves me reeling. Where do we go from here?

I stand by a fountain that doesn't flow on a campus I do not know, mulling my options, which are few. That's when two security guards approach. That's how they announced their presence anyway. Although only one of them speaks. Each is carved out of stone slabs, granite torsos with logger shoulders and longshoreman forearms, which stick out from coats two sizes too small.

"Got a complaint," the security guard says. A hint of an accent. Foreign? Eastern European? Or he could be from Massachusetts or just Worcester. "Man harassing students."

This would be a great time to summon a defense.

You can't flap your arms and fly away from this one.

"ID," the security guard demands.

I am happy to be handed a task I can complete, retrieving the wallet Frank returned to help a coroner identify the body.

The security guard offers a cursory glance at the ID, tucks it away, and then says, "We're going to need you to come with us."

I still can't place the accent. It's not New England.

By now, the quad has cleared, students rushing indoors to escape Nordic conditions.

I'm expecting a personal escort off campus, with a stern warning to get a visitor's pass next time, which I'll agree to for expediency's sake, but it's not like university police wield any real power. They're glorified mall cops. No one's getting locked up for stuttering in front of a pair of pretty girls. If campus patrol locked up every guy who floundered around a pretty girl, there wouldn't be any room left in the holding tank.

The two men walk ahead of me. With the swooshing winds and roaring gales, the distance between us, the hushed tones of their voices, I shouldn't be able to hear. *You* wouldn't be able to hear. My senses are enhanced. Low-end, high-, mid-, every wave and frequency in between. I catch every word.

I can't tell you what they say.

I don't understand Russian.

Every kid who grew up in the '80s recognizes the language, each consonant retrieved from hell's bowels, churned, regurgitated, spat out through an esophagus without articles. Even compliments in Russian sound like an insult.

And as a child of the '80s, I know a couple other things about Russians. One, they make for great stock villains. No one gets angry at a writer for choosing them as an antagonist. Can't get accused of racism. Stereotyping, maybe, but since most of us, in America anyway, grew up under the threat of complete and utter nuclear annihilation at the hands of the Red Menace, audiences tend to let the trope bashing slide.

This is what I'm thinking about, movies like *Red Dawn* and *Rocky IV*, the rest of my brain slow to make the connection to the second thing I know about Russians.

Their proven ties to Ari Fortman.

I start running. Security guards aren't pulling guns on a college campus. Then again this is America. Is there anywhere *more* likely to encounter a firearm?

Orders to "Stop!" fade with the heavy panting as I race, dart, and duck between tall, brick buildings. I run too fast for the big men to keep up. I don't hear gun shots.

By the time I make it back to the truck, which sits pristine beneath the halogen glow of a residential streetlamp, I am feeling silly for the needless theatrics. I can imagine how I looked to sorority sisters peeping out windows to glimpse a picturesque, snowy New England eve, only to catch sight of me, a dumb flightless bird, flapping his arms, hopping inept.

CHAPTER TWENTY-NINE

EVERYONE IS A HERO IN THEIR OWN STORY

I remind myself Freddie drives a car not a truck. Then again, the guy works in construction. Would it be *that* strange to have a truck for business and a car for the family?

If Lily doesn't call out Freddie by name, I'm thinking Paul. Both are on the shorter side, with darker, Italian complexions. Except Paul doesn't know Emily. Paul has no real ties to our family, save hiring Josh. And Lily *did* say Freddie, before implying she was taken against her will. I must be mistaken, heard incorrectly, inferred, assigned intent. I'm wrong about Freddie. I'm wrong about being tailed from the Best Buy and almost getting run off the road. And I'm wrong about secret Russian agents sent by Ari Fortman, the embattled former legal counsel and personal liaison to the goddamn president of the United States of America. Hired guns trying to kill *me*? After all the lunacy of the past twenty-four hours, that last statement proves both the most outrageous and ostensibly true.

Driving in my truck—I'm going to stop calling it Frank's—Frank is dead—I might not be great at math, but I can nail a good cliché; and possession is nine-tenths of the law—I ground myself in facts.

Provable, not-open-to-interpretation, beyond-a-shadow-of-a-doubt, facts.

There could be several reasons Freddie came up to see Emily. Three months have passed while I was in-patient. The world didn't stop spinning. That must've been hard on my niece, especially if she was fighting with her mom. Her dad just died. Freddie could've reached out to her, or her to him. I want to believe Freddie is a good man. I keep repeating this because he has reasons for revenge. Yet, there he was at the memorial, funeral, and reception, confiding in me how Josh reached out to him before he went missing to say he'd discovered dirt on who else?

No, there is one bad guy in all of this. You know his name as well as I do.

Knowing what you know about Ari Fortman and that family, are you surprised? When I started getting close, the Brothers showed up at Amy's to put me down like a dog, which is what started this wild, wild ride. Or maybe I should say: kicked it into overdrive. Ari and Andy orchestrated everything: those guys in the bar to harass me and light my short fuse; their man in the Olympia Diner to snatch Em before she could share what we'd both learned: the imminent inheritance. Blackmill. Fortman. An heiress in need of an ally.

What about the letters?

Frank read them. They expressed no cause for concern. Frank admitted working for Fortman. I can't take those letters at face value.

Which is why I must stick with the hard and irrefutable. Ari, with his political connections, ships me two states over to a mental ward, where he has his man under his thumb, my former friend Frank, try to assassinate me when I start putting it all together. Snakes in the grass, the Fortmans won't stop slithering until I cut off the head.

I need to think like a criminal.

When I was crafting my handyman detective back in Mrs. Virostek's class, I learned an invaluable lesson about writing bad guys. I was creating this villain, who was all twirling mustache and dastardly cackle, an unrepentant creep who committed sins for sins' sake. This propelled *my* narrative along, made sense for my hero. Mrs. Virostek took me aside and said, "No, you have it all wrong. Even the bad guy doesn't think he's a bad guy."

Everyone is the hero in their own story. It's true for fiction. It's true for real life. Ari Fortman justifies his actions. Manifest Destiny was a law of the land. The Civil Rights Act had to be passed in '64 because racist assholes believed they were preserving pure bloodlines, whatever the fuck that means, like those racist assholes in Charlottesville burning tiki torches, who believed they'd found a hill worth dying on. Of course, I think I'm right. Who am I to point fingers? I got my baby brother hooked on drugs, stole from my own mother, and now they're both dead. I've fucked over people, betrayed trusts, and broken hearts. I've used, cheated, lied, and stolen. I never ran out of excuses why rules shouldn't apply to me. I'm a bad guy, too.

Yeah, we might be bad, but we're not the worst.

Emily still has a chance to be better than the lot of us.

I don't believe in angels, and I won't believe in ghosts. Still, I look to the heavens, bless myself, and whisper a silent prayer. Give me *something*, Josh.

When my brain finally broke for good, my brother was the one person I could talk to. He understood me then. I need to hear him now. They say the wind is everyone you've ever known. I don't care how sentimental that sounds. Josh and I are one of two, and one can't be complete without the other. Divided, I've felt his presence guiding me on this journey, which has taken me from my home, the place that's been my sanctuary for the last thirteen years, only to learn everything I'd been taught is a lie; and I've endured his absence, hammering home just how alone I am in this world. I want the truth. Like Hemingway, one goddamn true sentence. I'm sick of being mystified by rudimentary basics ordinary men have mastered. I am never going to marry, raise a family, be healthy, whole. I had *one* thing: my brother.

My brother never let me down.

My brother always took care of me.

He's not leaving me now. Josh planted clues—he got me out here, opened my eyes to see people for what they really are, nothing but greedy, duplicitous pricks, present company included. Josh is not setting me up to fail.

What are we missing?

Talk to me, brother.

There's two of us…

There's two of us.

I don't leave when I die—I leave when you *die.*

Josh doesn't leave when he dies.

Josh leaves when I die.

I return to our mother's grave. It's pitch black now, not a star in the sky, like spilled pen ink blotting the heavens. Dark clouds hang low, like a curtain being drawn forever. A showstopper. I pull the flashlight, slap its head, bring the light back to life and tour the wreckage. Was her grave this trampled upon and desecrated the last time we were here? I dug up serious ground. When I was done, I tried to put things back. It's hard to replant dead flowers.

Like an animal, I sniff and detect the predators' scent. *I wasn't the only one here tonight.* The surrounding plot is freshly tilled, moist earth teething to the surface.

The humble headstone hits me. Again. It all hits me. What a lousy son I was to our mother, what a shitty brother I was to Josh. My entire life I've strived to do what I thought was right, follow a path I believed in. A righteous path. I thought I knew better than everyone else. This life is a study in contrasts, fools full of confidence, genius bogged down by self-doubt. I have no idea where I slide in along that spectrum. My entire life, I've followed a broken moral compass. Calibrated incorrectly, it's delivered me here.

How can I leave the door open for God but not angels and ghosts? At the same time, I understand this is my rational mind making sense of the nonsensical. How can we live any other way? My brain carries on nonstop internal dialogues, disagreements, arguments. With itself. Even when I win, I lose. We all lie to ourselves. You do it. I do it. That guy over there. Am I so unique? We all lie to ourselves, and we keep reinventing new lies until we receive the answers we want.

I'm sorry, and for so much more than sullying my mother's final resting spot or unburdening my grief on her grave. All my mom wanted was a happy family. She grew up in squalor with a single, alcoholic mother, and though I loved my grandmother dearly, I can't fathom how rough that must've been on her. It's why she took the first ticket out of town when my father, passing through with his motorcycle gang, asked her to hop on back. She was sixteen years old, a kid. Instead of landing in a pleasant '80s sitcom, she got our abusive, belligerent father, and two drug addicted screw-ups like Josh and me. When my father wasn't running around, sticking his dick in anything that moved or pinning Mom's head to the floor, screaming at her to shut up, her two sons were running around shooting junk, wreaking havoc, and adding additional strain. No wonder she died young.

You can beat yourself up later, brother. Right now, you need to open your eyes. Everything you need is in front of you...

I spray my flashlight over the cemetery, landing on the hole I tore up earlier. The daisy ditch is cavernous. I don't remember digging that deep. Maybe I went too far, opening a mouth to hell, unleashing the devil's rejects.

No, I don't believe in the Devil. I'm a Springsteen Catholic: I believe in the love that you gave me, and I believe in the faith that can save me…

That's when my eyes settle on the second set of daisies.

They are buried farther in the distance, beneath an isolated copse. One plus one equals two—two brothers, two tattoos. Two secret hiding spots.

Smart, Josh.

I run to the second set of daisies, falling to my knees. The ground is less forgiving at this hour, the earth more unwilling to share her secrets. My kneecaps feel cracked in half like stale ginger snaps. This time I'm prepared, bringing along the trowel, a prospector hoping to strike black gold a second time. I try—stabbing, scraping, scratching. Nothing. The ground is solid ice. Two-fisting trowel, my efforts yield little. I'm chipping flecks, flicking fragments of frozen. I don't quit. Like Andy Dufresne timing lightning to escape through a sewer of shit, I draw on my desperate determination. Eventually tenacity prevails. A small divot turns into a bigger dent, dent into scoop, scoop gouge, and then we have a hole. Soon, I'm tearing up chunks of rock, dislodging trunk roots attached to hunks of earth. I wretch free the abomination to unveil … another metal box.

Blowing off debris, I flip the lid to find a key, a scrap of paper with an address—Josh knows I can't read, but my brother was working with what he had—I know it's an address because words follow numbers and I recognize the formatting. I realize one page is actually two stuck together. The second page lists several sets of numbers, long series of them, which mean nothing to me. I understand including an address. Obviously, I am supposed to go there. I have a key to get inside, where more waits to be discovered. The other series of numbers? The longer sequential ones? Less elucidating. The first is separated from the rest. Perhaps, a security code. Like for a house. Okay. But beneath that, there are many more numbers, each set longer than the last.

If I am right and that first set *is* a security code, I can circumvent my illiteracy. Like a picture book, I must find the symbols and its corresponding match, punch them in, beat the clock. No different than physical therapy at the Institute when they ask me to point at the animal that says "moo." I'll have limited time before authorities are alerted—authorities who must be scouring all of New England and Upstate New York by now.

I remind myself Josh was staying up here for work. A cheap roadside motel. Is that what the key is for? Maybe the room has a safe? Those rooms are flea traps with doors made of balsam wood. No, the key and code is to get in somewhere more fortified.

I'm not going to solve this puzzle standing in a cemetery.

Staring down at our mother's grave, I try to summon those words I should have at my disposal, a simple apology, even a silent one. I used to be good at coming up with the right words for the right situation. When my speaking and writing grew more challenging, I gave up, lost it. Or maybe there are no words for moments like this. My head is an empty bowl.

I kiss my mom's headstone, letting my tears serve as a final goodbye.

We can only lie to ourselves for so long.

CHAPTER THIRTY

SHE'LL BE COMING 'ROUND THE MOUNTAIN

I hit gas stations for directions. With my limitations, minutes turn to hours, because I can't follow simple instructions like making a left at the right time. It's the street names that mess me up, every road up here a variation on St. Christopher—St. Christopher Road. St. Christopher Ranch. St. Christopher Ranch Road and Circle and Street and Way. I need to eat. It's teeth-chattering cold. Midnight cold penetrates the glass, hungry to devour important organs.

It's later now, and I'm running on empty. I find another all-night filling station, one with a Mom-and-Pop grocery mart attached. Closed businesses populate a sleepy boulevard, which gives me hope I'm getting somewhere. Up here, they trust you to pay for your gas after you pump, which affords using cash. I need food and caffeine. I can't remember the last time I ate.

Inside the mini-mart, I stock up on carbohydrates and fats, packages of white, powdered donuts, bags of mixed nuts, and greasy, fried potato chips, adding a pack of smokes to the bill of bad health.

I place the note my brother left on the counter for the cashier, an old man who grins, revealing a mouthful of rot where teeth fight for survival. "Like Antarctica out there, eh?"

I point at the note, rubbing my hands, making a show of how cold I am, blowing into fists, shivering, chattering. I bob in the affirmative, nod, wince, too cold to speak. He catches on.

The old man points down the road. "'Bout a mile. Off Saint Christopher Lane. First left is Cliffside. Seventy is at the end of the turnaround. Only house…" He pauses.

He wants to know why I am visiting this quiet town where everyone knows each other, especially so late at night. I need a reason to sell. I don't have one ready for him to buy.

I point at my throat, the same hapless gesture I've milked and mined most of my adult life. This time, the gesture lacks enthusiasm.

The old cashier stops smiling. I grab my smokes and hurry out to the truck. I don't look back. If an old man wants to call the cops on me because I didn't say goodbye, let him. I need to see this through. If tonight ends in a hail of gunfire with me centerstage, so be it.

On Cliffside Drive, the houses are spread out, separated by several acres of land. I don't know why but it reminds me of an annecdote I heard: you either have a naked neighbor or you *are* the naked neighbor. Maybe it's because out here I feel exposed.

I convince myself that no one is peeping out windows.

The house is empty, lightless, a pristine driveway covered in snow without tire tracks. I can't park in the driveway. Doing so would announce a visitor. No one needs to know I'm here. I make a U-turn in the cul-de-sac, and head back toward the gas station. When I find a road where other vehicles are parked, I leave the truck there.

Window's Peak is a small, quaint town with a small, quaint town center. Across the street from the nameless gas station and market, a shut-down Pizza Hut sticks out. I can't recall the last time I saw a Pizza Hut, let alone ate in one.

Walking back to Cliffside Drive, I pass a twenty-four-hour Dunkin'

Donuts, another lousy chain but it's open. Highway traffic races in the near distance. I didn't arrive via this freeway, reminding me how much time I wasted. I still have my coffee from the gas station, which beats Dunkin' Donuts, whose coffee sucks, but mine's run cold. I think of getting a refill.

Through the window, I see a television, and who else is on? Ari Fortman. Since it's FOX, I assume they are defending the sonofabitch.

My hands are chapped, raw—my escape didn't come with mittens or ear muffs. I've rationed remaining funds for essentials like caffeine, nicotine, and gasoline. The wind whips, nibbling, biting, gnawing my flesh. The walk back to the house on Cliffside Drive can't be more than half a mile but it feels much longer.

I've drained my cold coffee by the time I approach the dark street from the shadows, strolling down Cliffside like I belong at this ungodly hour. I reach the house, which is massive with several stories, tossing my empty Styrofoam cup in a near-by bush. A burnished wood plague hangs over the front door with more letters than a name requires, telling me it's a pithy saying, like "Home Sweet Home" or "Home Is Where the Heart Is" or "Solicitors Will Be Shot on Sight." The premise I'm operating under—that Josh stayed here and left something for me to find—feels foolishly optimistic. We've both been gone over three months. When Josh went missing, authorities would've checked *any* known residences first.

Up close, the home, which I only glimpsed during my drive-by, towers majestic. Being so close to Magic Mountain, the owners could rent it out, seasonal lease or VRBO. Unless they live here year-round and this is a trap. I'm too exhausted to care. The house is prime real estate, and must be worth a fortune on the open market. I force myself to be cautious, overriding the fuck-its, searching for signs of human occupancy. The garage doors don't have windows. I can't be certain a car isn't parked inside, fresh snow obscuring recent tracks.

What choice do I have? I take out the key Josh left me. The door unlocks. The security beeps. I have the flashlight out. It takes me longer than it would you, but I match up the symbols, punch them into the alarm keypad, beating the count before police can be alerted.

If Josh *was* staying here, he must've known the person. Given the nature of my brother's work, I immediately think Paul. I don't see pictures of Josh's last employer, or anyone, for that matter. Then again, it's dark. Whoever's house this is, I've alerted them someone is inside. I'll be fortunate if Paul owns the place. He won't shoot me on sight. I can't say the same about a stranger, especially when he—or she—asks what I'm doing here so late and I "refuse" to answer. Reasonable doubt. Just cause. A license to kill.

Before he went missing, Josh emailed me from motels in Bennington. He didn't direct me to a motel. He sent me to this place.

Now that I am inside, the first thing I notice is the smell. If you never met my brother—and why would you have?—you couldn't know Josh possessed a unique odor. Hard to describe. But somewhere between canned clam chowder, old gym shoes, and off-brand Old Spice. His scent lingers. That doesn't mean no one's stayed here since— it's been a *long* three-plus months. Judging by the mess, I'm confident my brother was here at some point. The big guy (God rest his soul) was a slob. The scent might not be as strong to a normie. Since smell is the sense most connected to memory, nostalgia creates a lump in my throat, a sad, final reminder I will never speak with my brother. At least not on this mortal plane.

I can't be sure what I am looking for. There is no big note on the counter, which I couldn't read anyway. With electronic communication, I have the option to let a robot translate. Physical copy is tougher.

There's a pile of mail with names. I've never been angrier at all these let-ters, which to me remain a mystery, swirling with their indecipherable configuration.

I'm not entirely powerless either.

There are only two ways to learn: inductive and deductive reason-ing. We either learn through inclusion of possibilities, by incorporating what could or should be, or by removal, excluding what doesn't belong.

That's when I notice the coffee mug. It matches one from Debra's house.

This isn't Debra's house. The mug is unique. Part of a set she and my father bought as souvenirs when they visited Arizona before he con-tracted the myelofibrosis. I know about the trip because Debra wrote me about it. She even sent one of these clay souvenirs to the Institute after Dad died.

I take the mug out of the cupboard to make sure I'm not mistaken, my memory flashing on an old poem or nursery rhyme about "Indians in a cupboard," or maybe I'm conflating, and Dr. Flynn and Kubica were correct about the confabulation. Plus, I'm pretty sure that nursery rhyme is considered racist now. I study the mug.

I am not mistaken.

The pottery is handmade, spun, baked in a kiln, each imperfection one of a kind. The hand-painted scene depicts a teepee and squaw. Debra probably gifted Josh one, as well. That would explain its presence here. Except the place is a mess and my brother never washed a dish in his life, let alone put one back where it belonged.

Josh gave me the security code to see something. And it wasn't a mug.

Whose house is this? I continue poking around, keeping off the lights. I don't think the hour is so late that no one would be up. I also don't want to risk announcing my presence. The flashlight is bad enough and leaves me feeling like G. Gordon Liddy opening and shutting drawers at the Watergate Hotel.

Patting my pockets, I feel the notes my brother buried beneath the daises. My eyes adjusting to the dearth of light, I set down the pieces of paper, staring at these series of baffling numbers. The first set was short and got me inside.

What are these other, longer ones intended for?

I see no safes, at least none out in the open. That doesn't mean one can't be hidden behind the many wall hangings and paintings.

Making my way into an office, I find another iMac, sit down, and power it on.

I need a password.

I grab the second set of numbers and begin typing, starting with the one up top, painstakingly matching what's on the page with corresponding figures on the keyboard.

I take my time, making sure to get it right, elated for the closure that has eluded me so long.

CHAPTER THIRTY-ONE

AND WE'LL ALL READ BOOKS TOGETHER WHEN SHE COMES

After my fifth attempt, I am locked out. I study the numbers carefully—and that's what they are are—numbers. Not symbols, not letters. I can tell the difference between, say, an asterisk and a seven. I'm not blind.

Exiting the spacious office, I retreat to a sprawling, sunken living room, taking a seat on the couch, kicking up my feet on the coffee table, making myself at home. Long list of numbers in hand, I attempt to solve for X even if I don't know Y.

Josh stayed north, Monday to Friday, to avoid lengthy round trips. The coroner said my brother had been dead for "as many as four days," *maybe* more. E-communication told me three. I've been so hung up on the math that I missed the point: neither number is absolute. Josh scoring drugs mid-week in Central CT disrupts his schedule. Why? Unless my brother didn't stop off to score drugs. He *was* drugged. That's what he told me.

That's what you imagined *you heard…*

Hallucination doesn't negate elucidating. It makes the most sense. A guy with a history of addiction? Who's questioning a fentanyl overdose? These days? Every time you turn around, a junkie is dropping dead from the shit. If Josh found vital intel, he could've been killed *anywhere*, including this house.

My lids grow heavy and my head flops forward. I resist the urge to sleep.

I'm so tired…

I wake with a start and search for clocks. There are plenty. All digital. Three figures and the shade of sky tells me it's after midnight. *So at least one, but not yet sunrise.*

I should've done this the second I stepped inside, secured the time. Lethargy pulled me under. I was exhausted, delirious.

I hop up, darting to the kitchen—I do my best thinking when moving. I've succumbed to a micro-sleep, like those days Josh and I did speed. We'd stay up days straight, and our bodies, in an attempt to override our poor decision-making, would auto-power down. Like then, we've passed the witching hour, crossing the threshold. Transition. End of the old, start of the new.

Tomorrow, tonight…

Today.

Today, my niece is eighteen. And a millionaire.

Freddie has her, and I don't know his plans.

Besides the microwave, there's a landline phone affixed to the wall. People don't use landlines much anymore—except my sister-in-law or people over seventy. I think back to what Freddie said about Josh calling him from a strange number—i.e., not his cell—a "Vermont area code." That could mean a lot of things. It could also mean he called from here.

It's been a long time since I tried this trick. I'm not even sure if it's still a thing. Six and nine are below three on the top, right-hand side of the keypad, diagonal from the star. Star sixty-nine. Moreover, my perfect auditory retention recalls the pitch, tone, and key of each.

Hardwired in my brain from childhood. Prank calls Josh and I used to make. Call back the last person you spoke with. Why not? I press the digits. A phone rings. I won't be able to say anything if anyone answers. It's a last-minute Hail Mary. I need a big play, and I need it now.

"Hello?"

I hang up.

I don't need more than one word to recognize Freddie's voice.

The phone rings back, and I retreat from the wall as if it were on fire. It keeps ringing. Rash, paranoid, I run and rip the phone out of the wall, immediately regretting my impulsive behavior. I don't know what Freddie's answering or calling back means, or why I'm assuming it's bad news. I look at the phone smashed on the floor, the giant hole I've excavated from the drywall, and rue my short fuse more than ever. I've lived my entire life this way. I am my father's son.

With cell phones and call forwarding, Freddie could be down the street. Moments of clarity tend to be reserved for alcoholics and addicts for a reason. We are slow learners. I've just broken into a house, in the middle of nowhere Vermont, and alerted the man I suspect of abducting my niece for her inheritance that I'm here, waiting. None of that sits right.

People don't answer the telephone that gleefully if they just committed a capitol offense…

I revisit these splintered, fractured thoughts, and if this sounds ludicrous to you, trust me, it sounds equally bizarre to me. I've written myself into a corner. Unless this has been mapped out all along. Which is the only way to tell a mystery: backwards. You start at the end, *after* you've solved the puzzle, working your way to the beginning, sprinkling clues throughout to make it look like you've been in control all along. This can only be done *after* the fact, which is what my brother did. He figured it out.

This thought hits me when the headlights pull in. I am too distracted to speculate who's behind the wheel, relived not to see primary colors like blue or red. A part of me wants to run. I also need to learn what Josh knew. When the front door pushes open and the foyer light flicks on, I'm not surprised to see Freddie. I just phoned and told him where I was, in so many words. We stare at each other, before he breaks into a grin and calls over his shoulder. "He's here."

Emily runs in, past Freddie, straight to me, throwing her arms around my neck. It feels wonderful.

Then she stops to look around, perplexed. "What are you doing at Grandma Debra's house?"

Debra's? Now that mug makes sense. And, yes, there *is* a familiar scent. You have to sniff through my brother's assorted odious offenses to get to the potpourri and lavender, but it's there. I also deduce Freddie and Emily were on their way, since, well, here they are. Why would they be coming to a vacation home my stepmother owns? I'm overpowered by these conflicting considerations, and slotting them in accordingly proves challenging.

Freddie steps all the way inside, closing the door, locking it behind him.

"What are you doing here, buddy?"

He doesn't wait for me to act out a response before pointing at the wall. "Jesus. What happened to the phone?"

No time to explain temper tantrums. I grab the paper Josh left for me, the one with the security code, and other, longer numbers, which still make no sense to me. Bank routing? Off-shore Cayman accounts? That's my last, best thought.

"Where did you get these?" Freddie asks.

I point at Emily, then raise my hand high.

"Josh?"

I nod.

"When?" Freddie asks.

I mime digging and shivering. He appears confused.

"Everyone is looking for you," Emily says, staring up at me. "I'm so happy we found you first."

Me? I mimic holding a phone, pantomiming trying to call her, how the number was out of service. More than Freddie, Emily understands how I communicate.

"That number was on my mom's plan. I didn't want—I needed a clean break."

I put my hand over my heart. *I've been worried about you!*

"I've been worried about you, too. They told me … you had yourself committed?"

I leave it there. A psychotic break. I've been in dual diagnosis facilities before. It's a logical assumption, plausible, and explains why Andy and Ari arranged it that way. I'd be distraught over Josh. Freddie isn't watching me. He's staring at the numbers on the page. Then he abandons us, hurries from the room, out of the house, leaving me alone with my niece. I have a lot of questions I want to ask him. I have more I need to ask her. She has a bunch for me, too.

"Why did you leave the hospital?"

I point at her. I'm trying to tell her I've been searching for her. I'd also like to understand who took her at the Olympia Diner, why she's with Freddie, and much more. I can't get out anything before Freddie is back inside, toting a shoulder bag with a laptop, which he extracts and drops on the counter.

"Em," Freddie says. "What's your grandmother's Wi-Fi password?"

I've never heard Josh refer to Debra as "mom," and I don't know when Debra earned the moniker of "grandma." It's the least confusing part of an equation that is far from adding up.

"It's on the back of the router," Emily says, pointing to an adjacent room. I can't understand what's happening, everything moving too fast.

"I come up and visit Grandma Debra sometimes," Em says, seeing my frustration. She sounds apologetic. I get it. Josh didn't share my favorable opinion of Debra. Emily's spending time with her must've felt like a betrayal.

"Ski season," Emily says. Then, almost as an aside: "Grandma's built a few houses up here. She puts the others on Airbnb. To earn extra income."

Built? Others? Extra income?

Owning more than one house is already rich in my book. Owning several and renting them out elevates stakes to a higher tax bracket.

Emily wraps her arms around my waist, hugging me tighter. "It's going to be okay."

I've never been good at hiding my emotions.

When her hand brushes against the metal, my niece pulls away, shocked, scared. Which is the last thing I want. I hate how large Em's eyes have grown. I am *not* a danger. Not to her, at least.

"They're license numbers," Freddie announces from the kitchen table, interrupting the tense moment.

Emily stops looking at me like I'm deranged, as we both turn to Freddie. It's the urgency in his voice. I'm grateful Emily's attention has been diverted elsewhere.

Emily stares at him, waiting for clarification.

"For permits to blast." Freddie furrows his brow.

The three of us have traded places. Freddie and Emily can't understand why Josh left me this information.

I might not be able to write, speak, or count, but right now I'm the only one in this room who can read the situation.

I know why Josh buried the USB stick, magnet, and blasting license numbers for me to find.

It took a while, but I now know how this story must end.

CHAPTER THIRTY-TWO

SAUT DE LOUP REDUX

I pull out the gas station map from my back pocket, the one the cashier gave me to help chart my path to this conclusion. In the kitchen where Freddie sits with his laptop open, I point at the pages Josh buried.

I mime further explanation of the blasting permit numbers. I need Freddie to fill in the blanks. He picks up on what I am asking. Freddie works in the same field Josh did, privy to a lexicon and vernacular I am not, although he probably wouldn't explain it in those terms. I need his words to speak for me.

"Each blasting site," Freddie says, panning between Emily and me, slowing down to simplify. "Every time a blaster drills, splits, or uses explosives—he needs a permit."

Of all the mysteries confronting me, I can't think of a bigger one than how Josh, who struggled with a publicly known addiction, managed to hold onto his blasting license. Then again, Josh was a country junkie. I, like Joe Walsh sings, belonged to the city. The difference: my sins may've been well documented, but I could hide in the crowd. In a small town, Josh's problems were relegated to rumors, gossip. There are only so many junkies in Berlin. Once he got his habit under control, my brother could keep it a secret. In other words, people were quicker to believe his bullshit because they *wanted* to believe his bullshit. Present company very much included.

I point between the gas station map and the blasting permit numbers. It takes Freddie a moment.

As a non-verbal communicator, I don't know many towns by their name. This is *my* special power. Each time Josh would email or FaceTime with me from another roadside, sharing details about his new job, I could mentally map it. Geographically picture it. Longitudinal and latitudinal lines don't compute for me the same way they do for you. You snap a picture. I *see* it. New England, *all* of it, this place I'm from, its topography burned on my brain.

With one finger on the Vermont/New Hampshire border, the other on those permit and license numbers, I groan, grunt, point. Words don't come, but Freddie follows.

Studying the numbers, Freddie types each into his laptop.

I stab, increasingly emphatic at the map.

"Hold on," Freddie says.

"What's going on?" Emily asks.

"This job was…" Freddie says, reading from his computer. "This license was for a site in Plasterville." He scrolls the web further. "Twenty fourteen."

I point at the next.

Freddie, catching on quicker, types and responds, "Bretton Woods, same."

More pointing at the gas station map. More clacking away at laptop keys.

Freddie reads, "North Conway," Wolfeboro, following year," and then we're into Vermont and flipping calendars.

Now that the lights are on in Debra's house, I have an easier time seeing what's been in front of my face all along. The pictures of my stepmother. There's even one of me. A couple of my father and her. Most of the photographs are of my stepmother and … my brother's boss Paul … posing in front of new houses, resorts, and ski lodges. High-end accommodations to lease out and make bank on.

I run and lift one of these pictures from the wall, carrying to the table, placing it near the townships and corresponding permit numbers, alternating a finger between picture and numbers, numbers and picture.

"Yes," Em says. "Grandma Debra has a house in North Conway and Wolfeboro. Plasterville, too."

Freddie's eyes light up. "Josh blasted the foundation for all these houses."

"Grandma's houses?"

To Freddie and Em, it's still a coincidence.

But in the world of investigation, there is no such thing.

And in the world of court-stipulated allocution of estate funds there is even less wiggle room. I pull the USB stick out of my front pocket, plug it into Freddie's laptop, and hit play. Freddie hits stop. He's not being mean. He can read, and it's faster than listening to the monotone robot who translates for me. Emily crowds in. I wait for their reaction.

There's a lot to read so I leave them to it, walking to the fridge and helping myself to some milk. I stand at the sink, watching the clear white moon high above Magic Mountain.

"Why do you think I went to pick up Emily?" Freddie says.

I get that now. I don't let on I doubted him. The part they are missing is *how* Debra got around the stipulation to pay Josh. Namely, she didn't. She paid him, all right. With his own money. Essentially, my brother was working for free. Which is a helluva deal. Until someone figures it out.

I point at the map again, motioning around Debra's house, my milk splashing with wild gesticulating.

When the milk splatters on the floor, it hits me: I'm drinking fresh milk. As in not expired. Someone has been here recently.

Freddie and Emily are watching me, but I've stopped moving, my eyes back out the window, fixed on the headlights pulling up the drive.

CHAPTER THIRTY-THREE

IF YOU WANT TO SING OUT

Paul pushes through the door. The three of us watch him nod at the security panel. "When you punched in the code, I got an alert." He sounds already bored by the conversation we've yet to have. "We were already headed up here."

Who's we?

At first I feel vindicated when the two Russian security guards, the ones I met earlier at the college, squeeze through the door. I'm not paranoid. Or maybe I am, but they're still out to get me. The Russians take a seat at the kitchen table behind Paul.

Validation gives way to confusion. Because if the Russians are working for the Fortman Brothers, why are they with Paul? Both giants, one of them was at the diner, having Em call him "Daddy" to throw me off the scent. It's one answer to an endless parade of questions.

I don't get any further speculating before my stepmother Debra steps inside. She stops beside Paul, who makes a show of grabbing her hand, tenderly, lovingly.

"Why don't you go upstairs and lay down, honey?" he says. "This might take a while."

When my stepmother turns my way and our eyes meet, I see what

I've been missing, the vitriol and disgust, her contempt for my very existence, the ire she directs at me for this long-con she's been forced to play. This woman I've thought of as a mother looks like she wouldn't piss on me if I were on fire.

Before Debra takes a step, Paul tightens his hold and pulls her back. In case we're missing the nature of their relationship, he plants one on her lips, and it's tough not to recoil. Paul is my brother's age. Debra is over seventy. People have done worse for less money.

Debra passes me without a condescending glance, before she ascends the main staircase. It's a long walk to the master bedroom. I hear a door fall open. It does not close. Debra isn't going to sleep. She's here to witness my fall, destruction, end.

"I wasn't going to let your brother steal from me, too," Paul says, walking to the fridge, grabbing a beer. "Want one?" he asks, the offer insincere. "Right," he says, shutting the door. Whether that "right" refers to my being sober or my inability to answer is as unclear as it is inconsequential.

Then, as if he'd forgotten Freddie and Emily are here too, Paul says, "Freddie, back me up. You know what a junkie Josh was. How much money did he steal from you?"

Freddie has every right to pile on. He can back out of this fight. Freddie doesn't take the easy way. "A lot," he says, before adding, "But he was my friend. And that meant more. We were working through it."

"Seriously?" Paul says, "That's adorable." Then sterner, waving a hand over the three of us: "Take a seat. All of you. You're making me nervous." His two Russian thugs stir to let us know it's not a request.

I turn over my shoulder, toward the couches sinking in the living room.

Paul looks at his phone. "Make yourself comfortable." Then to Freddie: "I see you pulled the blasting permits."

"Yeah," Freddie says, sneering. "You had Josh working for his own money."

"We *all* work for our own money, Fred."

Paul isn't stupid. He played the game. Found out what Debra was worth, got close to her, and they formed a mutually beneficial union.

Freddie didn't take Emily to get her money. He took her to keep her safe. From Paul and Debra.

And I led them straight here.

As I'm thinking this, Paul's stare traces the floor, from the smashed plastic pieces at my feet, to the cavernous abyss in the wall. He shakes his head. "I'll add it to your brother's bill."

Paul walks into the living room, descending the short stairs. Emily has taken a seat. Freddie and I remain on edge, eyeballed by the Russians. When Freddie and I don't move, Paul turns over his shoulder, and one of the big Russians lets his coat fall open so we can see the gun. Emily tenses. Freddie doesn't like it either. Any guy bedding a woman as ancient and decrepit as Debra to make a buck is already morally bankrupt. He's got a million reasons to make the leap to murder. That is if he hasn't gotten a head start. The Fortmans killed my father. I'm growing less certain about who pulled the trigger on my brother.

Freddie and I join Emily on the couch, if on opposite sides. It's a big couch, one massive rectangle. I'm on what's considered the ottoman section. Seriously, the couch is so big, we might as well be in separate zip codes.

Paul cracks his beer, takes a swig, follows it with an exaggerated, "Ahh," like I'm missing out on some great enjoyment in life. I might be. But I don't miss beer. Even when I drank, I wasn't a fan. Stuff tastes like cow piss squeezed through a dirty, old sock.

"I wasn't letting Josh pull the shit he did with Freddie." Paul cranes his necks, relaying a secret directive.

A Russian pushes himself to his feet and heads out into the cold. Whatever he's doing, I can't imagine it's helping our cause.

Paul turns his attention to the stairs, back up the well where my stepmother Debra waits, dramatically placing both hands over his heart. "True love is hard to find."

I want to rush him. I know I'll lose that fight, a bullet put in me first. I want one crack at breaking his jaw. After that, the rest is gravy.

"If your friend Frank had done his job instead of letting you run, we could've saved a lot of time."

And I'd be dead.

Paul groans. "I told Ari the old guy didn't have it in him. Frank had become institutionalized. He tell you about his kids? How they hated him? Frank didn't *have* any kids. Not anymore. Once Ari told me Frank killed the *entire* family, I knew it was a bad plan. Guy had nothing to live for. Poor bastard offed himself." Paul turns to the black night. "Found his body in the middle of the woods. Self-inflicted gunshot wound. Sacrificed himself to let you go."

I miss Frank. He was a good man.

"I think he *planned* to run," Paul says. "He dragged a deer into the back of the trailer, left a trail of blood." He shakes his head. "Throw authorities off the scent? Live off the land while you played hero? Who knows?"

He gave me *time, Paul…*

"Your brother found a clause in your dad's will." Another sip of beer. "But you already know that."

How stupid am I? Blinded by my hatred of the Fortmans, I missed the big picture. There was nothing secret about the settlement—it's public news. I kept wanting to find dirt on Ari and Andy, even Amy. I didn't have to find dirt on them. The brothers walk around covered in it, proudly. Men like Ari celebrate their filthy riches, rubbing your nose in their birth right. Ari Fortman serves presidents, and I, a mute moron, am going to take him down? Josh and I were prisoners. I can't say whether giving Josh a lump sum would've been a good or bad thing. That much money, maybe he overdoses. Or maybe he's able to pay back a friend, get his shit together, finally grow up. Either way, it wasn't Paul's, Ari's, Andy's—or Debra's—call to make.

"We got you to sign away your rights away in the loony bin. When you, for some reason, believed your brother was alive." This prompts the first sincere expression I've seen on Paul's face since he got here: pure, unadulterated schadenfreude. "What was it you saw in the guy? Why did you think your brother was so special? Like Josh could walk on water or something? He was a big, fat dope fiend. Used to be a good wrestler and lineman. In high school. What had he done since? Besides take drugs and burden people. You two are the same. Both pieces of shit. Users. Losers. Two garbage brothers not worth a damn. I guess it makes sense you were so close. Even when you were apart."

Up above, the floor moves. I listen. Footsteps patter across the hardwood. Debra looms, waiting for Emily to wave her rights, so she can stamp her seal and make it official.

Take in the scene. Read the room. Use all the senses you have left. Most of all, stay calm, brother. I've given you everything you need. Don't let him get a rise out of you. That's what he's counting on, your quickness to flash. He wants an excuse to shoot you. He already has his reason—you broke into his house. You're an intruder. This is his moment. Men like Paul can't just win, he needs to gloat, show off. Like the display of public affection, macking on your mom, stepmom, and he's doing it now. For Christ's sake, for once—stay cool...

"What's it like?" Paul asks me. "Living like that? I'm watching your dumbo eyes flit around your numbskull. You gotta be thinking some-thing. That's all you *do*. Think. It must drive a man insane." He snickers again. "No wonder you were committed."

The front door opens. Paul checks over his shoulder. The Russian returns with an attaché case, like Paul is 007, plopping back in the kitchen chair, glaring my way.

"Yeah," Paul says, laboriously. "Your rights. Weren't worried about that. But Emily…" He stops there. Doesn't say anything else, leaves me to infer. "Honey," he says to Em. "You know your dad owed a lot of money." Paul looks at Freddie, as if this plan helps him out too, before returning attention to Em. "You're eighteen. You have your whole life ahead of you. You're a Fortman. You think your mom and grandpa and family aren't taking care of you? This money isn't yours. It's your grandmother's."

Like Paul is a saint devoted to eldercare. He's been behind every-thing. I kept wondering how Josh got a new partner to take a chance on him after his well-known struggles with addiction. He didn't. He got a new owner, who doled out enough to keep my brother alive while he built these palatial homes for himself and Debra, breaking down my brother's body so Josh could earn what already belonged to him.

Paul grabs the case from his men, retrieving forms. He's flipping through them, barely paying attention. So cocky, so sure this plan will work. "Now, Em, you sign here. And in exchange, I am going to over-look your uncle being a pain in my ass." Paul spreads his arms. "What did he do, really? He left a hospital against medical advice. You know your Uncle Ari can make this all go away." Paul snaps his fingers. "Like that."

"Then…" Paul says, peering up the well, as Debra descends the stair-case. "My fiancé and I will send that one"—he flashes on me—"back to the Institute, keep paying his bills. You have my word."

"Ha ha."

Paul mocks being taken aback. "Did you … talk?" He whips his head left, right, all around, over his shoulder at the Russians. "You heard that, right? Dumbo said something, didn't he?"

"Ha ha," one of the Russians parrots.

Paul laughs, but it's not a real laugh. "Ha ha. Look at you." He faux claps. "I heard that doctor was working hard with you in the hospital. I suppose that's what they're *supposed* to do, help patients. Didn't think much of it. Figured you were beyond hope. Well, good for you. You should be proud of yourself, buddy."

"It's okay," Emily says to me. She sees me reeling, riled with rage. "It's just money. He's right. I have Mom and Grandpa. I'll be okay."

Freddie side-eyes me, startled as I move my hand toward my lower back.

See, Paul got most of that right.

Except the part about Frank.

Frank didn't shoot himself. Josh did. And since Josh is dead, it's time I stop lying to myself and accept what I've done.

There can be no happy ending for me.

CHAPTER THIRTY-FOUR

THE TAXI CAB RIDE TO FREIGHT ELEVEN

My eighteen-year-old niece takes me, her fifty-year-old uncle by the shoulders, shaking me straight, getting me to understand. "It's just money."

"Great, we all agree," Paul says. "Let's get this over with." He nods at his men. One of them reaches in his breast pocket, bringing back a pad and stamp. "Debra, darling," Paul calls.

When I hear my stepmother encroach, I know her inclusion is for theatrics. Emily is willing to sign away her money. Paul and Debra are already crooks. Not sure notary fraud makes them any eviler.

Emily sees me glowering at my stepmother, shaking me again. "It's just money," she repeats, as if I didn't hear her the first time.

Yeah, kid, just money.

How do you tell an eighteen-year-old that money is everything? Oh, you can say it's not, how the best things in life are free. Or how money doesn't buy happiness. In the beginning, you might believe that. I did. As a kid. We had it. I never worried about it. When my parents were getting divorced, I remember sticking up for my dad, a rare occasion— can't remember what prompted it—playing Devil's advocate maybe? I've always been captious. I brought up how at least our father provided for us. The guy earned a lot. Especially for someone who dropped out of high school in the tenth grade, and my mother replied, rather caustically for her, "Yeah, the state will pay for you, too."

She was right, of course. I'd later find out, firsthand, on the streets of San Francisco, where I leaned on social services. The Bay Area is notorious for its generosity in that department. There's GA—that's General Assistance—where you walk in an office and they hand you, like, six hundred dollars. All you had to do was ask. We're talking early 1990s. I can't recall the exact number. It was a lot of money for a homeless junkie. Then you work through the system, food stamps, welfare, social security supplemental income, and then further down the lonesome road, you can tack disability onto that. You do all right. If I wasn't spending it all on drugs, who knows, maybe I stash some away, get back on my feet. Instead, I waited in line for every dirty dime I could get my fingers on, banging dreams into my arm. That was my path. Like every aged gangster lamenting the regrettable end of the road, "That was the life I chose."

Choices are funny like that. Objective chance. I think about that one a lot. What would've happened if I took a right that one day and not a left? How would this have turned out if I never rode my bike off that ramp and hit my head? Do I end up on drugs? Would my brother still be here?

I would like to know how Josh died. I accept I won't get a definitive answer. Did he overdose on fentanyl or did someone supply a hotshot to get him out of the way? Paul and Debra had a good thing going. Josh found out. He left me evidence buried beneath our mother's tombstone to protect his daughter. Maybe he knew his end was coming. We all know when our end is coming.

I won't have to wait long now.

If Josh didn't put that hole through Frank's head… Ghosts—regardless of your opinion on the subject—are notoriously lousy shots.

Like Frank said. It was him or me.

I choose me.

I rise, pull the gun from behind my back, and take aim.

The first thing you do is slide off the safety.

Thanks, Frank.

Everyone freezes. I don't need to speak. When Emily accepts she can't stop me, a smile comes to her slowly. It's a sad smile, just the same.

"You didn't search him?" Paul says to the two Russians, who shrug.

Of course, they didn't. I'm too stupid. Too ineffectual. I'm a stuttering, stammering, drug-fried dummy on his best days. I was never a threat. They got me to sign away millions because I believed a fantasy, that I'd see my dead brother on the other side. Money does me no good. Being alive without my brother does me less. I'm no hero, martyr, or saint. I just want to know, before I go, I did one goddamn good thing with my rotten life.

I see Paul glance at Debra, who mouths a silent no.

It was a good fallback plan, Josh. But Frank and I got this...

The Russians stand, sandwiching a retreating Paul. I motion for Freddie and Em to get behind me. I study every movement, however subtle. Hands inch. There's two of them, each Russian with a gun. I won't be able to get both before one of them gets me. The layout is clear, next move calculated and emblazoned on my broken brain.

I cock the hammer. No, it's not necessary, but, man, it feels cool.

"You're going to shoot us?" Paul blurts a laugh. "Then you *will* go to prison or a real mental ward, and this time no will be watching out for you. You'll be locked up with killers and rapists and worse. You have your whole life ahead of you, buddy." Paul thwaps his head, hard. "Come on! Use what's left of your brain. Think! Right now, they got you for what? Assault in a Berlin bar and improper disposal of a deer. A slap on the wrist." He turns to Debra. "We'll get him a lawyer, right?"

"Of course," Debra says, returning to sickeningly sweet, as if none of this has happened. "You can go back to live at the Institute." She turns to Paul. "Or live with us. Isn't that right, honey?"

"Whatever you want, babe," Paul says.

Sure, I'll go live with my dead father's mistress and her boy-toy. We can all have dinner together. Will I be assigned chores? Do I get a new "Dad"? Christmas mornings will be a hoot. We'll sit around a big blue spruce and open presents purchased with the blood of my father and the blind trust of my brother, chugging eggnog, yucking it up, as bells ring out along Worthington Ridge for Christmas Day.

I'm not feeling the holiday spirit.

Paul, seeing this, turns to Freddie. "Talk to him!"

I take a deep breath, center, focus, and summon everything I have left.

I look Freddie in the eyes. "J-J-Josh is s-sorry."

So am I.

Unlike the retcon on Han Solo, I shoot first. This isn't my first time.

I hit one Russian square in his broad chest. It's a kill shot. To be fair, I have a huge target to work with.

Freddie cradles Emily, pulling her out of harm's way, as the second Russian and I point our guns at one another, squeeze, and fire at the same time.

We both hit our mark.

Falling backwards, I feel the pain all at once—the pain of everyone and everything—and then I feel nothing.

There's screaming and crying. I hear a loud thud. I might hear, "No!" A woman's voice. An old woman's voice.

I crash over wood. Fragile parts break. Blood spills like wine out my chest. I crack up, howling with laughter.

In the end, I was able to find my voice, after all.

I'm afraid it's too late to fix the rest of me.

Through fading eyes, I see Freddie already has out his cell. Debra stands shellshocked, covering her mouth. Paul hangs his head, accepting checkmate.

Emily rushes to me. She lets out a gasp. I understand why. It's more than the gunshot blasted through my heart. I've fallen over a wooden end table, whose leg has splintered off, its sharp end spearing my side, clear through my liver, impaling me.

My niece is sobbing. I manage to take her hand, holding it, squeezing.

I am out of words, Emily, but if I could speak, I'd tell you, it's all going to be okay. You are loved. I'm going to see your dad. He's proud of the woman you've become, and he's going to be happy to see me. Nothing feels better than blood on blood. You live your life, kiddo. It's a beautiful thing, this chance we're given. We get only one shot. But so many chances to get it right.

PART FOUR

THE END

JOE CLIFFORD

A DISSERTATION

"Did you finish?" Dr. Walker asks.

"I did," Jen says. "This weekend. Start to finish. One sitting."

"What do you think?"

"In terms of…" Jen isn't sure how to respond, so many aspects to address.

Behind her desk, Dr. Walker smiles.

It *is* a loaded question.

Beyond the cracked-open window, bluebirds twirp joyous, heralding the songs of spring. Southern New England is much warmer than Upstate New York this time of year.

Dr. Kubica takes Jen's hand, gives it a squeeze, let's her star student know it's okay if she doesn't have all the answers.

"I found it bittersweet," Dr. Kubica says, adding her take on the book. "In a twisted way. Very dark." She smiles. "Though not without levity. It's clear he retains a sense of humor. And if I'm being honest? I'm flattered to play such a prominent role."

The doctors laugh. It takes a second for Jen to join them.

This is Jen's first time here. For the past few months, her professor, Dr. Kubica, a speech pathologist, has been driving the two and the half hours from Upstate New York to the Central Connecticut hospital, trying to get the patient to speak. A graduate student, Jen has been privy to the notes from these sessions. An expert in the field, Dr. Kubica has only been moderately successful during her weekly visits, extrapolating grunts, syllables, but never words. She agrees with Dr. Walker that, from a physical point of view, there is nothing preventing the patient from speaking. Mentally, however…

Jen hopes this unique case of confabulation will formulate her doctorate thesis, which centers on the trauma caused by the loss of a sibling. It's more complicated than that—psychology often is—and this study stretches the definition of "complicated."

Listening to the two doctors discuss the case, Jen sits wide-eyed, taking it all in. Her studies thus far have been theoretical; a field practicum changes perspective. Jen holds an iPad, cribbing notes. A recorder sits on the desk, red button pushed, permission already asked and granted.

Dr. Kubica gestures at Jen. "She will be using this case as the basis of her dissertation."

"I can't thank you enough," Jen tells Dr. Walker.

"It's what we do," Dr. Walker responds. "This case *is* fascinating. I'm interested in your conclusion." Dr. Walker pats the manuscript on her desk. "What did you *really* think of it, Jen? It's okay to be critical. He's not in the room with us."

"I'm not a fan of the genre," Jen says. "Crime and mystery. It was an entertaining read though. Then again, I wasn't reading for pleasure…"

The two doctors stare, waiting for more.

Jen sighs. "I found some of it … overwrought, heavy-handed."

"The religious symbolism?" Dr. Walker says.

"The ending. Christ speared through the side. The sacrifice for mankind." Jen turns to Dr. Kubica, who smiles. "There *is* humor in there. You have to look for it." Jen's mouth crinkles. "Mostly? I felt bad for him."

"It's a danger of the profession," Dr. Walker cautions.

At NY's Uniondale School of Medicine, Jen has learned to avoid personal attachment, which leads to side-effects like transference, countertransference, and worse.

Buttery sunshine slips through the slats of the blinds. Dr. Walker's office reminds Jen of a country sunroom with its billowy, white curtains and soft, pastel hues. More therapist living room than psychiatric headquarters. On the wall behind her: all the awards, commendations, certificates, and degrees the doctor has earned. Jen hopes to be there one day.

"Tea?" Dr. Walker asks.

"Yes, I'd love some," Jen says.

"Only if it's decaf," Dr. Kubica adds. "Caffeine after noon keeps me up all night."

"You know," Dr. Walker says, standing, plugging in, and turning on the electric tea kettle. "We are only having this scene—according to *him*—to pass the Bechdel test."

Jen laughs harder than the joke warrants, before recounting, verbatim: "The Bechdel test. A way of evaluating whether a film or other work of fiction portrays women in a way that is sexist or characterized by gender stereotyping. To pass the Bechdel test a work must feature at least two women; these women must talk to each other, and their conversation must concern something other than a man."

"Very good," Dr. Walker says. "And we are three."

"Only," Dr. Kubica adds, "we are still talking about *him*."

Now the three laugh together.

"As a case study … for a dissertation." Dr. Walker turns to Jen. "Tell us: do you think this scene qualifies?"

Jen smiles. "Findings: inconclusive."

The women laugh harder.

Jen gazes past Dr. Walker, who stands at the tea kettle, out the window at the budding green fields and spring flowers sprouting through the thaw. "I appreciate your bringing me in on this."

"You don't need to keep thanking me," Dr. Walker says.

"It's her first time—" Dr. Kubica starts.

"Being a character in a novel?"

Jen's face waxes concerned. "Do you really think he'll add me as a character?"

The tea kettle boils, and Dr. Walker fills three mugs. "Do you intend on meeting him?"

"If possible."

"Then, yes, I'd say there's a very good chance." Dr. Walker delivers the tea, before settling back behind her desk. "He might change your name."

"Can we discuss that?" Jen pauses, catching the unique, handcrafted design of the clay mug. A Native American motif. Interesting...

"You mean why does he seem to change fact to fiction?" Dr. Walker says. "Fiction to fact?"

"Reading the case files," Jen says, " as well as this … I guess we must call it a 'novel'? I'm having a hard time deducing his criteria."

"That's a tricky question." Dr. Walker purses her lips.

"He hasn't been here long?" Jen pans between the two doctors. "If I am understanding correctly?"

"Yes," Dr. Walker answers. "Less than half a year. Five months, give or take."

"He wrote all that in five months?"

"Actually, he wrote two manuscripts," Dr. Kubica says, more familiar with the patient's background, history, and diagnosis.

"Yes," Dr. Walker confirms. "The first was quite different. Radically. In that one, he was raised by an uncle, there were missing twins—no brother. He called it 'true crime.'"

"Literally?"

"You mean did he *say* the words? Yes. When he first got here, he spoke. No issues there. He had an attitude, a chip on his shoulder, I suppose. Immature, but that's not uncommon for recovering addicts. They stop developing emotionally at the point they start using."

"That's another thing I'm confused about," Jen says.

"His age?" Dr. Walker anticipates her questions, because they are the same ones she's needed to address in order to treat the patient.

"That is a great observation," Dr. Kubica says to her protégé.

"Agreed." Dr. Walker sips her tea, face turning toward the high sun. "In his world, there was no pandemic, no new president. His world ceases to exist sometime around November twenty-seventeen."

"Sometime?"

Dr. Walker smiles. "Good catch. No. There is an exact date. November sixteenth, two-thousand seventeen. That is the date his brother Josh died."

"But not from a fentanyl overdose." Jen knows this. She's read the patient's chart, focusing on the clinical aspects of the underlying psychology, holding off on personal analysis until she spoke with Dr. Walker and met with the patient. There is no guarantee he will talk to her. Jen remains cautiously optimistic. Still, she is careful not to come across as too brazen, sounding like a know-it-all. Before entering the field, Jen thought this was a caveat to heed around men, especially older, established doctors and professors, whose fragile male egos were more easily bruised. That is still true. But as a graduate student, Jen acknowledges the hierarchy. Drs. Kubica and Walker have completed the steps she has yet to undertake. They've had their case study, written and defended their dissertation.

"Fentanyl is in the headlines *now*," Dr. Walker responds.

Jen winces, wondering if her playing dumb was the right move.

Dr. Walker's kind smile lets her know all is forgotten. She stands, walks to the window, her back to the others as she stares over the hospital's boundless fields, the budding cheery blossoms and rich smoky applewoods coming back to life. "The … not talking … took place after I called him out on being a character in his own book."

"That's when he started this whole … act?" Jen's prims her mouth, thinking. "Why does he claim to have this affliction in the … book?" Hands over iPad, she prepares to type.

Dr. Walker stares past Jen's shoulder, rolls her eyes. "Dysarthria."

"A form of aphasia," Dr. Kubica adds.

"Interesting timing," says Jen. "They just diagnosed that actor with that. What's his name? The one in all those *It's Hard to Die* movies?"

"Yes," Dr. Walker confirms. "Another incongruity? Perhaps. He sets everything five years previous but still uses current events such as—"

"—the examples you point out," Dr. Kubica finishes, clearly proud of her student. "Actor. Fentanyl." Pause. "The *former* president."

"Thank God," Jen says, which garners a genuine chuckle from all. "In what I just read he's forty-seven. So that would make him … fifty-two?"

"Thereabouts."

"His world—his *reality*—stops when his brother died." Dr. Kubica is guiding her student. She can't answer these questions for her. This is all part of the pedagogical process.

"That's the strange part." Dr. Walker returns to her desk, sitting, cupping her tea, which has cooled enough to drink. "The last book he shared with me—"

"The one about the missing twins," Dr. Kubica reminds.

"He called it true crime, but it was all fiction. This one—" Dr. Walker trails off.

Jen waits, transfixed by the details of this mesmerizing case study in madness. *She's not sure what to classify it as either.* The longer she listens to Drs. Walker and Kubica, the more Jen reconsiders, reevaluates the many directions her dissertation can take, whether she focuses on grief, general mental illness, or she couches it all under the giant umbrella of another form of insanity yet to be determined.

"This." Dr. Walker points at the unfinished manuscript. "This is masked as fiction but it's true."

"True?" Jen's mouth falls agape, as much from the twist as Dr. Kubica's keeping it secret the entire drive down, a fact that makes her mentor smile.

"Let's start with the antagonists," Dr. Kubica prompts.

"The Fortmans."

"Yes," Dr. Walker says. "Andy and Ari."

"Ari," Jen says. "Full name 'Arioch,' which is Greek for the devil."

"Very good." Dr. Walker scribbles on a pad, which she passes over. "It's all Greek to me…"

Jen reads, "A. Fortman."

"Both their initials."

"It's an anagram," Dr. Kubica says. "Rearrange."

It doesn't take Jen long. "Manafort?"

Dr. Walker waits.

"As in Paul Manafort?"

Dr. Walker places one finger on her nose, points the other at the grad student. It's a play on the charades within the book. The patient would not like to see this. He'd think they were mocking him. He would decide at that point, when Jen giggles, that he would not help anyone with their dissertation or answer any of their stupid questions.

"The same man who worked for the former president?" Jen's enthusiasm bristles. "Ari, special counsel—are you telling me his father worked for Paul Manafort? *The* Paul Manafort?"

"That's the part that is so bizarre," Dr. Kubica says. "All that stuff about workers being sent to die in poisonous fields? All true. His father, Neil, did die that way. He was a foreman for the Manafort Brothers."

"The construction company?" Jen says it like a question, but she's implying more, a fact Dr. Walker picks up on.

"Yes," Dr. Walker says. "It's complicated. Manafort is a made-up family name. Manafort Brothers construction company was started by Paul and Frank, Sr., whose sons Paul and Frank, the juniors, well, you know Paul. Paul went into politics. Frank runs the construction side of things. The rest, as they say… Now this subject matter, our patient in there—" At this, Dr. Walker glances past Dr. Kubica and Jen's shoulder, toward her door, where beyond lies the dayroom. There, inmates whittle away days, sitting in assorted chairs, staring out windows at big, black birds and tall trees, the pretty blue skies. The patients are so sedated, you seldom hear a word. Save the occasional squawk or bellow. Madness here suffers in silence.

"You're telling me this—" Jen points at the stack of papers. "This … happened?" Until now, Jen has been operating under the assumption that some characterization, about the brother for instance, would be factual, but that the most outlandish claims, such as Paul Manafort's family killing his father, would have no basis in reality.

"Yes," Dr. Walker says. "And no. The plot *is* fantasy. Made up. The storyline. His being at a facility out west—which by the way coincides with the death of his mother—"

"And father," Jen adds, abandoning her ruse of not having formed a thesis. She needs definitive answers. "Would you say, doctor, that his confabulation is primarily the result of profound grief?"

"Because he uses his brother's real name? Mother, father? Perhaps. But that's not the real question, is it?"

Dr. Kubica grins.

"So, he uses real names for his brother, father, mother—" Jen starts.

"Freddie is also a real person, a former business associate of Josh, who Josh stole money from."

A light goes off for Jen. "Is it possible, that's the whole point of this? That he wrote this as means to apologize on behalf of his dead brother? Josh stole from Freddie, but died too addicted to apologize for himself."

"My entire professional career…" Dr. Walker laughs. It's not a happy laugh, but it confirms Jen's hypothesis. "I haven't encountered a patient like this."

"I'm not sure I've come across *a story* like this," Jen says. "Fact *or* fiction."

"It's … something else," Dr. Walker agrees.

"That section, about 'Dr. Flynn' leaving the door unlocked? You're 'Dr. Flynn'?"

"I suppose so." Dr. Walker flashes on her computer. "That's where he writes. Every night. Most of the people in there are seriously compromised. Our friend? There's nothing wrong with him."

"Besides crippling guilt over his brother's death."

"Did he inject the fatal dose?" Jen is certain she's solved the case.

"Oh, no, nothing like that. His brother Josh died from cirrhosis."

"Wait. So … alcohol … not drugs killed him?"

"Officially? Yes. But our patient *did* inject his baby brother with heroin for the first time. He never forgave himself for that."

"Was the brother using before then?"

"Like Freddie says in the book. Josh was getting drunk at twelve. So yes. And no. Addiction runs in the family." Dr. Walker points at the manuscript. "It's all in there."

Jen feels so turned around.

"Like the Fortman name," Dr. Kubica says. "You have to rearrange what is on the page and put it in order to find it."

"Find what?" Jen asks.

"The truth," Dr. Walker says. "The Manafort Brothers knew the Milford Power Plant was contaminated, and they, Frank, Jr., did pay an out-of-court settlement to the stepmother, who *was* left with all the money."

"Their father left them nothing?"

"He left two Harley Davidson motorcycles to an illegitimate half-brother."

"That must've stung."

"According to our friend in there, it's what pushed Josh over the edge. After that, the drinking and drug use got worse. Josh snapped."

"Like—"

"Exactly."

Jen reaches for the stack of papers. "May I?"

"By all means."

Jen picks up the manuscript, leafing through, wishing she'd known all this the first time she read it. "You said you've read all his works?"

"Before and *after* he checked himself in."

"Wait. He can walk out anytime he wants?"

"He's here voluntarily."

Jen puts back the stack.

Dr. Walker checks the clock on the wall, a sign her generosity with time is winding down. "I *do* have to start rounds soon. Is there anything else, specifically, you'd like to ask me?"

"Confabulation is your area of expertise…" Jen trails off, before perking up. "Do you think recovery is possible?"

"I'm hopeful for a cure, yes," Dr. Walker says. "Right now, I think we need to focus on repetition, patterns. Which can be found in his writing. I believe they are paramount to helping him. That's how he communicates. Through his work. Yes, he can speak, read, count. And he can obviously write."

"That *would* be one big plot hole," Jen says.

"If a first-person protagonist can't write, then, yes, how are we reading his work? As for this narrative? It goes beyond that."

"You said he covered this material before." Jen pauses. "What did you mean by that?"

Dr. Walker points at the printed-out stack. "In there he talks about the 'start' of a mystery series. Well, he wrote it. Five books. A fictional account of what he spells out more clearly here."

"The Manaforts and the death of his father."

"Yes. It's why we have a "Frank" and a "Paul." As character names. Although they are not 'Manaforts' in the book. What's interesting is Josh did have a stepdaughter and he *was* married to a Manafort cousin, but here, Emily and Amy, are not those people. They are original creations. It's like he wanted to steer clear of that arena, out respect for that part of his brother's life. Emily is a fictional character, and Amy, I believe, is an ex-girlfriend from Josh's high school days. The New York State Asylum for Lunatics closed in the seventies, if memory serves."

"But the parts about Frank and Paul Manafort are true."

"Put it in a Google search engine. Frank knowingly sent men to die, placing profit over person, and Paul Manafort? We all know what happened to him."

"What are the repeated patterns? In his published works?"

"Quite a few. One, a short sidekick. I'm not sure why having a short sidekick matters in these mysteries, but they all have one. This time it's Freddie."

"Perhaps our patient's inferiority complex about his size."

"Very good," Dr. Kubica says. "He's six feet, but compared to his brother and father, he's reduced to a small man. Emasculating."

"Which adds to the violence, the physical bravado. Being a fighter."

"I'm not sure being a fighter is the same as having anger issues, but our patient *is* guilty of one of those. Repeated instances of lashing out, physically. Police have been called in."

"What about the bicycle accident?" Jen asks. "Any truth there?"

"Not a bicycle," Dr. Walker says. "Though he *did* suffer a near-fatal motorcycle accident while in grad school."

"I thought the father left the Harleys to a half-brother?"

"He did. Different bike. Honda. Interesting side note? That mystery series? It's based on the half-brother, who did do estate clearing in the cold New Hampshire mountains."

"Fascinating."

"I'm sure he'd say so."

"Delusional, grandiose. Christ-like." Jen can't help but laugh. "Can we just go with fucked up." She pauses, hesitant, unsure if the joke lands.

It does. Dr. Walker and Dr. Kubica erupt.

"You're right, Mary," Dr. Walker says. "I *do* like her. Yes. Mountains. Cold. Snow. Why is this so imperative?"

"I think he wants to mimic how difficult it is to survive. For people like him. He envisions himself in *Call of the Wild*. Man vs. his very nature. Hardscrabble, infertile, hostile landscapes. Cut off. By beating these odds, he's shows he won't quit, never surrender, that he's going to be … fine."

"Go on."

"Except he's not 'fine.' He's mentally ill. Long history of substance abuse, possible brain damage from this … motorcycle accident?"

"Before shutting down his speech completely, he was complaining about a stuttering problem. Apparently, he had one as a child. Stress, anxiety brought about by his father, who was violent, abusive. It had gone away, the speech impediment, only to return with a vengeance."

"After his brother died?" Jen asks but she already has her answer as she types onto her iPad. She can't rely on the recorder, risk its battery dying. This is the meat she's been after. "What else?"

"Odd bits. The most grandiose parts…"

"Like taking over for a world-famous rock singer?" Jen laughs. "Obviously fabricated."

"Wrong."

Jen's jaw drops.

"You know the band The Counting Crows?"

"Of course. Who doesn't?" Jen's face contorts, slow to catch on. "Wait. You're saying that's *true*?"

"It is. When Adam Duritz, lead singer of the Counting Crows, left his previous band, the Himalayans, our friend in there *did* take over singing duties with some of the remaining members, the guitarist and drummer anyway."

"And proceeded to run the band into the ground with his drug use?"

"Among other things, yes. Also, he repeats phrases, the big one being, 'In the world of investigation, there is no such thing as coincidence.' " Dr. Walker points at her bookshelf. Several covers with the patient's name stand out. "In virtually every one of them, characters utter that precise phrase. The sum, you might say, is greater than the whole."

"We're not looking at several separate books. Instead, we have one mammoth tome."

"For instance," Dr. Walker says, extracting a small paperback. "The Benny character."

"The gigantic, catanionic, bald, man-child he references?"

"Another book." Dr. Walker taps the cover, before slipping it back. "He's adopted Benny's malady—and physicality—to a certain degree. But mostly it's the lyrics."

"Lyrics?"

"Song lyrics. To pop songs. He sprinkles them throughout. Liberally."

"Allusions?"

"Still clinging to his rock-and-roll dreams?" Dr. Walker suggests. She waves a hand to signal, Who knows? "Amidst myriad other pop culture references." Dr. Walker stops, check the clock again. "I really do need to be running. Would you like an introduction?"

Jen doesn't need to answer that. She wouldn't miss this opportunity for the world.

The three women stand and walk to the door.

Dr. Walker holds the door wide for her colleagues. "After you."

*

I hear the door open, which interrupts my watching the big, black birds. My hearing, of course, picks up everything. I know they are coming. I know what they are saying about me. They've gotten some of it right. No one ever gets it *all* right. Most of it is wrong.

"That's why he shaves his head," I hear one of the doctors whisper.

"Simpatico?" another responds.

The other patients around me caw, flapping their arms like flightless birds.

The three women come to rest behind my chair.

"There's someone here to see you," Dr. Walker says.

I don't move, don't turn around. Everything they need to know? I've already put on the page. Read it. Figure it out.

A mystery writer plants the clues. It's up to you to find what they are and make sense of them, not me. My job is done.

"Hi," a female voice says. "My name is Jen. Jen Hillier. I've read … your latest book. It was … very entertaining. It offers me a fascinating glimpse into that mind of yours. I inferred a great deal from it— answers I believe we can use to help you. But first, I have a few more questions. I was hoping you could help me complete the puzzle?"

Of course, I can help complete the puzzle. It's my story, *my* world. I control who lives, who dies, so no one I love ever has to get hurt again. My brother isn't going anywhere without me. I could explain it all, put it in terms so black and white, no mystery would remain. I can resurrect the dead, and I can stay hidden in the shadows with the ghosts. It's all up to me to decide. Me. Not you. Not God. Me. You have questions? We all have questions.

I can answer whatever the hell I want.

But I won't say a word.

ACKNOWLEDGEMENTS

TK

ABOUT THE AUTHOR

Joe Clifford is the author of several acclaimed novels, including *Junkie Love* and the Jay Porter thriller series. He lives in the San Francisco Bay Area with his wife and two sons. Joe's writing can be found at

www.joeclifford.com.

www.ingramcontent.com/pod-product-compliance
Lightning Source LLC
Chambersburg PA
CBHW022115310726
48972CB00007B/2053